I0667837

Breaking the Barriers

A Breakin' in the 80s Novel
Book 2

B.B. Swann

DEDICATION

This book is dedicated to everyone out there
who has ever strived to reach for their dreams.
Keep striving because sometimes, we make it.

CHAPTER ONE

Mike

Mike Ryan never wanted to be a stalker, but he sure rocked the job.

Glancing at Cindy Wilson across the classroom, he caught his breath. Maybe he should feel special. Lucky. Call Guinness. Not many guys had permission to spy on their girlfriends. But damn, he felt like a creep following her around.

Hide their relationship at all costs. Nobody could know. Not that he cared, but she did—even if he didn't understand why. Aside from their best friends, Hayden and Molly, nobody else in the Elkwood High class of 1986 knew they were dating.

And it totally sucked.

Mike tapped his pen against his notebook, one smack for each tick from the clock above the door. Five minutes. Five more minutes until biology ended, and he'd follow her—again. Looking at the teacher as he droned on about DNA in his gravely pack-a-day voice, Mike leaned back in his chair. The molded blue plastic dug into his muscles, and he sighed.

Cindy turned her head at the noise, making eye contact, but ended it before he could react.

Three minutes. Tap. Tap. Tap.

Two minutes. Tap. Tap.

She brushed a stray hair from her face and Mike flexed his fingers. He forced his gaze back to the teacher.

"Don't forget," said their teacher, "your third quarter project outline is due tomorrow."

The ear-splitting final bell rang, and everyone talked at once. Chairs scraped and sneakers squeaked against the tiled floor. Two guys squeezed past Mike, bumping into him on their way to the door as they raced toward freedom.

Mike gathered his books, peeking again at Cindy from the corner of his eye. She laughed at something Molly said, and he swallowed down the lump of jealousy that clogged his throat.

Melissa, a girl he'd dated a few times last year, patted his arm. "Later, Mike."

He smiled, sparing her a glance. "Yeah, see ya."

He turned his head back in time to catch Cindy's glare. She shoved a book into her bag and stomped out the door. Grinning at her reaction, he followed.

It had been so long since he'd been on an official date, even his self-absorbed mother asked him why he never went out. It was a bogus concern. She only noticed because she had to stay home when his dad nixed her requests for the two of them to *get away*— again.

Mike rolled his eyes. If his dad would take her somewhere, she'd leave him alone about his lack of a social life.

Weaving through the crowded hall, he focused his gaze on Cindy's athletic form gliding between the big-haired girls with their padded shoulders. Cindy stood out in a crowd, and not because she was the only black girl in their small, Illinois town. Her don't-mess-with-me attitude and talents on the track made her special.

She stopped at her locker and Mike slipped to the opposite side of the hall to take a drink from the water fountain. A pair of white Keds appeared next to his feet, smooth-skinned legs starting inside the sneaker and extending past his view.

"I've been looking for you, Mike."

He muffled a groan, wiping his mouth with the back of his hand and standing to face the shoe owner. To his left stood Jenny, a junior from his trig class. Across the hall, Cindy frowned.

Jenny walked her fingers up the sleeve of his jean jacket. "A few of us are going for frozen yogurt. Want to come?"

She flashed her dimples, flipping her long blonde hair. She liked to point out that it was the same shade as his whenever she badgered him for a date. As if matching hair meant they should be together—like Barbie and Ken.

2

The echo of metal on metal hit his ears as Cindy slammed her locker.

"Sorry, got plans." He bit back a smile and moved his arm from Jenny's reach to scratch a fake itch on his head.

"Are you sure?" She leaned closer and put both her hands on his chest. A cloud of perfume encircled his head, and he blinked his watering eyes. "If you keep telling me no, I'll think you don't like me."

He opened his mouth as Cindy bumped into Jenny's side, knocking her away from him.

She smirked at Jenny. "Oops, sorry. Got pushed. Crossing the hall is like playing Frogger."

"Right." Jenny rubbed her shoulder.

Cindy stepped between them and shot a wide-eyed glance at Mike before bending to get a drink from the fountain.

Her hip touched his leg and he pressed back slightly. He shook his head at Jenny. "Already have plans."

Cindy stepped back from the water fountain.

Jenny yanked her foot from under Cindy's.

"Excuse me," Cindy said.

Jenny turned her back and smiled at him. "Maybe next time." She slid a hand up his arm and Cindy's eyes widened again.

"See ya later," Jenny said with a tap of her finger on his nose.

Mike smirked as Jenny brushed past Cindy, chin raised, and eyes narrowed.

Cindy glared back then turned her gaze to him.

He gave her a small grin.

"Hmph." She strode toward the door.

He chuckled as he followed her, but the fun ended as they walked through the parking lot. For all the attention she gave him, the twenty feet between them could have been fifty miles. She didn't make eye contact, didn't look in his direction, didn't flip him off. Nothing. Just like every other day.

Sunlight reflected off the cars in the dusty gravel parking lot, and Mike squinted against the glare. Unlocking his red Camaro, he tossed his backpack in the back seat and glanced once more in her direction. His blood heated just thinking about touching her. Shiny black hair pulled into a curly ponytail, smooth brown skin glowing in the sunshine—he'd committed its softness to memory during their secret interactions.

Sucking in a breath of cold spring air, he hopped into the driver's seat and revved his engine. *Obsession* blasted from the speakers he'd left up too loud.

"Tell me something I don't know," he said to the radio. He sang along while he drove, following her blue Escort to the running trail outside of town.

Pulling into the lot right behind her, he parked next to her and cut the engine. With a blast of cool air, Cindy opened the door and slid into the passenger seat. Her sweet scent enveloped him, and he was home.

"Hey." She leaned toward him.

"Come here. I've waited all day for this." He held her face and kissed her, long and deep. He touched her shoulders, sliding his hands from her arms onto her waist. He pulled her closer, and she sighed.

She played with the spiky hair on top of his head while her lips moved softly against his.

When he finally let her go, her brown eyes twinkled in the sunlight streaming through the windshield. "How was your day?" she asked.

"Lonely." God, he sounded pathetic, but each day got harder and harder.

"Well, you had company after bio." She pressed her lips against his again.

He pulled away shaking his head. "Just ignore her. I do."

"I'd like to, but she's always trying to talk to you."

"I never should have gone out with her sophomore year." Mike squinted. "It was only one date. Girl doesn't know how to take no for an answer."

"That's not all I've heard about her."

"Oh?" He raised his eyebrows. "Didn't know you listened to gossip."

"It's hard to ignore when everyone talks about it."

"About what?"

Cindy shook her head. "I don't spread rumors. But she'd better keep her hands to herself." She touched his leg and heat raced across his thigh. "Next time I won't be so nice. I'll push her *into* the Frogger lane."

4

"Her hands aren't the ones I want touching me." He wagged his eyebrows up and down and grinned. "But you can touch me anywhere."

She giggled and caressed his cheek. "Come on. It's a nice day. Let's take a walk before I have to practice."

Mike's stomach tightened. Great. Another walk in the woods. Their relationship had become a freaking fairy tale. Snow White and Prince Charming, kissing in the trees.

He held her hand as they walked the ten feet through the gravel lot to the trailhead and stepped onto the uneven path. The leafless trees allowed the sun to reach them, making the cool breeze more bearable. A large branch from a broken maple tree hung across the trail. Jumping in front of Cindy, Mike held it back and wiped away the spider webs. She passed through with a smile and took his offered hand again.

After a few minutes of listening to the conversation of the birds, they walked toward a large flat boulder set back under the trees. His white Converse sank into the squishy leaves of last summer, sending the smell of wet earth up from the ground. They sat on the rock. Wrapping both arms around her, he pulled Cindy into his warmth.

She relaxed against him. "Are you excited about joining track?"

"Yes," he chuckled. "I can't believe I let you talk me into it. Senior year, most people drop out of sports, they don't join a new one."

Mostly he looked forward to not missing out on time with her because she had practice. Not that he'd tell her that. He sounded pathetic enough without letting her know how obsessed he was with her.

"You'll do fine."

"Why do the girls start practicing before the guys?" He glanced around at the woods. They only met here so she'd be able to make it to practice on time on the other side of the park.

"Because," she said, straightening the lapel of his jacket. "We have a shot at going to state with our relays this year. Gotta condition."

"I hope you don't hold me to that standard. I've never even been to a meet. I might get smoked on the track and make an ass out of myself. Or get out-thrown in the field events."

She raised her eyebrows and tucked in her chin. "You better not. No boyfriend of mine can suck at sports."

"Keep up that attitude and I'll lose on purpose."

"That is the most ignorant thing you've ever said." She giggled as he tickled her. "Take it back."

"Only if you promise not to laugh at me tomorrow when I drop the ball on my foot."

"It's called a shot, and no way. I claim laughing rights anytime you do something *that* stupid."

"You're mean." He rested his cheek on the top of her head. "Maybe I should go home and practice. Want to come and help me?"

"I have to practice."

"How about afterward." He held his breath waiting for her answer.

Her shoulders stiffened. "I can't. You know that."

"I know you *think* that. Nobody's there. We'll be alone."

"I want to." Cindy frowned and dropped her gaze to the ground. "But I can't."

He blew out a frustrated breath. "No, you *won't*. There's a difference."

His body ached to sit with her on a couch, watch TV, listen to music, anything but walk in the trees or kiss in his car. As romantic as it *should* sound, it wasn't.

"I don't like this either." She pushed off the rock and sloshed through the muck back to the trail.

Mike pursed his lips, staring at her back, then jogged to her side. "The only thing stopping us from telling everyone we're dating is you." He gently grabbed her shoulder and turned her toward him.

"Do we have to argue again?"

"No," he said with a shaky grin. "You can just agree with me and then we can act like a real couple."

She gave a sarcastic laugh. "If I agree with you, I won't be around to *be* a couple with you. My mom will kill me and barbeque my remains on the grill."

"C'mon, Cindy. She can't be that bad."

"When we moved here, Mama told me no dating until after high school. Her words were, *Boys are nothing but trouble, and I'll whoop you into tomorrow if I catch you with one.* I don't want to cross Mama."

Mike smirked. "You moved here when you were twelve. Maybe it's time to revisit that conversation."

6

"No, it's…" She glanced at her feet then over his shoulder. "It's not the right time."

"Why not? Is it your brother? Are you afraid Elijah will get mad?" Chuckling, he stuck his hands in his pockets. "I mean don't you two have that weird twin bonding thing? You know, *Wonder Twin powers, activate.*"

"No," she said with a snort. "I can handle Elijah. That's not it."

Avoiding his eyes, she walked on toward the lot. Mike kicked a stone into the brush and followed. They reached their lonely cars in the sun-filled dusty lot.

He held her hands and pulled her toward him, staring into her eyes. Acceptance, belonging, passion, understanding, floated in those melted chocolate depths. He drew a shallow breath. It should be so easy. Why did she make it so hard?

"I want a real relationship, Cindy. Where we go on real dates and do real things together where everyone can see us and know we're together."

"You know I want the same things."

"Then let's *do* them." He held her hands to his chest. "If we both want things to change then why not change them?"

She stared back, biting her lip.

His heart jackhammered against his ribs.

Then Cindy shook her head, and his hopes landed in the dirt at his feet.

"We graduate in a few months. Once I'm at college and out of the house, we'll be free."

Months. More waiting. More hiding. More sacrifices for reasons he didn't even understand. Maybe she didn't really share his feelings. Maybe she didn't like him as much as he did her.

"Right. Let's keep hiding in the woods." He ignored her frown and walked to the Escort, pulling the door open. "Better get to practice, before you turn into a pumpkin."

"So, that's it?" She raised her eyebrows. "You don't want to be with me?"

"Of course I do. I always want to be with you. But not here."

7

He glanced around at the trees, bare branches clacking in the wind, last year's nests visible without the leaves to hide them. Sad reminders of families long gone. He returned his gaze to hers, blinking against the sting in his eyes. "I can't do this anymore."

"You mean you *won't*. There's a difference," she mocked.

"I guess so."

"Fine. Then we won't." Cindy sniffled. She crossed her arms and turned to glare at the trees.

Staring at her profile, Mike swallowed the boulder from his throat. He'd gone too far this time. "Are you... are you breaking up with me?"

She gasped, whipping back around to face him. "What? No."

He lifted his gaze to hers, hands shaking at the rare tears that sparkled in her eyes. His stomach tightened and he ran a finger across her cheek.

She whispered, "Are you breaking up with *me*?"

Was he? Could he go back to meaningless dates with girls who didn't matter but would at least be seen in public with him? No, he could no sooner end this than he could solve a Rubik's cube without pulling off the stickers. But things had to change, or he'd go insane.

Cindy closed her eyes, and the tears slid down her face. "You are."

"I don't want to break up, but I can't keep hiding." Lifting his trembling hands, he wiped her tears away with his thumbs.

"Mike, what if... if people don't like us being together? There aren't any couples like us here."

"So? The difference in our skin doesn't matter."

"To some people, it will."

"Since when do you care what people think?"

"Since I have something they can ruin."

"You stand up to everyone who pisses you off or looks at you wrong. What makes this any different? Isn't this important enough to fight for?"

"Of course." She squeezed his hands. "But that's what scares me. People are assholes."

Mike leaned his forehead on hers. "If someone has a problem with us, they can deal with it."

"Yes, but..." The tremors in her bottom lip sent vibrations to his stomach.

"Let's start slow. Just tell our friends and the assholes at school. Your parents won't have to know, but everyone else will know how I feel for you." He forced a grin. "Then maybe Jenny will leave me alone."

She gave a soft laugh, tears spilling onto her cheeks.

"I promise," Mike said. "Just at school. I won't call your house or come to see you there. Just... please."

This was it. His last argument. Slumping his shoulders, he swallowed back the bile rising in his throat. A no this time would send him over the edge.

The chirping of the birds ticked away the longest ten seconds of his life. His chest constricted, sweat trickling down his back despite the coolness of the day.

"You're right. I *do* want people to know." She pressed her face into his neck. "Okay, we'll start slow. Just at school."

He pulled her in for a kiss. "Thank you," he whispered.

She shook her head. "Thank me if we survive tomorrow. With the stupidity of some of our classmates, you might change your mind."

"Nah. I can ignore them as long as you don't make me follow you around anymore."

A slow smile spread across her face. "I'll break the news to Jenny."

"Be gentle."

"Right." Cindy rolled her eyes. She kissed him on the cheek then laid her head on his chest. "I have to go. I'm gonna be late."

"Okay." He squeezed her then gestured to her open door. She got in, her body rocking back and forth as she rolled down her window. Mike leaned through to give her one last kiss. "I'll see you tomorrow. I'll wait for you by the door."

"Okay. See you at school." She touched his cheek and he stood back, waving as she drove away.

Driving home, relishing the warm feeling in his chest instead of the usual cold loneliness, he worried about Elijah's reaction to their relationship. Mike wasn't afraid of him, but he didn't want to have her brother mad at him. And he didn't want Elijah to narc on them to her parents.

He'd trust Cindy to take care of her brother and he'd focus on the others. This relationship would turn their little rural school upside down.

But Mike would do whatever it took to be with her. How hard could it be?

CHAPTER TWO

Cindy

As soon as her red ranch-style house with its front porch deck came into view, Cindy sighed. Pulling up to the curb, she turned off the car and leaned her head back on the seat.

The tension in her shoulders from the last hour seeped away into the light of the setting sun coming through her side window. Normally practice was fun but with Mike on her mind—and what they decided to do—she just wanted to get home and convince herself she'd made the right choice. Maybe she'd even take Mike's advice and bring up the topic of dating again. Maybe. She sat straight and rolled her head from side to side, wincing as the tense stress bubbles popped and cracked.

She got out and walked along the driveway on the side of the house to enter through the back door. Climbing the steps of the back deck, she went inside to the kitchen and tossed her keys into the bowl sitting on the white Formica countertop. Cindy laughed as a scrawny pair of arms encircled her knees.

"Cinny," her youngest brother cried.

She lifted him onto her hip. "Hey, Benny. Did you miss me?" She blew a raspberry on his chubby cheek and rubbed his fuzzy cropped hair.

He giggled.

She set Benny on his feet and one-arm-hugged the other little boys sitting at the round oak table. Joshua, eight, and Gabe, six, both pushed her away but smiled. They stopped running to her when they turned four. Benny had a year left to worship his big sister.

Her dad appeared from around the corner of the living room. He grabbed the silver handles on his wheelchair and pushed himself closer to the table, his thin arms and legs shaking from the effort. "Hey, baby girl. Just in time for dinner."

She gave him a smile and glanced at Mama as she set a steaming bowl of green beans on the table and took her seat across from Cindy's dad. Cindy sat between them, frowning at the tired slump to her mom's shoulders and the bags under her eyes.

She'd seen the old pictures. Mama was a "looker" as Daddy had told them. Even after five kids, she still had a slim figure and only a few gray hairs. But battling Daddy's illness was sure to add a few more—that and dealing with her stupid brother.

"Where's Elijah?" Cindy asked. Her mom answered.

"He's at the library studying with his friend Jamal."

Right. The only thing Elijah studies with Jamal is beer.

"I thought we had to Huxtable it for dinner every night." Cindy snorted and grabbed the nearest bowl. "Why does he get to skip?"

"Your brother is trying to make better choices," her mom said. "You should support him."

Avoiding the eye roll that would earn her a grounding, Cindy replied, "Oh, I do. He knows it, too."

He knows I'll kick his butt for hanging out with that thug. Cindy spooned potatoes on her plate, gritting her teeth. Now she'd have to deal with that tonight, too. Why couldn't her brother get it together?

"Mama, she ain't taking green beans." Gabe complained.

"Ain't is not a word, Gabe. And I am, so quit tattling." Cindy put a scoop of beans next to her ham. She took a bite and made a face at Gabe, green beans hanging out of her mouth. He grinned and threw a bean at her plate.

Her dad laughed. "Hey now, you're supposed to eat your food."

His hands shook as he lifted his fork toward his mouth. The green beans he'd scooped fell back to the plate.

Stomach swooping, Cindy put her fork on the table and held her dad's hand, helping him spear the beans so they wouldn't fall off.

"Thank you," he mumbled.

"No problem, Daddy." She choked down another bite herself. The shaking had gotten worse. She swallowed her beans and smiled at her dad. "Track officially starts tomorrow."

"Any new talent this year?" Her dad lifted his cup with both hands. He still spilled water on his chin.

Cindy bounced her knee under the table, taking her dad's timely question as her cue to pass the baton.

"Well, there's a new guy joining the team. Mike. He's the boys' soccer goalie and Hayden's friend. He's strong." And funny. And cute. And an excellent kisser. And... She grabbed her water glass.

"I think your daddy meant are there any new girls. The boys aren't your concern." Her mom cut into her ham and speared a piece with her fork. Chewing, she pointed the fork at Cindy. "You focus on *your* goals."

Cindy's face burned. "Yes, Ma'am."

"Wait until college is through, then you can find a good one," her mom said.

"There's plenty of good kids here, Shirley." Her dad winked at her, and Cindy gave him a shaky grin.

Fight for him, you big chicken. Keep trying! "Well, Mike is really nice. What is your idea of a good one, Mama?"

"Someone who won't knock you up like half the girls today."

"Mama!" Cindy glanced at her little brothers, glad they seemed more interested in building mashed potato mountains than listening to talk about boys and girls.

"I hear about it every day at the factory. Seems like all the ladies know at least one pregnant teen. I don't want that to happen to you."

Her dad laughed. "Mama's right, baby girl. That's not the future for you."

"I agree, but I think I'm smart enough to date without letting *that* happen." She met her mom's raised eyebrow with one of her own. "Why don't you let me try it and I can show you how responsible I am?"

Her mom shook her head, glancing at her husband. "Absolutely not."

"Why not? You let Elijah date last year."

Clearing his throat her dad said, "That's true. We did."

13

"That's different," her mom said. "He's a boy."

Cindy gritted her teeth. "So? Just because he can't *get* knocked up doesn't mean he can't do it to someone else."

"Watch your mouth, young lady." Her mom nodded to her little brothers. Their wide eyes focused on Cindy. "You need to set a better example."

"Right, I should just accept the double standard."

"Why this sudden interest in dating?" Her mom squinted. "Is there something you need to tell us?"

"Only that you're being totally unfair and sexist." She stabbed her ham with her fork. "Why can't I go out with someone? I'm the only senior girl not allowed to date. I'm not a baby."

"No, but you're acting like one," her mom said. "And those other girls aren't my daughters, you are. And you'll do as I say."

"I thought this was America, the land of the free. Not the land of Shirley's dictatorship."

Her mom's hand connected with Cindy's cheek, echoing through the silent room. Cindy rubbed away the sting, glaring at her mom. Gabe stared at Cindy. Benny sniffled and Josh grabbed his hand.

Throat tight with angry tears, she glanced at her dad. He frowned, looking from Cindy to her mom. His head bobbed like Stevie Wonder and his left eye had partially closed. The knuckles on the hand holding the fork turned white while his mouth opened and closed, a low moan the only sound.

Cindy dropped her fork to her plate with a clatter.

"Daddy? I'm sorry, I'm sorry." She hugged his shoulders. "I didn't mean to upset you."

He continued to shake, but patted her hand, his left eye twitching as a tear rolled out.

Her mom pushed out of her chair and rushed to his side.

Cindy glanced at her little brothers. "Why don't you guys go get ready for your baths. I'll be in there in a minute to help you."

They exchanged a look with each other and nodded, running toward the bathroom.

Cindy drew a shaky breath. "Mama, I'm sorry. I shouldn't be disrespectful."

Her mom ignored her and reached for her dad. "It's okay, Carl. Don't worry. Cindy and I can handle this." She patted his cheek and stroked his graying hair, staring into his watery eyes. "Shhh. It's fine. We're fine."

She continued to reassure him until his shaking lessened and he relaxed his death grip on his fork. Once his eyes were again equal-sized, he took a deep breath, sinking back into his wheelchair.

"I'm okay," he said. He patted Cindy's knee. Only half of his mouth smiled. "Don't you worry."

Face on fire, Cindy stood and picked up her plate. "I'll go help them with their baths. Mama leave the dishes. I'll do them for you." She set her plate on the counter and stepped into the living room, suppressing a sob.

Her mother followed. Looking back at her husband, she whispered to Cindy, "I'll ask you again. Is there *something* you need to tell me?"

Mike was wrong. Her family wasn't ready. She swallowed. "No, Mama."

"Shirley?" her dad called.

"I'm coming, babe." Wrinkling her forehead, she patted Cindy's cheek. "I'm sorry I hit you."

Cindy lied again. "It's okay. The boys are waiting. I'll go take care of them. Then I think I'll go… study with Elijah."

Her mom returned to the kitchen and kissed Daddy on the cheek.

Sadness seeped through the anger as Cindy watched them. Sometimes her parents' love made her sad. The disease was taking its toll on Daddy, and Mama suffered the effects, too.

Cindy could only do so much to keep him healthy and reduce his stress. Helping with her little brothers, keeping Elijah out of trouble— and hiding her relationship with Mike.

****

Sometimes Cindy wanted to kill her brother. If he wasn't almost twice her size, she'd at least tie him down so he couldn't get himself into these messes. Instead of going to Molly's and calling Mike without her

15

family overhearing her, she was in this dumpy neighboring town to get the world's biggest idiot out of trouble—again.

She parked her beat-up Escort in front of a dirty gray, shotgun house. With the engine off, the beats from Run DMC exploded from the house and punched their way through her closed windows. The bass sent vibrations into the review mirror, ripples on liquid metal, and her dark eyes quivered in the reflection.

Scanning the street between her car and the house, she shivered. Moonlight fell on the unkempt yard and rickety porch, creating the perfect scene for a horror movie. She half expected Freddy Krueger to scratch his blades on the side of her car.

"Elijah, if I get robbed, I'll kill you twice." Cindy took a deep breath, grabbed the keys, and stepped out into the chilly air, mashing down the lock with her thumb before she slammed the door.

She couldn't hide the goosebumps crawling over her skin but strode toward the house with her chin held high. Showing fear only invited trouble.

As she reached the front sidewalk, the pungent scent of weed hit her, and she grimaced. Before she reached the porch, the door opened. Jamal stepped out, and Cindy curled her lip.

His eyebrows lifted over his watery black eyes. Not much taller than her, he still had at least fifty pounds on her, all muscle. Red parachute pants, black t-shirt, and hair cut in a perfect fade, he looked like a break dancer, but his body moved to the beat of the music pounding behind the front door with the rhythm of a toddler. He grinned, the gold tooth on his upper gum glinting.

"Hey, baby. Here for the party? Maybe I'll stay." He raked his eyes over her jeans and sweatshirt. "Whatcha got under dem clothes?"

She hopped up the steps. "Shut up, Jamal. I'm here to get my brother."

He grinned and reached for the door handle to push it open. "C'mon in."

"You think I'm stupid?" she asked. "Go get him. I'll wait here."

He laughed and crossed his arms. "Why? Afraid to have fun?"

"Getting high isn't my idea of fun."

Jamal chuckled. "Someday you'll cave." He groped her with his bloodshot eyes and shook his head as he closed the door.

Cindy bounced on her toes, her gaze roving over the deserted yard and quiet street. She rubbed her hands up and down her arms to smooth out the goosebumps. Her mind wandered to Mike, of course. What if he'd heard Jamal talking to her like that?

"Hmph. He'd kick his ass, that's what." Better not to tell him anything.

Although, after watching Jenny with Mike, maybe she should tell him, let him get jealous for once. Knowing his temper though, he'd come here to find Jamal. With his blond hair and sea blue eyes, he would only become another victim in this neighborhood.

The door flew open, and Cindy jumped. A large-shouldered boy emerged, glaring at her with bloodshot brown eyes the same color as his skin. Hands clenched in fists and muscles bulging in his thick arms, he took a step toward Cindy and curled his lip.

She pushed his chest with both hands. "What the hell are you doing?"

"Damn, Cindy." He darted a glance toward the house, then snarled in a rough whisper, "What are *you* doing here?"

"I came to bring you home. You know you shouldn't be here, Elijah." She poked his chest with her finger. "Mama and Daddy told you to stay away from these punks."

"Whatever." He mimicked her stance and smirked. "You run back home. I can take care of myself."

Cindy leaned closer. "You come home with me now or I'll tell Mama and Daddy."

She couldn't do that and risk upsetting her dad, but their parents moved them away from the city to give them a better life. Even if her brother didn't appreciate it, she did, and she wouldn't let him jeopardize it.

Elijah's face darkened. "You crazy? They'll send me to that stupid boot camp."

"You need to find new friends. These guys are nothing but trouble." She grabbed his arm and pulled him toward the steps. "Come on, let's go."

"Dammit." He yanked his arm from her grasp, glancing again toward the door. "Leave me alone. I ain't goin'."

"What's wrong with you? Can't you see these guys are bad news? They aren't your friends. They're using you."

"Nah, they get me. They…"

"They know they can *get you* to do what they want and make you think they care. But they don't."

He leaned into her face. "You don't even know 'em."

She waved away the smell of beer from his breath. "I don't want to know them, and you shouldn't either. They'll get you in trouble again, just like last year."

"That ain't my fault." Glaring, he ran a hand over his short-cropped hair. "I didn't know they'd be hitting that store."

"Ugh, isn't not ain't. And it doesn't matter. You still got busted." Angry tears prickled her eyes.

"What, you want me to make some nice boring friends like you did? Keep me out of trouble?" He shook his head. "I've seen the way they look at me, like I'm about to attack them or somethin'. I don't… I don't fit in with anyone at our school."

"You haven't even tried to." Her stomach dropped at his confession, but she wouldn't give up. "What about Hayden? You like him."

"He's alright. But…"

"But what?"

Elijah stared out over the darkened neighborhood. "You don't get it."

"Get *what*? That you keep doing the same stupid shit? Daddy worked hard and sacrificed to get us here." She ignored the pain in her chest and its echo on Elijah's face. "You gonna throw it away 'cuz you can't say no?"

He kicked the porch rail. "It's just a party."

"Daddy needs us." Her voice cracked. "Him stressing about you will only make things worse."

Elijah stared at her, his forehead wrinkled. Then he bit his lip and nodded. "Fine. Be back in a minute. Get in your car." He looked around the darkened neighborhood. "And lock the doors."

Cindy smirked. "Just hurry. I wanna get out of here." Her brother disappeared into the house.

Back in the car, she bounced her knee against the steering wheel until he emerged and sauntered toward her. She leaned across the seat and unlocked the door. He folded his huge frame into the passenger seat and Cindy sped away from the house.

"What'd you tell them?" She glanced at Elijah from the corner of her eye.

He shrugged. "That you had to fight a bitch that messed with your best friend. Needed me for backup."

She snorted. The trouble her best friend Molly'd had with Andrea, a girl on their cross-country team seemed easy compared to Cindy's current predicament with Mike. "I definitely didn't need back up to deal with her. But thanks for making me look tough so your *friends* won't mess with me."

He grinned. "Got your back, sis."

They drove in silence for a while. Then she asked, "Why do you hang out with guys like them?"

His grin faded and a belligerent smirk took its place. "I guess it's just what I do."

"Well, do something else."

"Maybe I like my life the way it is."

"You know the things they do. The things they want you to do for them." Cindy laid a hand on Elijah's arm. "Don't *you* want to decide your future?"

She sure did.

Elijah patted her hand but simply stared out the window into the night.

CHAPTER THREE

Mike

Leaning his back against the cold bricks of the school, Mike bounced his knees and scanned the busy parking lot for Cindy's car. This was it. Their first walk through school as an official couple. He bounced his knees faster.

John, his soccer teammate, jogged up the steps. "Hey, Mike."

"Hey." Mike nodded but kept his eyes on the lot.

"Dude, *pleeease* tell me your parents are going out of town this weekend." He stopped in front of Mike. "We need a party. You know, release some steam."

"Nope. Your turn to host." Mike's mom had talked dad into a trip, but he didn't want to have a party. He'd rather spend time alone with Cindy.

"Damn, my parents'll be home," John said.

The sun glared off the window of Cindy's blue Escort and Mike grinned. He pushed himself off the wall, yanking his backpack further onto his shoulder.

Focusing on her car, waiting for the first glimpse of her, he almost missed Elijah coming toward him on the steps.

Almost.

He met Elijah's stare.

"What's up?" Elijah said, brushing past Mike.

Mike smirked. "Not much."

Either he accepted the news of them dating better than Cindy thought he would, or she didn't tell him. Since Elijah didn't bury his fist in Mike's face, the second was probably true.

After Elijah passed, John whistled low. "That dude is creepy."

Mike frowned. "You think?"

"He hangs out with losers from that alternative school, EHS South." He shook his head. "Those guys are messed up. I heard one stabbed a cop."

Laughing, Mike said, "If he stabbed a cop, he'd be in juvie, not alternative school. Elijah isn't creepy. He's quiet."

"Whatever. I wouldn't want to meet him in a dark alley alone."

Mike bit back a laugh. Neither would he after Elijah heard about him and Cindy.

"Well, gotta jet. Let me know if your parents leave." John wiggled his eyebrows. "I know someone who can get us a keg at a discount."

"Sure, see you later." John's words barely registered. Mike smiled as Cindy walked toward him wearing his favorite faded jeans and a purple sweater that hugged her tight waist. About to close the distance, Jenny jumped in front of him, and he jerked back.

"Hi!" She wrapped her arms around his waist and leaned into him. "Guess what? *We* are going out tonight. This time I won't take no for an answer."

"Uh, nope," he said, pulling her arms away. "I'm busy."

He glanced back to Cindy. She increased her pace, glaring at Jenny's back.

"Come on, Mike. We'll have fun." Jenny rubbed his chest, frowning when he batted her hand away.

"Already got a date."

"With who?"

"My girlfriend." He smiled at Cindy running up the stairs.

Jenny's eyes narrowed. "You don't have a girlfriend."

"Yeah, he does," Cindy said. "So back off." She slid an arm around his waist.

Mike laid his arm across her shoulders and kissed her cheek.

"You're dating Cindy?" she sneered. "Uh, lowered your standards a little, didn't you?"

Cindy stiffened in his arms, but Mike held her back with a squeeze. He cocked an eyebrow. "If I'd lowered my standards, I would have said yes to you."

After glaring at Cindy, Jenny pressed her lips together and stalked toward the building.

Mike watched her for a moment, then met Cindy's gaze. "Sorry, that was mean, but she deserved it."

"I agree."

"Forget about her. Today is about us. Okay?" He kissed her softly, sliding his fingers from her chin to the smooth skin on her neck.

"You're right." The bell rang and she groaned, jerking her head toward a group of sophomores who watched them with wide eyes. "Let's go. I think we've put on enough of a show. You better watch out for Elijah in the hall, too. Sorry. I didn't warn him."

Mike squeezed her hand and glanced around. "You never know, he might be fine with it."

Cindy's laugh sent a warm glow through his chest.

"Right. Like Jenny." She led him inside and kissed his cheek. "I'll see you later."

She walked into her class, and he jogged toward his at the opposite end of the hall, grinning ear to ear. For the first time since he'd told Hayden he liked Cindy, their relationship was real. And he had the stares and whispers to prove it.

****

After school, Mike rushed to his first track practice, relieved to be away from the idiots in his classes. Maybe they thought he couldn't hear them gossiping about him and Cindy. Or maybe they didn't care. Whatever, their opinions didn't matter. Still, he squeezed the metal ball in his hand, imagining it hitting a few of the faces he'd seen.

The bright spring sun warmed the skin on Mike's neck as he stood with Hayden by the shot-put circle. He held the shot in his hand, rubbing the smooth metal and testing the weight. He smirked at Hayden. "Definitely heavier than a soccer ball."

Hayden laughed. "Let's see what you've got." He stepped away into the grass and crossed his arms.

The throwing coach, Mr. Ebbs, cleared his throat. "Try the glide technique first. It's easier to execute. Then you can work up to the spin." He gave a quick demonstration and Mike bit back a laugh. Mr. Ebbs may still hold the school record, but his paunchy stomach, gray temples, and creased eyes were more suited for a barstool than a track.

Mike shrugged, and placed the shot on his right collarbone, touching his neck. He faced the back of the circle, pivoted toward the toe board, wobbled, and released the shot. It arched into the air and landed—ten feet away in the grass.

They all stared silently at the shot.

Mr. Ebbs wiped his forehead with his hand. "Ahem. Well, that was a good first try."

Hayden nodded. "Sure, the first time's the hardest, right?" He pinched his lips together.

With clenched teeth, Mike picked up another shot and took his stance again. Ignoring his audience, he thought of Cindy. She would chew him out if she saw that pathetic first attempt. And he'd deserve it, too. He closed his eyes and took a slow deep breath, picturing her face.

He released the breath and spun. When he let go, he knew it was a better throw. The shot sailed through the air and landed twenty feet further than his last.

"Wow." Coach raised his bushy eyebrows. "That was... much better."

"Thanks." Mike muttered to Hayden. "Cindy would kick my ass if I sucked."

"Definitely," Hayden said with a chuckle.

"Looks like the spin is your technique. Keep practicing." Coach slapped Mike on the shoulder and walked toward the discus group.

After a few more practice throws, they headed to the track to join the runners. It wasn't until they jogged a warm-up lap together and then met up with the sprint coach that the knots left Mike's stomach. At least he knew how to run and wouldn't make an ass of himself.

"Let's see what we have this year." Coach Miller yelled. "Line up for hundreds. When you've finished, you can clock out."

The guys shifted toward the line. Mike followed, trying to look like he knew what he was doing. He leaned his head toward Hayden. "What're hundreds?"

Hayden pointed to the other end of the track. "At the whistle, just run that way as fast as you can." He led Mike to where the group stood at the end of the track waiting for their turns to run.

Standing behind the crowd, Mike glanced around, meeting the amused stares of two seniors he didn't know well. One mumbled something like *"that's the guy"* to the other, and they laughed.

Heat pooling in his chest, he met the speaker's gaze. "You got a problem?"

Hayden followed Mike's glare. "What's up, Gavin?"

"Nothing." Gavin smirked. "Just talking to Matt."

Mike clenched his fists. "Got something to say to my face?"

Gavin and Matt exchanged another smile.

"Nope," Gavin said. "Why don't you mind your own business?"

Mike took a step toward them, but Hayden held him back with a hand on his arm.

"You guys are up," Hayden said. pointing to the line. "Run your feet instead of your mouths."

"Whatever, *Captain*." Gavin laughed. They took their positions on the start line, bolting away when the whistle blew.

"Assholes," Mike said. He glanced at Hayden. "Go, team, right?"

Hayden shrugged. "If you really want to screw them over, run fast and get a spot on the 4X1. They've been trying for a year to replace me *and* our anchor graduated, so I'll bet they have their eye on making the cut."

Mike glanced at the end where Gavin and Matt high-fived the coach. "Looks like they think they've done it." The burn of adrenalin tingled in his gut and he smiled at Hayden. "For now."

Mike lined up with Hayden in the next group. He gave him a sideways glance. "Don't cry when I blow by you. It's nothing personal."

"Good luck with that," Hayden replied, laughing.

Mike focused on the coach. Despite the cool breeze blowing across the cinder track, sweat dripped down his back. The whistle blew and they lurched forward with the others. He finished just behind Hayden and a second in front of the rest. The coach checked his watch.

"Well done, Ryan." He slapped Mike on the shoulder. "Looks like we've found a new anchor, Bishop."

"I think you're right, Coach," Hayden said.

Mike smirked at the glares from Gavin and Matt. He elbowed Hayden as they walked to the infield to stretch. "Mission accomplished."

"Good. I'd hate to run with either of those pricks." Hayden pointed across the grass toward the other side of the track. "Here go the girls."

Mike followed his gesture and watched as Cindy, Molly, and several girls ran their hundreds. He'd seen Molly run the state cross country race last fall with a broken arm and a concussion and she *still* got second. He knew she was good. But seeing Cindy's long lean legs flashing in the sunshine as she blew past them all, Mike's chest filled with a glowing heat.

She was better. She was incredible. And she was *his* girlfriend.

Better yet, now everyone knew it.

Panting at the finish line, Cindy high-fived Molly. Hands on her hips, she turned toward him and waved.

He returned it, the heat spreading from his chest to his lower gut. "Damn, she's fast."

Hayden laughed. "Yeah, don't ever challenge her to a race. Not sure your manhood could handle losing to her."

"I could take her. Besides," Mike grinned, his eyes following Cindy as she walked toward the locker room with Molly. "If I threw the race, she'd kill me."

"Truth," Hayden said with his eyebrows raised. He waved toward the building. "C'mon. let's get cleaned up and get some food."

They met the girls outside the locker rooms.

"You guys want to get something to eat?" Hayden asked.

Cindy glanced at Mike. "I can't. I'm supposed to watch my little brothers. My mom has to go to the store."

Dammit.

"That's okay. We can go next time." He held Cindy's hand. "Right?"

She smiled "Of course."

"Now that you guys aren't hiding, let's go somewhere together for dinner on Friday." Molly said.

"Sure, we could try that new Chinese restaurant by the mall." Hayden brushed a strand of hair off Molly's face. "Is that okay with you?"

Molly nodded. "Perfect," she said.

Hayden kissed her fingertips.

Mike exchanged a glance with Cindy. "How does that sound to you, *daaarling*?" He held her hands to his chest.

"Oh, Mike," Cindy gushed in a breathy voice. "I would *love* to go to dinner with you on Friday."

He hugged her and replied in a fake, teary voice. "You've made me so happy."

Molly and Hayden laughed.

"We are not that bad," Hayden said, punching Mike on the arm.

Molly snorted. "Well, I'm not, but you are. Remember, you're seventeen going on seventy."

He tickled her waist. "You have no respect for my romantic nature."

She giggled and pulled away from him.

Mike put an arm around Cindy's waist. "She's right though. You make the rest of us look bad."

Cindy shook her head. "You look pretty good to me."

Hayden winked. "Nice one."

Groaning, Mike said, "Not you, too." He kissed her cheek but pulled away and cussed under his breath.

"What's wrong?" Cindy asked.

"Elijah," Mike mumbled, and Cindy turned to face her twin.

Staring down opponents on the soccer field was nothing new. As the goalie, he was the last man to beat, and he knew how to handle the pressure. But now, his stomach tightened. Elijah wasn't about to blast a soccer ball at his face. Instead, it would be one of his huge fists and they would cause more damage. And pain.

Still, showing fear wasn't an option. Mike straightened his shoulders and pulled Cindy to his side with an arm around her waist.

"Hell no," Elijah yelled. "Get your hands off my sister."

Cindy pushed herself in front of Mike. Hayden stepped up to Mike's side.

"This ain't your business, Hayden," Elijah said. He glared at Cindy. "What the hell are you doin'?"

She shoved Elijah's chest. "It *ain't* your business either."

"Stop, Cindy." Mike pulled her back with his hands on her shoulders.

"I said, don't touch her." Elijah brushed Cindy aside and pushed Mike.

Mike stumbled back a step and held up his hands. "Chill. I don't want to fight you."

"You ain't got a choice." Elijah stepped forward and bumped his chest into Mike's.

Cindy elbowed her way between them again. "Knock it *off*, Elijah. He's my boyfriend."

"Like hell he is. Get your ass home. And he'd best stay away from you." He pulled Cindy by the arm.

"Ow, let go!" She yanked it from his grip.

Wincing at Cindy's words, Mike moved between them this time, leaning into Elijah's face. "You keep *your* hands off her. That's her decision, not yours."

Hayden grabbed Mike's arm and pulled him back. "C'mon, Elijah. Mike's cool. Give him a chance."

Elijah shook his head. "He ain't dating my sister."

Cindy groaned. "Shut up. I can date whoever I want. You're not my boss."

Mike locked eyes with Elijah.

"Mama is." Elijah lifted his chin. "She told you no dudes."

Cindy laughed a humorless laugh. "Right. Just like she told *you* not to hang out with those idiots you call friends—drinking and getting high. What if she found out about that? Remember the boot camp?"

Mike bit back a laugh. Boot camp?

"You better not say anything." Elijah darted a glance at Mike then glared at her.

She took a step toward her twin, hands on her hips and head bobbing from side to side. "Then stay out of my business. Don't say anything about me either."

Elijah nodded but pointed a finger at Mike. "You better watch yourself."

Mike raised his eyebrows. "Meaning?"

"Meaning, if you hurt my sister, boot camp ain't gonna stop me from kicking your ass."

Cindy rolled her eyes. "Whatever, Elijah."

But Mike shrugged. "Point taken. But I won't ever hurt her." He pulled Cindy by the hips until her back rested against his chest.

Elijah pressed his lips together. "You got balls, man. Just remember, I'm watching."

Elijah strode away and Hayden blew out a breath. "Damn."

Cindy turned and hugged Mike. He put his arms around her and rested his cheek on her head. "Think he'll tell your mom?"

She shook her head. "He's scared to death of that boot camp. Mama isn't kidding about that."

Molly sighed. "I get it, your mom scares me, too. Come on, let's get changed. I'm starving." She kissed Hayden, and they went into the locker rooms.

Judging by Elijah's reaction, their mom was a definite threat to this relationship. Maybe he *shouldn't* encourage Cindy to tell her mom about them.

Mike kissed Cindy's cheek. "Will I see you later?" His stomach already ached from missing her.

She shrugged. "I don't know. If I can slip out after Mama gets back, I'll call you." She laid her head on his chest and he rubbed his hands up and down the warm skin of her bare arms.

"Okay, then maybe." He smiled, glad he could at least say a real goodbye in public this time. Leaning in, he kissed her soft lips.

The door opened and Andrea walked into Cindy's back.

"Oh, sorry I didn't…" She gaped at the goodbye scene she'd barged into. "Uh, I guess the gossip is true."

Cindy stared back, hands on her hips.

Mike frowned. "You got a problem, Andrea?"

Her eyes widened. "No, but you guys do. Everyone's talking about you." She glanced around the empty area. "And it's not all good. Just thought you might like the heads up."

Cindy squinted. "You can tell everyone I said to mind their own business."

"Hey, I told you. I don't have a problem. Do what you gotta do. I'm just telling you what I've heard." She waved and walked toward the parking lot.

Cindy pinched the bridge of her nose. "I told you this would happen."

He grabbed her hands. "And I told you, it doesn't matter what other people think."

"Okay. But you better get ready for a whole lot of stupid coming at us." She raised her eyebrows. "And with our tempers, that could cause problems."

"I promise to keep it in check." He drew an x on his chest.

"Heh. Me, too." She stood on her toes and kissed him. "I have to go."

"I know. I just don't want to say goodbye. I'll talk to you later."

She squeezed his hand and went into the locker room.

He pushed the boy's door open and went to his locker. Several guys watched him pass, not bothering to hide their smiles. He'd promised to keep his temper in check, but heat filled his face and he looked away—so he wouldn't start swinging.

Hayden sat on the bench putting on his street shoes. He glanced around at the others then met Mike's eyes. "You going to eat with us?"

Mike opened his locker and stared inside. "Looks like I have a snack right here." A package of Oreo cookies lay on his shoes. He gritted his teeth, ignoring the not-so-quiet laughter behind him.

Hayden grabbed the cookies. "Good, I'm hungry." He opened the package and bit into a cookie, then held them out to Mike. "Want one?"

Mike *wanted* to slam his fist into someone's face. Instead, he took an Oreo and turned to his left to toast Gavin with the treat. He held the cookie up into the air. "Thanks."

Gavin glared back, and Mike took a bite.

Hayden stood and grabbed his bag. "Get changed, I need real food." He waited for Mike and they left the locker room.

Outside Mike said, "Thanks. Your idea was better than fighting."

"They're idiots." Hayden threw his bag in his trunk and slammed the lid.

Mike dropped his bag into the passenger seat of his Camaro. "Why the hell is this such a big deal?" Anybody could see how great Cindy was.

Hayden shrugged. "People don't like change I guess." He waved at Molly walking toward him.

Mike's stomach burned. They had it so easy. "Don't tell anyone about this. I don't want it to upset Cindy."

Hayden nodded. "Gotcha."

"So, let's go eat. I'm starving." Molly asked Mike, "Are you coming?"

Hanging out with them would be like watching a romantic movie alone. Mike shook his head. "No, you guys have fun. I'll eat at home."

"You sure?" Hayden asked.

"Yeah. I have homework to do, anyway. I'll see you tomorrow."

"Alright, later."

Mike got into his car and leaned his head back on the seat. "Damn."

He started the car and pulled from the lot. Hayden was right, he needed to ignore his classmates for Cindy. But when he turned the corner, the Oreos rolled out of his open bag and onto the seat to mock him.

"Uhhgg!" He picked up the package but stopped before he threw it out the window. Using ignorance to fight ignorance would make him an idiot, too. Gavin put them in his locker to hurt him, but it would only work if Mike let it. Besides, he smiled and grabbed another cookie, he loved chocolate.

CHAPTER FOUR

CINDY

Cindy drove home with a death grip on the wheel.

"Dammit. Elijah," she said to herself. "You had better not say anything."

By the time she reached her house, she'd thought of ten-thousand ways this could backfire. They all ended with Cindy on house arrest from her mom until she turned fifty.

Inside, her little brothers sat with her dad in the living room. Josh lay sprawled on the black leather couch, one skinny leg thrown over the back. Gabe hugged his knees, sitting on the floor in front of the TV, his eyes glued to the cartoons. He moved slightly side-to-side as He-Man battled Skeletor, their voices blaring from the speaker.

But Benny curled up on Daddy's lap, holding his favorite stuffed teddy bear, with one hand and sucking the thumb on the other. Her daddy's head shook back and forth slightly, the movement taking Benny's little body with it.

A warm slash of pain hit Cindy's chest and her breath hitched. She could almost pretend her dad was just rocking her brother. Almost.

They all looked up at the sound of her feet on the linoleum.

"Hi, Cinny," Benny said from his place on their dad.

She grinned. *Can't compete with Daddy.*

"Hi, Benny." She fell onto the couch and grabbed Josh's foot, tickling it with her fingertips.

He laughed, kicking into the air. "Hey! Stop!"

"I just wanted to see if you were awake," Cindy said. "You were all so quiet I thought you were napping."

Gabe shook his head. "We aren't babies like Benny. We don't take naps."

Cindy and her dad chuckled, but Benny sat up, removing his thumb from his mouth with a wet squelch. "I not a baby. Right, Daddy?"

"No, you aren't. You're a strong man. Gonna do great things in this world." He kissed the top of Benny's head and met Cindy's gaze. "You and Elijah make sure of that for me, okay?"

Cindy rubbed her neck. "Daddy, *you* can make sure of that. You'll be here for it."

Before he could do more than give her a sad smile, Elijah came through the front door.

"Hey, son. Thought you had studying to do tonight with your friends."

Elijah frowned at Cindy, then nodded to their dad. "Change of plans."

She crossed her arms. *Right. He came here to give me a hard time.*

Mama rushed into the living room, slipping her arms into her windbreaker. She smiled at Cindy and Elijah.

"Oh good, you're both here. Take care of the boys while we go to the doctor. There's a casserole in the oven for dinner. It should be done in half an hour." She moved behind Daddy's chair and grabbed the rubber-coated handles.

"Sure, Mama. Need help?" Elijah dipped his head toward the wheelchair. "You know, getting outside and into the car?"

"I can still walk some." Their dad said, his smile fading. He kissed Benny's cheek, then lifted him off his lap and onto the floor. "I'm not that bad yet."

Elijah shook his head. "I… I didn't mean that, Daddy. I just thought, you know the chair is heavy going down the ramp and—"

Cindy pressed her lips together. *Way to go idiot.*

"We got it." Their mom pushed their dad toward the front door. "We should be back in a little over an hour."

Cindy stood from the couch. "Don't worry, I'll take care of everything." She glared at Elijah.

"Thank you, baby girl." Her dad waved as her mom pushed him out the front door toward the ramp.

Elijah shut the door behind them and turned to Cindy. "We need to talk."

"Don't." She scooped Benny up and sat with him in her dad's recliner, settling him in her lap. "I told you, it's none of your business."

Sighing, he sank onto the couch by Josh.

Cindy pretended to watch the TV, but He-Man wasn't enough to distract her. She knew what Elijah would say and it was bogus. He didn't even know Mike, so how could he say anything about their relationship? From the corner of her eye, she caught Elijah bouncing his knee, crossing and uncrossing his arms.

After his fifth heaving sigh, Cindy glared at him. "Don't blow a gasket. Say what you want so I can get back to ignoring you."

"C'mon, Cindy," Elijah said. "There's stuff you need to know."

"Ha! You think you know more about him than I do?"

Benny turned in her lap. "Who's him?"

She kissed his cheek. "Nobody. Why don't you go wash up for dinner? Josh and Gabe, you, too."

Benny slid from her lap and ran to the bathroom in the hall. Groaning, the other two followed him. Cindy stood just as the timer on the oven beeped.

"I'll get it. You get the plates." She headed for the stove.

"I know how you are." Elijah glanced toward the hall and spoke in a lower voice. "You like him, so you'll believe anything he says."

"And why shouldn't I? He's never lied to me." She grabbed the oven mitts and opened the door, squinting as the wave of heat washed over her face. The spicy scent of Mama's bubbling cheeseburger casserole joined the heat and sent her stomach rumbling.

"Maybe not. But guys talk. I've heard things, and I don't like 'em."

"Right. Like they talked about Hayden, lying about him and Molly?" Cindy rolled her eyes and set the hot dish on the table. "You shouldn't believe everything you hear."

"He's a player, Cindy." Elijah laid a hand on her shoulder and frowned. "I don't want him to play you."

33

"He's not playing me." Mike's face rose in her mind. The one in the woods when she'd agreed to expose their relationship—the insecurity, the hope, and the joy—that wasn't the face of a player.

"Yeah, says *every* girl who thinks they changed the jerk." Elijah snorted.

"You don't know him. I do. End of story."

"You know 'bout him, too. Don't lie to yourself. You've seen who he dates."

"What's that supposed to mean?"

"Man, he only dates girls like him. Rich and white. He don't know 'bout our life."

Cindy clenched her teeth. "*This* is our life. We live in the suburbs. It's no different than his."

"You know what I mean."

"Yeah," she said with her hands on her hips, "and I think that's a shit way to look at this."

"Why does he want to date you?"

"Oh, I'm not *datable*?"

"No, I mean, yes but… you don't fit his shallow mold."

"White and rich?" Cindy said with a sneer.

"Exactly."

"You're an idiot." She grabbed the milk from the refrigerator and poured three glasses for the boys. "Maybe you should try getting to know Mike before you judge him."

Elijah sat in his chair, leaning back and stretching his legs. "Pass. I ain't hanging out with him. You know what he's after. Same thing he got from the other girls."

"That…" Cindy cleared her throat. "That's not true. And he knows I won't."

She wasn't ignorant. She'd heard the rumors. And Mike had never denied that he had… experience. But he knew she wasn't ready and had never pressured her to do anything. Still, in moments of doubt…

"You better not."

"That's none of your business either."

"How many?"

She smoothed the napkins. "How many what?"

"How many girls he been with?"

"I'm not talking about this with you."

Elijah snorted. "You don't know."

Her cheeks prickled with heat. She returned the milk to the fridge and slammed the door. "Besides, people change."

"They don't change *that* much," Elijah mumbled.

The boys ran back into the kitchen, jumping into their seats around the table. Cindy dished a serving on each of their plates then filled her own. She jammed a bite into her mouth, burning her tongue and adding to the heat in her chest.

"All I'm saying is, I'm watching. One mistake and it's over." Elijah sat and scooped three heaping piles of casserole onto his plate.

"Not your call." She met Benny's curious stare and pointed at his plate. "Eat. Be careful. It's hot."

"What are you talking about?" Josh asked.

"Nunya," Cindy said with a forced smile.

"What's that?" Gabe said with a frown.

"Nunya business. Now eat so you can take your baths." She took another steaming bite, watching Elijah's face. "You sure this isn't a color thing?"

"Nah. Well…a little. But I could deal. If he had a clue 'bout us." He shrugged, pushing his food around his plate.

"So you're saying Jamal is a better option because he *has a clue*?"

This earned a laugh from Elijah. "That boy don't have a clue about *anything*. He's a hoser."

"Believe me, I know." She took a sip of her milk and eyed her little brothers, hoping they wouldn't understand any of this. "So *my* choice is the better option. You just need to give it a chance."

He was quiet for a moment, then his breath whistled out his nose. "I don't want you to get hurt."

Her insides twisted and she struggled to swallow as she met her twin's gaze. His opinion mattered, more so than anyone else in her family. But how could she convince him to accept this?

"I won't." Cindy sighed. "Look, it's been six months. Things are good. *Really* good. Don't worry."

"Too late." Elijah smirked. "You know I won't lie to you, right?"

She scrunched her eyebrows. "Of course."

"Then don't get mad later if I get the 411 and say something you don't wanna hear."

"As long as you never say *I told you so*, we're good."

"Deal." He grinned. "I got your back."

"Thanks." She scooped another cheesy bite and swallowed it with the lump in her throat.

Elijah frowned for a moment then looked at the boys. "Eat up dudes. I'll take you outside for a while."

"Can we play team tag?" Benny asked, wiping his hamburger-smeared face with his hand.

"You can't cry when you get tagged," Josh said.

"I don't cry." Benny lifted his little chin.

Gabe nodded. "Yeah, and Mr. Boo Boo can't play."

Benny hugged his teddy bear and looked at Elijah.

"Leave him inside. You're on my team, 'lil man. I got *your* back, too," Elijah said.

Benny clapped his hands while Josh and Gabe argued with Elijah about the teams. Blinking away the tingle in her eyes, Cindy finished her dinner.

Got your back should be their family motto.

****

Later that week after track, Cindy followed Mike to their cars. She threw her bag in the back seat and turned to hug him. Head on his chest, she breathed in the musky smell of his shirt.

"So, what do we do now?"

He tickled her back with his fingertips and his chuckle rumbled under her ear. "I have an idea. But I'm not sure you'll agree."

"Try me."

"Will you come to my house for dinner?"

"Uhm, will your parents be there?"

"Yes."

Her heart jumped to her throat. "You want me to meet them?"

"Mine don't care if I date, so we have nothing to hide from them."

She chewed the inside of her cheek for a long moment.

"Is it too soon?" Mike asked.

"No, but… are you sure they'll be okay with… me?"

"Mom will ask you a hundred questions and Dad'll tell bad jokes. They'll love you."

"Well, okay." She sucked in her lower lip. "Mama thinks I'm going to Molly's."

"She'll cover for you, right?"

Cindy nodded. She caught Molly's eye and pointed to Mike then herself. Molly gave her a thumbs-up.

Mike smiled and pushed off the car. "Come on, follow me." He kissed her, then got into his car.

She followed him to his house, deep breathing to keep from totally freaking out. The mansion-like houses of his neighborhood did little to ease her anxiety. It was easy to ignore their different economic classes when they were at school but faced with the ornate homes and professionally landscaped lawns, reality slapped her in the face.

Mike pulled into his wide driveway, continuing into the three-car garage. Cindy parked in the space behind him and he ran back to her car, smiling like a five-year-old at Christmas. She got out trying to return it, but her lips only quivered.

"What if they don't like me?" she whispered.

He hugged her slim shoulders, kissing her neck then her cheek and lips. She responded with a soft sigh.

"Everything will be fine."

They walked along the brick sidewalk toward the front door, her hand in his. She lifted her chin as he opened the ornate wooden door.

Breath caught in her throat as they stepped inside. She gulped to push it back to her lungs where it belonged. It wasn't the house that made her palms sweat and her knees shake. Unbeknownst to her parents, she'd gone to a few of Mike's parties, and the rooms looked the same, minus the drunk teens making out or dancing.

A voice called out from the kitchen. "Mike? Is that you?"

Cindy froze on the ceramic-tiled foyer.

"It's okay." He kissed her fingers and gave them a squeeze. "Hey, Mom," he called back. He pulled her toward the kitchen, still holding her hand and grinning like he'd just won the lottery.

Cindy tried to melt into the floor.

He led her through the lavish front room with pale peach walls and cream-colored carpet so soft it felt like walking on marshmallows. Past the green leather sectional which probably cost as much as her car. A huge wall of windows across from the entry flooded the room with sunshine and warmth.

Despite the fresh flowery scent from the candle burning on the table and the calm quiet of the room, the butterflies in her stomach twisted like they were on speed.

In the kitchen, Mike's mom stood at the sink, rinsing lettuce in a colander. Her long blond hair fell in a perfect sheet to the middle of her back. Cindy gaped from the perfect hair to the statuesque figure in the skin-tight, Jordache jeans and light blue cashmere sweater. His mom stood every inch of six feet tall, almost as tall as Mike. Facing away, she hadn't noticed Cindy yet.

"Mom, I have someone for you to meet."

Cindy tried to take a deep breath but only managed a short gasp. What the hell? With her big mouth, she never had trouble talking to people. This shouldn't be so freaking hard. She tightened her hold on Mike's hand, hoping the one he held wasn't as sweaty as the other one trembling at her side.

His mom turned from the sink and smiled.

"This is my girlfriend, Cindy. This is my mom, Renee."

Cindy smiled back. But three things happened at once—his mom's gaze fell to their joined hands, her smile became robotic, and Mike sighed.

Cindy gulped. *We are so screwed.*

She tried to pull her hand from Mike's, but he squeezed tighter.

His mom raised her startled eyes and nodded. "Hello, Cindy. It's nice to meet you." She held out her hand.

"Hello, Mrs. Ryan. It's nice to meet you, too." Mike had to let go so Cindy could shake, but he slid his arm around her waist. She wished he wouldn't touch her so his mom would stop staring.

"Please call me Renee." She glanced at Mike. "This is a surprise. I didn't know you were dating anyone."

Cindy hid a grimace. Did she always know when Mike dated? She sure didn't keep up with the parties he threw at their house when she and his dad were out of town.

Mike glanced at Cindy. "Well, now you do."

"Thanks for letting me in the loop," Renee replied with a laugh. She picked up the bowl of lettuce. "Will you join us for dinner, Cindy?"

"Yes, thank you."

Rene pointed toward the French doors on the other side of the large kitchen. "Your father is grilling out back. Why don't you go introduce Cindy?" Smiling, she set the salad on the kitchen table and returned to the cabinet.

Mike pulled Cindy by the waist toward the back yard. He whispered in her ear. "Come on. I promise, he'll be easier than my mom."

"Hmph. Are you sure?"

He placed a kiss on her cheek. "Yeah, he's cool. Mom's high maintenance."

"She and my mom would get along then."

He held the door open, and she stepped outside onto the back patio. Flat gray stones stretched along the entire back of the ranch-style house. They extended twenty feet out until they reached the concrete surrounding the huge kidney-shaped in-ground pool. Grass, mostly filled in with the green of spring, began at the edge of the far side of the concrete along the pool and stretched about twenty feet until it met the woods bordering their property.

Groupings of padded seats and lounge chairs dotted the patio. The rose bushes were just sprouting leaves, and the flower beds were still bare, but Cindy could imagine the beauty of this yard on a sunny summer day.

She hoped she would still be alive to see it. Doubtful if her mother found out about Mike.

The "grill" was part of an outdoor kitchen, complete with a sink, refrigerator, and granite counters. Mike's parties had never extended outside so she had never seen the backyard. She cleared her throat and wet her dry lips with the tip of her tongue.

Mike's dad flipped a burger and glanced up. His eyes widened for a moment, then he winked at Mike. He set the flipper on the counter and wiped his hands with the apron he wore over his jeans and polo shirt.

"Hello there." The warmth in his smile melted the icy feeling in Cindy's chest.

Mike led her over. "Dad, this is Cindy."

She expected him to extend his hand. Instead, he pulled her by the shoulders and gave her a hug.

"Nice to meet you, Cindy. You can call me Greg."

When he released her, she swallowed—hard. "Uh, well, thanks. It's nice to meet you, too, uh Greg."

Mike laughed. "Dad, give her time to get used to you." He held her hand and scooted her closer to him. "My dad is an old hippy. You know, peace and love, that stuff."

"I'm not a hippy. I'm just friendly." He winked at Cindy. "I hope you're hungry. Burgers will be ready in ten minutes."

Cindy said, "Thanks, I'm starving."

"Ahh, a girl who's not afraid to eat. Today it seems like everyone is always on a diet and drinking Tab." Greg punched Mike's arm. "I doubt she'll eat like you and your brothers though. I better make a couple more, just in case."

Mike asked, "Is Tony home?"

Pointing to the grill full of burgers his dad chuckled. "He came home for the weekend. Why do you think I have so many burgers?"

Cindy's stomach dropped. *Looks like I'm meeting the whole family.*

Mike squeezed her shoulders. "Cindy can have one of my burgers. I don't mind sharing."

"He must be serious about you. My boys rarely give up food," Greg said with a grin.

Cindy smiled at Mike.

"She's the only one tough enough to put up with me."

Heat prickled her cheeks, and she chuckled, glad the blush wouldn't show too much. "You aren't lying." When Mike hugged her in front of his dad, the prickle became a flame.

"Later, Dad." Mike pulled her by the hands. "I have someone else you need to meet."

"Okay." Her stomach flipped at the serious look on his face. "Why do you look nervous?"

"Well, his opinion is important, more so than my parents."

"Who is it?" she asked.

His lips twitched. "You'll see."

They walked along the back of the house and entered through another set of doors that led into the living room. Then they headed toward the basement stairs. At the bottom of the steps, Mike turned right, and they entered a cozy den, complete with overstuffed black leather couches, a huge entertainment center surrounding a 32-inch console RCA TV, and a turntable and stereo that any professional DJ would drool over.

She looked around the empty basement. "So, who am I meeting?"

"Hold on," he whispered. "That can wait."

Mike pulled her to him and kissed her so long, she forgot she was waiting for an answer to her question. Then, something rubbed against her ankle and she yelped, jumping away from Mike.

"What the…?" She looked at the gray and black cat weaving between Mike's legs.

He lifted the cat. "This is who I wanted you to meet. Bonkers."

For such a small cat, it had a loud purr, like a small lawnmower. He rubbed his chin on Mike's face.

"I didn't know you had a cat. How come I never saw it at one of your parties?" She held her fingers out and Bonkers sniffed them with his little black nose.

"I always lock him away, so he doesn't get hurt." Mike rubbed Bonkers' head, and the purring increased. "Right, dude? Don't want you to get lost."

She smirked and Mike's face turned red. "I mean, my mom would kill me if something happened to him."

"Uh-huh." She tried to hold back her laugh, but Mike's face looked hot enough to light a match. She covered her mouth to stifle her giggle.

Mike smiled. "Fine, laugh it up. But if you tell anyone, I'll deny it *and* show up at your house to tell your parents who I am." He held Bonkers toward her. "Want to hold him?"

She nodded. "Will he let me? I've never held a cat before. My dad's allergic and my mom isn't a pet person." She and Elijah had begged for a dog when they were younger to no avail.

Mike shrugged. "That's the test."

"Oh, without his approval we're done, is that it?"

"He's a good judge of character." Mike's lips twitched again.

She reached for Bonkers and Mike passed her the warm ball of fur. When Bonkers purred and snuggled into her neck, she rubbed her cheek against the soft fur of his head. "Do I pass?"

Mike scratched Bonkers behind the ears. "I knew you would. He likes anyone who holds him."

"Jerk." He reached for the cat and she pulled away. "I think I like him better right now." She sat on the couch, holding Bonkers on her lap. He curled into a ball and closed his eyes.

Mike sat next to her and put his arm around her shoulders. "Sorry, I was just teasing." He kissed her ear.

Cindy closed her eyes, stroking Bonkers to the rhythm of Mike's kisses. "Maybe I'll forgive you."

"Thanks." He nudged her with his shoulder. "I'm sorry if this was weird. My parents aren't normal."

She giggled. "Does your dad always hug strangers?"

Mike chuckled. "Yep. He doesn't believe in handshakes. I'm not sure how he and mom ended up together. She's uptight."

He placed a line of kisses along her jaw.

Goosebumps covered her neck, and the speed infused butterflies migrated back to her stomach. Cindy pulled away and Bonkers jumped from her lap. She stared back into Mike's sea blue eyes. "Won't your parents come down here?" Catching them as they made out on the couch wouldn't endear her to his mom.

"No. This space is for me and my brothers. Why?" He ran a finger along her collar bone. "You have something else in mind?"

She slapped his hand. "No, it wouldn't be a good idea for us to get caught together." She raised her eyebrows. "Your mom doesn't like me."

He frowned. "Why do you think that?"

"You saw her face when she met me."

He shook his head. "She liked you. She invited you to dinner."

"I heard you sigh when she looked at me."

"That's because she looked at us the same way she always does when she sees me with a girl." He traced her lips with his finger. "She thinks I should still be seven and playing with cars."

"I didn't realize you'd brought so many girls to meet your parents."

He tilted his head and frowned. "Only a couple. And I never introduced them as my girlfriend. Those girls weren't important. Not like you."

She cocked one eyebrow. "Am I more important than Bonkers?"

"Well, I don't know if I'd go that far." He moved his hands to her waist and pulled her closer.

"Thanks. It's nice to know I rank below a cat." She wrapped her arms around his neck.

"No, you don't," he whispered. "I couldn't do this with Bonkers."

He leaned back onto the arm of the couch, pulling her chest on top of his. Kissing her, he put one hand behind her neck and squeezed her against him with the other on her lower back.

She pressed closer still, her body tingling. "Mike," she breathed against his lips.

"Hmm?"

"You know I've never... I mean..." *Oh shut up*, her body said.

"I know." He stopped kissing her and raised back up, smiling. "I was just showing you the benefits of dating you over Bonkers."

Cindy tried to grin, but Elijah's comments came back to her.

"What's wrong?" Mike whispered.

She shook her head. "Nothing."

"Something," he replied, raising his eyebrows. "Talk to me."

Inexperience filled her face with heat. Holding his hand, she lowered her gaze to their fingers. "It's just... I know you've done it. And I haven't and I was just wondering..."

She looked up. Red stained Mike's cheeks.

"That's not why I'm dating you." He rested his forehead against hers. "I just like being with you."

A tingling sensation crept across the back of her neck and onto her face. She cleared her throat and gave a nervous laugh.

"That's not it. Like… how many *times* have you..."

"Oh." He rubbed the back of his neck. "Why do you want to know that?"

"Don't you think I should?" She stared at his chest, unable to look him in the eye. "You know my side. I want to know yours."

"Well, I… guess that's fair but—"

A scream tore through the basement, echoing off the paneled walls.

"Mike! Mike! Let's play Donkey Kong! We have a few minutes before dinner's re…" Mike's little brother raced around the corner, then skidded to a stop in front of them.

"Perfect timing, Drew." Mike groaned, but a smile lit up his face.

Cindy frowned. *Relieved much?*

Drew wrinkled his nose. "Eww. Why are you holding hands? Girls are gross!" He stuck out his tongue and made gagging noises.

Sagging against the couch, she mock glared at the miniature Mike in front of her and ruffled his blond hair. "Hey, we aren't that bad. You don't mind playing Nintendo with me."

"Oh yeah, during the parties I'm not supposed to tell Mom and Dad about. That's different." Drew smiled at Mike and his blue eyes turned impish with his smile. "Is she your *girrrlfriend*?"

Cindy snorted and Mike reached out. Drew tried to dodge his grasp, but he caught him and pulled him onto the couch.

"Come here, dude." He rubbed his knuckles on Drew's head while Drew laughed. "For your information, yes, she is my girlfriend, so be nice."

"I am nice. And Cindy's cool, I guess, for a girl," Drew declared.

Cindy smirked. "He's only six. Isn't he too young for you to be teaching him your pick-up lines?"

"Never too young to start." Mike hugged Drew to his chest, poking him in the stomach. "And I'm glad you like my girlfriend."

The huge smile on Mike's face erased the rest of the sex-talk tension and stirred the butterflies in her stomach again. Drew liked her. His dad liked her. His mom, well, at least she didn't kick her out right away.

Maybe sharing their relationship *would* work out. Maybe it wasn't as bad as she thought. Maybe it would be easier than she expected.

"What the *hell*?"

The booming voice exploded the happy bubble she'd blown around herself. She spun around toward the stairs and met the dark eyes of Mike's oldest brother.

Just as tall as Mike but opposite in every way from Drew and Mike's fair coloring, Tony glared at them. His dark eyebrows made one straight angry line over his brown eyes as he glanced between her and Mike. She lifted her chin and stared back, but inside her chest deflated.

So much for easy.

CHAPTER FIVE

MIKE

Mike let go of Drew and he ran, bouncing on his feet in front of Tony.

"This is Cindy. She's Mike's girlfriend." Oblivious to Tony's angry face, Drew continued in his excited voice. "She's super good at playing Nintendo."

Cindy tried to pull her hand away, but Mike held tighter. He raised an eyebrow and met Tony's eyes.

Tony sat in the recliner across from them. "Hey, Drew, go see if dinner's ready. I'm hungry."

"But I want to talk with you guys." His bottom lip jutted forward.

"We'll be up in a minute. Save me a seat."

"Okay!"

Mike smirked as Drew ran up the stairs. He'd do anything for Tony's approval—like Mike used to before he learned his brother was an asshole.

Tony gazed back and forth between them. "So, you're dating?"

"Got a problem with it?" Mike asked.

Tony smirked and looked back at Cindy. "Kind of."

"Sucks for you." He stood and pulled Cindy with him. "Let's go eat."

She clutched his hand and nodded. He wanted to punch his stupid brother. Tony's sarcastic laugh increased the urge.

Tony shook his head. "I always knew you had idiot potential, but I'd hoped you'd be more like Mom than Dad."

Mike turned back and took a step toward Tony. "What the hell does that mean?"

"Mike." Cindy clutched his hand and held him back.

"You always do what you want and never think about how it affects anyone else."

"Who I date doesn't affect you. And it's none of your business either."

"I think it is." Tony curled his lip.

"Oh really? Why?" If he said it, the punch to his face would be his own damn fault.

Cindy pulled on his hand again. "Come on, let's go upstairs."

"Listen to your *girlfriend*. You don't want to start something with me you can't finish." Tony crossed his arms. Muscles bulged underneath his sweater and one twitched in his jaw.

"Finishing wouldn't be a problem."

"Mike, don't. Let's… let's go."

The uncharacteristic tremble in her voice stopped him. He glanced at her face, his stomach aching with guilt. Damn his stupid brother. And damn himself for putting her through this. "Okay."

He ignored Tony's chuckle and led her up the stairs. At the top he hugged her, whispering in her ear. "I'm sorry. He's way out of line."

She sniffled. "Yeah."

"He's wrong, he's the idiot for not giving us a chance."

"This was a bad idea. I should go." She pulled away and wiped her eyes.

"No, I want you to stay. Tony can piss off. His opinion doesn't matter."

"It should matter. He's your brother."

He rubbed a finger on her cheek. "So, if Elijah hates me are you going to dump me?"

"Well, no. But family is important."

"You're important." He kissed her, holding her soft cheeks in his hands. "And your opinion is what matters to me. We got this. You and me, together."

"I don't want you to fight with your brother or anyone."

"I can handle him."

"But you shouldn't have—"

He covered her mouth with his hand and gave her a crooked grin. "We. Got. This."

Taking a deep breath, she nodded. "All right. Yeah. We do."

"Good. That's the stubborn girl I love. Now let's go eat. I'm starving and my dad's burgers *are* the best." He took a step toward the kitchen, but Cindy jerked his hand again, stopping him.

"What did you say?" She stared at him with wide eyes.

He wrinkled his brow. "My dad's burgers are the best?"

"No, before that," she whispered.

The words rewound in his head and he smiled. "You heard me."

"I'd like to hear it again." She took a step toward him.

A warm bubble filled his chest and the words came easier than breathing. "I love you."

"Have you been taking romantic line lessons from Hayden?"

Heat prickled his cheeks. "No, it sort of slipped out. But I meant it."

She wrapped her arms around his waist and laid her head on his chest. "You know what?"

"Chicken butt?"

She laughed. "No, I love you, too."

"Then this should be a piece of cake."

"Or maybe a pie in the face. You haven't met my family."

"Yet," he said.

She pulled back, frowning. "Yet."

The smell of grilled burgers wafted from the kitchen and Mike took her hand. "Now that this is all cleared up let's go. If we hurry, we can get the biggest burgers."

In the kitchen, his parents sat with Drew at the farmhouse table.

His mom looked up. "Is Tony coming?" She dished salad onto Drew's plate then added some to hers.

"Who cares? More burgers for us if he doesn't." Mike scooted out a chair for Cindy, then took the seat next to her. He met his dad's curious glance with a frown, put a burger on Cindy's plate, and took one for himself.

Tony entered the room and smirked at Cindy, taking the seat next to Drew.

Mike glanced at her, wanting to give her encouragement. But she stared back at Tony with her chin up, and a muscle twitching in her delicate jaw. Tony looked away.

Their dad asked, "Did you meet Cindy, Tony?" His gaze bounced between the three of them.

"Yeah. We met downstairs."

Sounds of chewing filled the air and Mike nudged Cindy's leg with his own. She side-eyed him then took a drink of her water.

Drew broke the quiet. "Do you eat burgers at your house, Cindy?"

"Sure." She smiled at his dad. "Ours aren't ever this good though."

"Thanks," his dad said, beaming.

"I told you." Mike laughed. "Why did you ask, Drew? Did Dad want you to set him up for a compliment?"

Drew shrugged. "I thought maybe chocolate people ate different things."

His mom gasped and his dad's burger fell to the plate. Mike felt the heat spread from his forehead to his neck. But Tony openly smiled.

"Drew, that's not a nice thing to say." His mom's face matched the ketchup bottle on the table.

"It's okay, Renee." Cindy laughed then smiled at Drew. "Maybe some chocolate people do, but burgers are my favorite. Chocolate *and* vanilla people eat weird stuff."

Mike relaxed with her choice of adjectives. His mom, guzzling her water, still looked like she wanted to crawl under the table.

Drew chewed his burger, nodding his head. "I know. My friend likes to eat peanut butter and mayonnaise sandwiches. That's disgusting."

Cindy pointed her fork at Drew. "Oh, I have one better than that. I had a friend who put ketchup on their mashed potatoes."

"Ewww. Gross." Then he tilted his head. "But... French fries come from potatoes, so maybe they were onto something."

"Next time Mom makes them you can try it," Mike said.

"Stick to butter," their dad interjected. "I don't think your mother would like to see her potatoes become an experiment."

She shook her head. "No. Save the ketchup for the fries."

Tony made a disgusted noise in the back of his throat. "Can we talk about something else?"

Drew giggled. "Why? Are you grossed out?"

"Yeah," Tony looked at Cindy with narrowed eyes. "Totally."

Mike clenched his fist under the table.

Cindy smirked. "I guess Tony and I are different, Drew. I don't get grossed out as easy."

"That's not the only difference," Tony muttered.

"Right, she's way better looking than you, too." Mike smiled at Tony's glare. "And she can run faster."

Drew laughed, but Tony curled his lip.

Their dad sighed. "Speaking of vanilla and chocolate, who's ready for dessert?"

Drew and Cindy raised their hands.

Mike grabbed another burger. "Not me, I'm still hungry."

His mom rolled her eyes. "Tell me something I don't know."

"I'll go get the ice cream." His dad saluted, casting a glance between Tony and Cindy before going to the kitchen.

Cindy said, "Wait until track gets going. He'll be hungry all the time. My mom says the school should give extra meals for the runners to make up for it."

"That would cut down the grocery bills, wouldn't it?" his mom said, giving Cindy a smile.

Tony barked out a sarcastic laugh. "Mike doesn't need a free meal from the school."

"Dude," Mike said. "It was a joke."

"Tony knows that." His mom frowned at Tony. "*Don't* you?"

"Sure, Mom." He pushed his seat back and stood. "I'm going out for a while. I'll see you later."

Drew watched him leave then turned to Mike. "What's his problem? He's being a jerk."

"Drew," his mom scolded.

But Mike laughed. "Yes, he is. Guess he can't have ice cream."

"Good, more for me." Drew rubbed his hands together.

His dad came back in carrying bowls and balancing two gallon-sized frosty containers. He set them on the table. "Okay, open for business."

After ice cream, and one round of *stories about Mike when he was little*, his parents said their goodbyes and Mike led Cindy to the front porch. Pulling her next to him on the swing, he buried his face in her neck. "I wish you could stay longer."

"Me, too. But I gotta get home. Mama's probably been wondering where I've been."

"What will you tell her?"

"Another lie." She looked at their hands. "I hate that."

"There's something you can do about that."

"It's not that simple." She glanced at her car.

"Are you ever going to explain that?"

"There isn't time." She pursed her lips for a second and met his gaze. "We can talk about it later when you have time to answer *my* question, too."

"Yeah, I guess you're right." His gut churned though. The answer to her question was probably more complicated. Or at least would complicate things.

"I have to go."

"Alright. I'll see you tomorrow." He kissed her and she kissed him back, but he sensed her restraint. But what was it in response to—Tony or him?

She touched his cheek and stood from the porch swing. "See you tomorrow."

A hollow feeling filled his chest as he watched her walk to the car. She turned to wave as she got in, and he lifted his hand. The familiar ache set in and he took a deep breath to ease the pressure then went back inside—at least there he had ice cream.

CHAPTER SIX

CINDY

Driving home, Cindy grabbed her New Order cassette and shoved it into the player on her stereo. Cranking the volume up, she sang along for a minute then laughed.

"We might not have a love *triangle*, but it sure has been bizarre."

Cindy parked in her spot in the driveway. Inside, her mom waited at the kitchen table holding a mug of steaming coffee between her hands. She had the newspaper spread out across the table, eyes closed, and her head resting on the back of the chair. She still wore her factory uniform, dark jeans, and blue polo shirt. Molly's mom worked at the same factory and made the uniform look like Paris' latest gift to the fashion world. But her mom, with five kids and a sick husband, just looked tired.

"Hey, Mama." Cindy hugged her around the neck from behind.

She opened her eyes and patted Cindy's hand. "Hey, baby girl."

Cindy kissed her cheek. "You want me to do anything for you, Mama?"

"No. I'm fine." Yawning, she stretched her arms above her head. Her mom blew on, then sipped the coffee. Cindy sat next to her.

"You were at Molly's a long time."

"Yeah, we just wanted to hang out, you know. Girl time." Cindy chewed on her thumbnail.

"How was school?"

"Same old same old." Cindy sighed, eager to change the subject. "Can't wait to get outta there."

"Don't wish your life away. It'll pass fast enough on its own."

"Maybe, but high school is boring." And she could be free with Mike.

"Well, I have something that might make it more fun."

"What is it?"

"Some good news." Her mom set the cup on the table and turned to take Cindy's hands into hers. "Your daddy and I talked about it and we both think it's time to let you date."

Dating? As in boys? As in Mike "Uh, what?"

A smile filled her mom's face. "It was your daddy's idea. He finally convinced me."

Adrenaline rushed to Cindy's head, but she shook it back down. There had to be a catch.

"You said boys were nothing but trouble."

"I know. And maybe some boys are." Her mom dropped her gaze to the table. "But your daddy's worried about the time he has left, and he wants to see that you find someone to treat you right. To take care of you when he's gone."

A flood of emotions crashed down on Cindy. She clung to the anger to pull her back to the surface. "First of all, I don't need anyone to take care of me. And daddy has lots of time left."

She pushed back her chair and walked to the sink, glaring at the sunny backyard beyond the window. Jeez, it wasn't like she would get married at seventeen.

"Cindy, you know that isn't true. No sense in lying to yourself."

"I'm not lying."

"Yes, you are."

"He's going to be fine. It just takes time to heal. That's all."

Cindy bit her bottom lip. She wouldn't give up hope—even if her mom had.

Her mom stood, pulling Cindy into her arms.

"You're strong. Just like I wanted you to be. Taking care of everyone." She held Cindy by the shoulders. "But it's time you faced the future and took care of yourself. And that means preparing for what's to come."

"Mama—"

"Let's talk about this later." Her mom smiled and wiped the tear from Cindy's cheek. "I have a surprise. You are going on a date."

"A d-date?" Had they found out about Mike? Did Elijah tell them?

Her mom's smile grew. "He'll be here in an hour, so you better get ready."

"Who'll be here?"

"Your date. His name's Tavis. I work with his mama."

"What?" Cindy opened her mouth. "You set me up?"

Her mom laughed. "Yep. You can thank me later."

Thank her? More like kill her. "Mama, I'm not going on a blind date!"

She pulled away from her mom and paced the kitchen. *This can't be happening.*

"You are. Now go shower and get ready."

"But, Mama, I have a…" In her panic, the forbidden word almost slipped out. "I have a test tomorrow. I need to study."

"He can bring you home early." Her mom clapped her hands. "You're gonna like him. He's in college and has a job."

With a huge effort, Cindy restrained from rolling her eyes. He could be a millionaire like Donald Trump, and she wouldn't care.

"Shouldn't I get to pick who I go out with?" She struggled to draw a breath of the thickening air.

"Hmph. You don't go to school with anyone like him. He's a good man. Your daddy approves, too."

The creek of the wheelchair wheels on the kitchen tile made Cindy jump. She spun around to face her dad.

"Daddy approves what?" he asked with a knowing smile. "Tavis sounds like a nice young man. Perfect for my lil' princess."

Unable to speak past the lump in her throat, her gaze bounced between her parents' smiling faces.

Elijah entered the kitchen and jerked to a stop. "What's up?"

"Don't ask," Cindy said with a groan.

Her mom answered. "Your sister has a date tonight."

Cindy met her brother's stare. *Please get me out of this.*

He raised his eyebrows. "Really? Is it with…?"

Cindy snapped her reply through clenched teeth. "Mama set me up."

"No shit?" He laughed.

"Watch your language," their mom said. "And yes, I did. She's going with my friend's son and they'll have a *great* time." The frown she gave Cindy added the *or else*.

Her brother laughed and she clenched her teeth. "You do know this is *1986* not 1886, right? Parents don't make arranged relationships anymore."

"We thought you'd be happy." Her dad squeezed her shoulders with a trembling hand. "But if you don't want to go you don't have to."

Throwing her hands up, her mom replied, "What's she going to do? There's nobody like Tavis at her school she can date."

Cindy looked at Elijah again.

"True. Ain't no brothers there." He crossed his arms and raised his chin as if to say *told ya*.

Their mom frowned. "That's not what I'm worried about. The boys here are too immature. Unless you have a friend for her."

Elijah scratched his head. "Uhh."

"Yeah, Elijah," Cindy said with a sneer. "Tell Mama 'bout your friends. Anyone you want me to date?"

"Ahem. Well, no. None of them are good enough for my sister." His protective comment earned a smile from their parents, but Cindy narrowed her eyes.

Her mom pointed to the clock. "Go on. Get ready. If you don't like him after this date, don't go again. But I bet you'll want to."

Cindy's gaze whirled between them. Her mom's stern face, her dad's hopeful smile, and Elijah's smirk. She didn't see a way out without telling them about Mike. And she knew that was a can of worms she couldn't open tonight—maybe not ever.

"Fine. But I can guarantee this will be the only date with him."

She shrugged out from her dad's hold and stomped to her bedroom to get ready. Whoever Tavis was, he'd better be ready for a shitty night. And if he laid one hand on her, he would learn the real meaning of pain.

She showered, then threw on jeans and a gray track sweatshirt. Undoing her ponytail, she smoothed her braids onto her shoulders. Glancing at her reflection she squinted. No make-up, casual clothes, bead-less braids, she looked at least fifteen.

"Good. I hope he feels like a pedophile."

A soft knock echoed on her door. Elijah's muffled voice followed. "Can I come in?"

Cindy opened the door.

"Come to gloat?" She flopped onto her bed and crossed her legs.

"No." Elijah sat next to her. "You okay?"

"What do you think?" She hugged her pillow to her chest. "I know you don't care, but I can't do this to Mike."

"You're right. I don't care about him." Elijah blew out a breath and rubbed his hand over his hair. "But I don't want you to be upset."

"Too late." She wiped her eyes. "And Mike's a good guy. I wish you'd give him a chance."

Elijah put his arm around her, and she leaned her head on his shoulder for a minute.

"Why don't you give this *brother* a chance? Maybe you'll like 'em."

"Ugh! I already like Mike." She pushed away, leaning back on the headboard of her single bed. "Why does color matter to you? You'd get pissed if someone didn't like you because you're black."

"That's different."

"No, it's the same thing."

Elijah chewed on his lip for a minute then nodded. "Whatever. I don't want people giving my sister crap."

"Why do you care what people will say?"

His forehead wrinkled. "My friends have been talking about it."

"Tell them to mind their own damn business."

Now she had to worry about what his stupid friends thought? College couldn't come fast enough.

Elijah shrugged. "Dating him is asking for trouble."

Cindy pushed him with her foot. "Don't worry. I can handle trouble. I drag you away from it at least once a week."

"True." He laughed.

"This is so unfair! I can't believe Daddy talked Mama into it." Cindy pounded her fist on the mattress. "Well, if anything, maybe after I sabotage this set-up, they'll let me go on a real date with Mike."

The silver lining in the nightmare of Mama's blind date.

Elijah furrowed his forehead. "It was good to see Daddy happy at least."

The lump returned to her throat as she got off the bed. "Guess I gotta get this over with."

"You want me to follow you? If he gets out of hand, I can take care of it."

"No. But thanks for having my back."

"You know I always do."

She held his hand as they walked into the hall. "Come on. Let's go wait for Mr. Perfect to get here."

"You better now?" Elijah asked.

Better? Better was Mike ringing the doorbell and her parents greeting him with approval. Her dad shaking Mike's hand while her mom smiled. Mike's arm around her shoulder as they waved goodbye and left for dinner and a movie.

Cindy met Elijah's gaze and snorted. The odds of *better* happening were as good as Donald Trump being elected President of the U.S.A.

CHAPTER SEVEN

MIKE

In the den, Mike let Cindy invade his every thought. Her eyes, her smile, her lips. He leaned back on the couch and closed his eyes. He'd give anything to have her here, sitting next to him, holding hands. No, kissing. Yeah, that would be better.

He grinned, remembering earlier before Drew interrupted them. Her fingers on his skin, her arms around his neck, her legs in her track shorts. Heat spread from his head to just below the belt. Mike swallowed, still tasting her kiss on his tongue.

A pillow landed on his face and he jumped. "What the hell?"

Tony laughed. "What are you smiling about you book nerd? Gettin' off on trig?"

"Shut up." Mike sat, tossing his book on the coffee table.

"Man, you're uptight." Tony sat on the couch, eating from a bag of potato chips. He held the bag toward Mike. "Want some?"

"No." Mike rubbed his eyes. "What do you want?"

Tony frowned, chewing a handful of chips. "Nothing. I just came to hang out with my little brother. Find out why he's being an idiot."

Mike rolled his eyes. "I don't want to talk about Cindy with you." As worked up as his nerves were, having that conversation could have severe collateral damage—and his mom just remodeled the basement.

"That's not what I'm talking about. Though it does make you more of an idiot, I'll admit."

"Then what the hell *are* you talking about?"

58

Tony crunched on more chips, watching Mike's face. "You. You've changed, and not in a good way."

"Changed?"

"Yeah. You used to have fun, now you're just miserable." Potato chip crumbs fell from Tony's mouth as he added another scoop.

"Damn, that's disgusting." He grabbed the bag of chips and set them on the end table out of Tony's reach.

"See?" Tony waved to the bag. "A bag of chips sends you over the edge."

"I'm not miserable. You're just annoying, and you eat like a slob."

"No, you're definitely miserable. When's the last time you went out and had fun? When's the last time you had a party?" He chuckled. "Or got laid?"

"Geez, Tony. What the hell?" His lower gut tingled again though. Tony did have a point.

"Mom has dad talked into taking a trip this weekend." Tony chuckled. "Let's have a party and get someone to relieve your pressure. Here."

He reached in his pocket and tossed something to Mike, bouncing it off his face.

Mike winced and picked up the flat square of foil, reading the words printed over the ridge of the circle inside.

Extra Lubricated. "Nice. I'm not looking for a hookup. I have a girlfriend."

"That never stopped you before."

Heat prickled Mike's cheeks. "This is different. *She's* different."

"Have you done her yet?"

"Shut the hell up." Yep. He needed to get away from his brother.

"I'll take that as a no." Tony put his feet on the coffee table and crossed his arms over his chest. "Is that why you're chasing her? She hasn't put out yet?"

Mike gritted his teeth. "She's not like that, and I'm done talking to you about her."

"Why?"

"You don't like her because she's black," Mike said.

"That's not why I don't like her."

"Right."

"I don't like her because she's using you. And you're too stupid to see it."

This should be good. "What do you mean?"

"Think about it, dumbass. She knows you have money, that's all she's after."

Mike furrowed his eyebrows. "Money?"

"She's a gold digger."

"You're crazy." Mike shook his head. "She doesn't care about that."

"Like hell she doesn't, every girl does. Her parents probably put her up to it. And you fell for it."

"Did you take *Bigoted Assholes 101* this semester?"

Tony's sarcastic laugh rang through the room. "I'm not a bigot, just a realist."

"Saying that my black girlfriend and her parents are plotting to get money is pretty racist."

"That's not what I said."

"Then what the hell *are* you saying? You've never cared before about other girls I've dated or worried that they were looking for money."

"Usually you date girls with money. They don't need yours." Tony shrugged. "Like you said. This is different."

"Yeah, because she's different and you can't handle it." Mike glared. "She's not using me and she's not a gold digger. Her parents don't even know about me, so they didn't put her up to anything."

"Wait, she's hiding *you* from *them*?"

"She's not allowed to date."

"You're a bigger idiot than I thought." Tony shook his head. "She's lying."

"How the hell would you know?" Mike stood and picked up his books.

"Hiding that she's dating a rich *white* kid? She's just playing with you until she finds one of her own to take home to her parents." Tony stretched out on the couch and grabbed the chips. "You need to dump her before she dumps you. Keep your streak going. Find a different piece of ass that won't cause as much trouble."

"And that's my bullshit limit. You don't know her, so *kiss my* ass. And stay out of my business."

Tony's laughter followed him up the stairs. Mike stalked to his room and slammed the door. Throwing his books on the small wooden desk under his window, he crossed to his bed and fell across the mattress.

Cindy wasn't using him. She said she loved him. Tony didn't know what he was talking about. He unclenched his hand and glared at the stupid condom Tony threw at him.

"Idiot." Sitting, he opened the drawer on his nightstand, dropped the square inside, and slammed it shut.

But as he lay back on the bed, his mind once again focused on her, Mike couldn't help thinking that maybe his brother's idea wasn't *completely* crazy. If she loved him, really loved him, she should want to tell her parents. She'd agreed to let everyone else know about their relationship, but until she told her parents, it wasn't official. It wasn't real. Right?

And *why* wouldn't she tell them? Her mom sounded like a hard ass but so was Cindy. Was Cindy embarrassed of *him*?

No. Mike rubbed his face. Tony's idiotic comments made him doubt her. They belonged together, and soon everyone would know. There was no way Cindy cared that he was white, no way she wanted to hide him while she looked for someone else. No way.

As for the other problem his brother pointed out, he couldn't argue with that at all.

Sighing, he closed his eyes again, picturing Cindy's face. Yeah, he wanted her. But not just to have sex. He wanted her because he loved her. In an ironic twist, that's why he hadn't made a move. It wasn't her way, and he respected her. And despite his messed-up past, he'd never take Tony's suggestion. Cindy was too important.

But respecting her didn't help at times like this where he couldn't stop thinking about her. He smirked, every guy from the dawn of time knew how to take care of business on their own. Maybe he'd have to rely on his male instincts for a while. Or take lots of cold showers. Long tight legs and soft lips flooded his memory. He relaxed onto his bed and gave in to his thoughts—and instincts. He'd always hated cold water.

B.B. Swann

CHAPTER EIGHT

CINDY

The tinkling chime of the doorbell sounded, and Cindy closed her eyes. To her, it rang more like the gong of doom. She sat on the couch with a crossed-armed Elijah. Her dad napped in his recliner, snapping awake at the ring. He rubbed his eyes while her mom answered the door.

"Hello, Tavis. Come on in." She stepped back and held the door open.

Cindy glanced at Elijah one last time and stood. The faster she could get this over with, the better. She walked toward the door.

Tavis stepped around the open door and Cindy jerked to a stop.

Not sure what she had expected, she knew this wasn't it. Tall, like Mike, he was slim but muscular with smooth, light brown skin. The dark blue, long-sleeved t-shirt he wore stretched tight across his chest, revealing more muscles underneath. His dark hair cut in a flat top, framed his handsome face and his beautiful gray eyes.

Elijah stood too and walked toward Tavis. He pursed his lips and stuck out his chin. "What up?"

Mama twisted her hands. "Tavis, this is Cindy and Elijah. That's Carl." She pointed to her husband in his chair.

Cindy's dad tried to stand.

"Please, don't get up, Mr. Wilson." Tavis rushed over to shake her dad's hand. "It's good to meet you."

When he smiled, Cindy felt like joining him—which pissed her off.

"It's good to meet you, too." Her dad grinned like he'd won the lottery.

Tavis turned to Cindy. "Hey." A dimple peeked out on his left cheek.

"Hey." Cindy jammed her fingers into her jean pockets. "Well, let's go. I need to get back and study."

Tavis smiled, but her mom didn't. She cleared her throat and put one hand on her hip.

"See ya later. We're out." Cindy grabbed Tavis by the hand and pulled him out the front door into the late afternoon sunshine. Then she froze on the front porch.

"Uh, is everything okay?" Tavis asked.

"A red Camaro?"

"Yeah. I got it for graduation last year."

They walked toward the car and Tavis glided a finger over the top of the shiny hood. "Do you not like it? I mean, if you want, we can take your car."

"No, it's beautiful." Heat burned in her cheeks. It wasn't his fault her mom was wacked about dating and she missed her boyfriend and this guy drove the same car. "Sorry, about rushing you out. If we'd stayed, my brother would get weird and my mom might have us engaged."

He laughed and led her to the passenger side door. Opening it he waved her in. "I promise not to propose tonight."

"Thanks."

They drove toward the main strip of restaurants in town. "Are you hungry? We could go eat."

A flash of panic punched through her chest. "There's nothing good in town. Let's go someplace else."

"Okay. There's a great pizza place not too far." He glanced at her. "Is that okay?"

"Sounds great." Not like she'd eat anyway. She relaxed back into the black leather seat. "So, you're in college. What are you studying?"

"I'm a theater arts major."

"What kind of job would you get with that?" She wondered if her mom had bothered to ask his mom that question.

"Someday I'd like to be a director. You know, for stage productions, not movies."

64

"That sounds like fun." Then she remembered Molly's ex-boyfriend, Trevor, and his theater friends. They had turned out to be assholes, trying to keep Molly and Hayden apart with a bunch of lies. She'd hate to work with people like that.

"What about you?" Tavis asked. "Any plans for the future? Besides marrying me of course."

She fought back a smile.

"My only plan is to get out of here." And be with Mike. "Well, after my daddy gets better."

"What's wrong with him?"

"He's… he's just a little sick, that's all." The familiar hollow feeling whenever she thought about her dad's illness filled her chest. "But he will get better."

"I'm sure you're right." He gave her a small smile.

"I am." She leaned her elbow on the door and stared out the window at the trees flashing by. They were silent for a few minutes and then Cindy chuckled.

"You probably think I'm a total bitch."

"Nah. You love your daddy. I get it." He flashed her that dimpled grin.

"Yeah, I do." Tavis really did seem like a nice guy. But as she glanced over at him, she ached to see blond hair and blue eyes instead of black and gray.

He pulled into a gravel parking lot in front of a run-down brick building. Neon signs every color of the rainbow hung in the darkened windows. The surrounding buildings were better kept and looked safer, but this parking lot had the most cars. He drove around until he found an empty spot.

"Wow. It sure is crowded," Cindy remarked.

"They have the best pizza." He cut the engine and held up his finger, motioning for her to wait. He jumped out and ran around to her side of the car to open her door.

"You don't have to do that." She got out and smiled. His friendliness was hard to ignore.

"I treat my dates with respect. My daddy taught me that."

"He sounds like a good daddy."

Inside, the hostess led them to a table in the back of the dimly lit room. The red hooded lights were almost dark enough to hide the dingy brown tiled floors and graffiti-covered tables. Cindy slid into the booth across from Tavis, resting her hands on the scarred wooden tabletop.

She laughed. "They'd better have good food because the atmosphere is terrible."

"I know. It looks like something straight out of a horror movie, doesn't it?" He wiggled his eyebrows. "Michael Meyers from *Halloween* works in the back. I hear he slices the pizza with his bloody knife."

"That's disgusting," Cindy said with another laugh. "But I think I'd believe it."

Their waitress arrived, and they ordered a large deep dish and two sodas. After she left, Cindy glanced around—and slapped a hand over her mouth.

Molly and Hayden sat at a table across the room, paying their bill.

"Omigod." She leaned back in her seat and hid her face behind her hand.

Tavis frowned. "What is it?" He followed her gaze and looked around.

"Nothing." *Oh hell.*

"You look like you saw Michael." He smiled, but a wrinkle formed between his eyes.

His joke fell flat on Cindy's ears. She tried to breathe and—

"Cindy?" Molly's voice was higher than usual.

Cindy looked up at her best friend.

"Hey, Molly. Hayden." She glanced between their surprised faces. "What's going on?"

She cringed at her lame greeting.

Molly raised an eyebrow, glancing at Tavis then back to Cindy. "Nothing. What's up with you?"

Cindy tried to swallow but ended up coughing. "Well, I'm just out with my friend, Tavis." She waved a hand in his direction. "Tavis, this is my best friend, Molly and her boyfriend, Hayden."

God, just kill me now.

Tavis stood and shook Hayden's hand. "Nice to meet you both." He smiled at Molly.

Cindy blinked and held a hand to her eye.

"Darn these contacts. Molly, can you help me for a second?" She smiled at Tavis. "I'll be right back.'

Tavis nodded, smiling when Hayden took Cindy's place across from him in the booth.

In the bathroom, Molly grabbed Cindy's arm and glared at her. "What the hell are you doing here with another guy?"

"God. This is a disaster." Cindy threw her arms up. "My parents told me I could date."

"So, you decided to go out with someone else and leave Mike at home?"

"No! Mama set me up with her co-worker's son." Cindy leaned against the wall and rubbed her temples. "I didn't know what to do."

"Did you think about saying *no*? What about Mike? Did you think about how he would feel?"

"Of course, I did." Cindy glared back. "What was I supposed to do? Mama all but threatened me, and Daddy looked happy and I didn't want to upset him and risk him having an episode, and Elijah was there and..." Her throat finally released the tears she'd been holding back all night.

Sighing, Molly hugged her. "I'm sorry. I know you always think about other people. But maybe this time you shouldn't have."

"Girl, what am I gonna do?" Cindy sniffed. Grabbing a paper towel from the dispenser, she wiped her eyes. "I don't want Mike to find out."

Molly shook her head. "You have to tell him. He'll be more upset if he hears it from someone else."

"I know, but, how can I? He's gonna be pissed. And I can't blame him."

"Just tell him the truth."

Cindy's stomach churned. "Alright. I'll tell him. Promise me you and Hayden won't say anything?"

"Okay, but you need to tell him tomorrow."

"I will. Come on, let's get back out there. We kinda left Hayden hanging." Cindy pushed the door open and led Molly back to the table.

Hayden got up to let Cindy have her seat. "Everything okay?" He looked at Molly.

"Yep, all fixed." She held Hayden's hand. "We need to go. It was nice to meet you, Tavis."

Tavis tilted his head. "Maybe I'll see you around. Good talking to you, Hayden."

After they left, Cindy took a drink of the pop the waitress had delivered.

"Your friends looked a little surprised to see me." Tavis stirred the ice in his drink, his long fingers gently holding the straw.

"Oh. Yeah. Uh, I don't get out much." She took another drink.

"I see." The smile left his face, and for the first time, he looked hurt.

Why did these things always happen to her? If ever someone was hurt or needed help, they always seemed to find her. And she felt compelled to help them. She was like Florence freaking Nightingale for the needy and broken-hearted.

Cindy sighed. Unbelievable as it was, her mom had set her up with a great guy, and she was about to crush his hopes.

"I have to be honest with you, Tavis." She dropped her gaze to the table. "You seem like a nice guy and I can see why my mom wanted me to go out with you. But you see, my mom doesn't know that I... have a boyfriend."

Tavis leaned back in his seat. "A boyfriend?"

Biting her lip, she nodded. "His name's Mike. So, I shouldn't have gone out with you, but I couldn't tell my mom the real reason I didn't want to go."

"*Now* I see." Tavis slowly nodded his head, then he laughed. Not just a polite laugh, a full-bellied laugh that brought tears to his eyes.

The longer he laughed, the more Cindy considered slapping his dimpled cheek. "What the hell is so funny?"

Tavis took a deep breath and wiped his eyes with his napkin. "It's just, the girl my mom sets me up with has a secret boyfriend and is worried about him finding out. Then we run into her friends in another town."

"So?" There was nothing funny about this. Mr. Perfect apparently had a big flaw, he was insane.

"So, you haven't heard the best part." He smiled so big that both his cheeks had dimples. He glanced from side to side and leaned forward on the table. "The funny thing is, *I* have a secret boyfriend, too."

"What?" She stared back with her mouth open. "You're... you're gay?"

He nodded. "His name is Brett. We go to school together."

Good thing it *wasn't* 1886, her mom was a terrible matchmaker. It was her turn to laugh. "Why did you agree to go out with me?"

"Well, my parents don't *know* that I'm gay. I agreed to this date to keep them in the dark." The light in his smile dimmed. "Mom's been bugging me about bringing home a girlfriend. I thought going out with you would keep them happy for a while. Until I get up the courage to come out."

"Oh my god. I can't believe it." Cindy gave him a wry smile. "I'm sorry, hiding things is hard."

"Why don't your parents know about...?"

"Mike."

"Mike. Don't they like him?"

"Uhm... it's complicated." She glanced at the table.

The waitress arrived with the pizza and set it on the table. Cindy's mouth watered and she grabbed a slice, biting into it before she set it on her plate. "You were right. This pizza is awesome."

"I told you." Tavis laid a hand on hers. "We don't have to talk about Mike if you don't want to."

"It's alright." She wiped her mouth with her napkin. "Mama doesn't want me to date at all. Especially not with anyone she doesn't approve of. And I don't want to upset Daddy. Stress causes him to have... episodes. So I haven't told them about it."

"How have you been hiding it from them?"

"We only just recently let it out to the kids at school." She chuckled. "Running into Molly and Hayden was a fluke."

"They know about Mike?"

"Yeah. They set us up actually." She smiled at the memory. "They also cover for us. I tell mama I'm at Molly's so if she asks, Molly helps me out."

"She doesn't mind lying?" He took another slice of pizza.

"Well, she doesn't like it, but she understands. You saw the nice side of Mama. Molly has met the real one." Cindy raised her eyebrows. "She wants to look out for us but doesn't like being disobeyed."

"I know what you mean. I love my parents, and you'd think the struggles they faced as a biracial couple would make them more accepting of differences, but it didn't. Instead, they just want me to take the safe route and find a girl that won't raise any eyebrows."

"What about you? How do you keep Brett a secret?"

"It's easier to hide when you don't live at home."

"Mike and I are going to the same school, and I can't wait to get there. We can be free."

"No, you won't." Tavis shook his head. "It's just a new place to hide. At the risk of sounding like a hypocrite, find a way to tell them about Mike before you go. You'll be both happier."

Tears prickled her eyes. Mike had said the same thing, going to school to hide wouldn't change anything. But, was her happiness worth hurting her dad? Was Mike's? She couldn't say yes for sure.

Trying to lighten the mood, she teased Tavis. She squeezed his hand and chuckled. "Is this where you propose?"

"I told you I wouldn't. Though I will admit I am a great catch."

Since the pressure of liking him was lifted, his cuteness didn't piss her off anymore. "You are. Cute, smart, career-oriented, everything a girl could want." She raised her glass and took a drink. "Except for the gay thing. But you'll be a great catch for Brett."

"He's the catch," Tavis said pushing his plate away. "He's cute *and* going to med school. But at least tonight my parents think I'm on a straight date with a beautiful girl."

"Thanks. And mine think I'm dating an incredibly attractive and eligible black man."

He winked, pulling bills out of his wallet for the check. "Come on, I'll take you home. You can tell your parents I was too hands-on if you want. That way your mom won't try to set us up again. Who knows, maybe I'll clear the way for your man."

She shook her head and slid out of the booth. "I don't want to make you look bad."

He shrugged. "It's all part of my plan. If they think that's the reason your mom doesn't want us going out, my parents won't bug me either."

He held the door for her, and they stepped outside into the night.

Cindy walked alongside him to the car with an empty feeling in her stomach. As difficult as her situation was, his was worse. With all the talk about AIDS, anyone who was gay had it rough. She'd seen on the news how gay people were treated like lepers, even if they *didn't* have the disease. She hated that Tavis had to deal with that kind of treatment when he was such a caring person. He didn't deserve it. Nobody should be punished for love.

After arriving at her house, Tavis parked in the driveway and cut the engine.

She said, "Thanks for the pizza."

"Anytime." His eyes sparkled in the glow of the streetlamp. "Hey, if we ever both come out to our parents, we could always double date. I could meet this cute man of yours."

"I'd like that." She kissed his cheek. "Thanks for helping my parents get used to me dating. Maybe if they found out you were gay Mike would look like the better option for me."

"True. But I'm probably better looking, so they might still consider me."

"You're cute, I won't lie. But not like Mike." She pictured his lips and her belly quivered. "You don't make me shake inside."

Tavis's cheeks imploded with his dimples. "Maybe not, but I'll bet Brett would disagree. I make him shake like j-e-l-l-o."

She laughed as he sang the jingle from TV. "Thanks, Tavis."

For a clandestine, unwanted, and unexpected date, it was a good one. But even though Tavis told her to do it, as she prepared to go inside and lie to her parents, her gut churned. Reaching for the door, she wondered if she'd even know the truth when she saw it, or if she'd forever get stuck in the circle of lies she'd created in the name of love.

Regardless, she stepped inside and added Tavis to the loop.

CHAPTER NINE

MIKE

T he next day after school, Mike stood in the throwing circle for his first ever shot-put throw at his first ever meet. A bead of sweat traced his spine, dripping slowly along the skin on his back. He tuned out the distant sounds of kids laughing and yelling in the stands, the crowd cheering, the coaches shouting encouragement, and tried to focus on the eight-pound metal ball he held in his hand.

The bright sun overhead added to the heat, and he wiped his free hand across his forehead. Determined not to make an ass out of himself at his first meet, Mike squeezed the shot to his neck and closed his eyes. He took a deep breath. Visualized the throw. Leg muscles tightened with anticipation. He exhaled and spun toward the toe board. Then, pushing all the tension and frustration he'd felt this week into his arm, released his throw.

The shot arced through the air, glinting in the afternoon sunshine. It landed in the dirt and Coach Ebbs clapped. "That's the way to do it! Well done, Mike."

The judge measured the distance and raised his eyebrows. He called out the result. "Fifty-five feet, two and a quarter inches."

Mike ignored the smattering of applause from the spectators. He glanced around and disappointment tightened his chest. She'd missed his first throw. He stepped out the back of the ring and went to where Hayden stood waiting for him.

"That was an awesome throw. Only five more feet to qualify for state."

Mike shrugged. "Yep."

"What's wrong?" Hayden asked with a grin. "Not every throw can be state qualifying."

"Yeah." Mike scanned the area again.

Hayden smirked. "Don't worry, she isn't ditching you. She and Molly are warming up for the four by one."

Heat filled his face. Damn, was he that obvious?

"Still think I'm bad?" Hayden joked.

"Yes. And I think you've infected me with your wussiness."

"Hey, there's nothing wrong with expressing your emotions."

Mike snorted. "Not if you're a girl."

"This wussy can still outrun your ass."

"Good thing. That will help when you need to outrun my fist." Mike laughed, punching Hayden on the arm.

"Asshole." Hayden laughed.

They watched the competitors for a while and Mike completed his next two throws, gaining an inch with the last one. After he finished, they walked toward the track to wait for the girls' race to begin.

Mike searched for Cindy, smiling when he found her on the infield practicing hand-offs with Molly and the rest of their relay team. Focused on her warm-up, she didn't see him, but *he* couldn't look away.

"Final call, girls' varsity 4X100 meter relay." The announcer's voice blared from the PA followed by the crackle of static.

"Come on. Molly is lead leg and Cindy is anchor. Let's go stand by the finish so we can yell at them." Hayden jerked his chin toward the track.

Mike followed Hayden through the crowd along the fence surrounding the track. They squeezed into a spot just before the finish line. Leaning his arms on the fence, Mike stared at Cindy, waiting for her to make eye contact. She looked everywhere but at him.

"What the hell?" Mike muttered to himself.

Molly waved to Hayden and tapped Cindy's shoulder, pointing to Mike. Cindy glanced at him.

He waved to her, but his stomach clenched. "Fuck."

"What's wrong?" Hayden asked.

"I don't know. Cindy's looking at me like I'm the stupid *I want my two dollars* kid in *Better Off Dead*."

"You're imagining things," Hayden said, looking across the infield. "You know, you girls are emotional."

Mike smirked at the joke. "Takes one to know one."

The girls walked onto the track and his gaze followed Cindy. He tried not to stare at her body while she slid off her warmup pants. Tried. Swallowing hard, he raised his gaze to her face and caught her laughing as she jogged to her mark at the other end of the track.

He shook his head but couldn't help peeking again at her warm skin shining in the sun.

"Let's go, Molly!"

Mike jumped at Hayden's yell. On the track, Molly bounced in lane four in front of the blocks. She ignored Hayden, staring straight ahead while she hugged her knee to her chest.

Maybe he was being too sensitive about Cindy. Hayden didn't whine about Molly not looking at him.

"Runners, on your mark."

Molly jumped, raising her knees to her chest, then knelt and set her feet in the blocks, planting her fingers behind the line.

Mike glanced sideways, laughing at Hayden as he bit his thumbnail. "Need me to hold your hand?"

Hayden exhaled. "Only if you want to, honey."

"Set."

The crowd hushed for a moment and Mike's stomach flipped. Their soccer games were noisy, no time to get nervous.

The gun fired and the noise returned. Parents, teammates, coaches, everyone screamed at the runners. He found himself caught up in the hype, screaming at Molly as she bolted out of the blocks.

"Go, Molly!" He joined Hayden's shouts. He could hear their teammates hollering from the other side of the track as Molly flew past them. She handed off ahead of the other teams to the second runner, a junior named Lexi, who took off down the straight on the other side.

"Damn, Molly's fast," Mike said. "I've only seen her run cross country."

Hayden nodded. "Wait until you see Cindy. Her race pace is faster than you've seen in practice."

Lexi reached the exchange zone in the lead and passed the baton to Andrea, the newest member of their relay team. She ran through the curve, arms swinging, teeth bared in a determined snarl. She pumped her legs, struggling to maintain the lead. As she approached Cindy, her pace slowed slightly.

Cindy took her lead off steps and reached back for the pass. Andrea all but fell into her outstretched hand. Mike cursed under his breath as the girl in lane five pulled ahead of Cindy.

Mike screamed, "Dig, Cindy! You got this!"

Lip curled, arms and legs pumping fast, Cindy narrowed her eyes and dashed toward the finish. Hayden was right, Cindy was faster than Molly. She closed the gap with the leader and pulled ahead with fifty meters to go. She blasted past and crossed the finish line a second ahead of lane five.

The crowd cheered and Mike joined in.

"Did you see that? She kicked ass after that bad handoff." Mike slapped Hayden on the back.

He laughed. "She's tough. She wasn't about to let that other girl win."

"Yeah, she *wants* to win, that's for sure." Mike watched Cindy hug Molly. She turned and met his eye, giving him a thumbs up. She pointed at him and Hayden like they had better win, too.

He nodded and laughed.

"Hey there, Hayden."

They turned and came face to face with a woman pushing a man in a wheelchair. If the deep brown color of their skin wasn't enough of a clue, Mike knew they were Cindy's parents from Cindy's smile that laid on her dad's face. Mike returned it.

"Hello, Mr. and Mrs. Wilson." Hayden held his hand out to Cindy's dad, glancing at Mike. "This is my friend, Mike Ryan. Mike, these are Cindy's parents."

Trying to keep it from shaking, Mike held out his hand. "It's nice to meet you."

Her dad grasped it and Mike's hand shook more from the extra tremors. Why hadn't Cindy told him her dad was not well?

"Good to meet you too, Mike." He smiled. "You must be the goalie Cindy mentioned."

"Uh, yeah. That's right." She'd told them about him?

Her mom nodded. "She said you were new to the team. You like it so far?"

Mike met her direct gaze. "It's different than soccer, but I like it."

She didn't seem too scary. But then, she didn't know he made out with her daughter whenever he could.

"Mike's great at the shot-put. He has a solid chance at going to state this year." Hayden said.

Mike glanced at Hayden from the corner of his eye and raised his eyebrows.

Cindy's dad gave a low whistle. "That's impressive for someone new to the sport."

"Thanks. I still have a way to go, but I'll get there."

"I like that determination." Her dad patted her mom's hand. "Just like Cindy."

"Good luck," her mom said. "Cindy's goal is to get to state, too. They might make it if they keep focused. Right, baby?" She returned her husband's gesture.

"Well, she's still gotta have fun. She's a kid, too."

Mike agreed. Cindy should bypass her mom and just tell her dad about them. He seemed to be more reasonable.

"You know how I feel about that. Fun can come later, once she's done with school."

Mike and Hayden exchanged a glance.

"Mama? Daddy?" Cindy approached them with wide eyes. She met Mike's gaze and her head bobbed as she swallowed.

"Great race," Mike said.

She nodded then hugged her dad. "Hey, Daddy. What are you doing here? Are you sure you should be out? It's kind of chilly. Where's your jacket?"

"Quit fussin'. I'm fine, fine." He patted her back and nodded at Mike. "Hayden, introduced us to the next shot-put record holder."

Mike laughed. "I don't know if I'd say that."

"Yeah, he's good." Cindy glanced between him and her dad then bit her lip. "Thanks for cheering us on guys."

"That's what boy...teammates are for." Hayden's cheeks reddened and he glanced at Mike. "We're here to cheer on the girls' team."

Mike bit back a laugh. "Right. So they do the same for us." He met Cindy's wide-eyed stare.

"Go team." She raised a fist in the air.

Cindy's mom cocked an eyebrow, pressing her lips together.

"Hi, Mr. and Mrs. Wilson." Molly hugged Cindy's mom and dad, then went to Hayden's side. He put an arm around her waist and kissed the top of her head. "Good job."

"Thanks." She smiled at Cindy's parents. "Did you see our race?"

Cindy's mom put her hands on her hips. "I did. Andrea better get her stuff together if you want to make it to state this year."

Cindy frowned at her mom. "She will. You know, first-time jitters. She'll work it out."

"Hmm mmm," was her reply. She pursed her lips at Hayden, and he let go of Molly.

As Molly talked to Cindy's dad about the details of the race, Mike tried to catch Cindy's eye. But she bent to the ground, untying and retying her shoe. He drew in a slow breath, lost in memories of her soft skin. Imagining those fingers in his hair, in his hand, against his lips, he grinned.

Not the place to fantasize about your girlfriend, idiot. Track suits don't hide much.

He raised his gaze—right into her mom's watchful stare. His face burned.

Her mom crossed her arms. "Did you tell Tavis about the meet, Cindy? Is he coming to watch you?"

Mike's gaze flew to Cindy's face. A cold tingle ran along his neck.

"No, Mama," she stammered, glancing at Molly.

Mike did, too, and got another punch in the gut. Molly blushed and Hayden glanced at the ground. Who the hell was Tavis?

"Well, I'm sure he wanted to come. He probably had to work. You can call him later and tell him how you did." Her mom turned to Mike and Hayden, her gaze on Mike's burning face. "Good luck with your season boys. I'm taking Carl to the stands where we can sit."

Mike met her steady gaze. Her comment still ripped through his chest like a bullet—and she knew it. He no longer doubted Cindy's reason to hide their relationship from this woman. But apparently, he wasn't Cindy's only secret.

Her dad smiled at them. "Yes, good luck boys. I hope you do well, Mike."

"Thank you, sir," he managed to say with his tight throat.

With one last look at Mike, Cindy's mom smiled and grabbed the handles of the chair, wheeling her husband away.

Mike stared at Cindy, the heat in his face doing nothing to melt the ice forming in his gut.

Molly said, "Come on, Hayden."

Mike ignored them, looking only at Cindy's trembling lip. They knew. They knew and didn't tell him. But as Hayden stepped away, their gazes connected. Mike glared back and clenched his fist.

Hayden winced and Molly pulled him away.

Alone with Cindy, the anger spiraled away, leaving nothing but a hollow pit in his chest—one she'd fill it with her latest excuses.

CHAPTER TEN

CINDY

After Molly and Hayden walked away, Cindy raised her gaze, flinching at the hurt on Mike's face.

"It… it was just a blind date. I wanted to tell you. I d-didn't know…" She swallowed the lump in her throat.

"Didn't know I'd find out?" He crossed his arms. "Who is he?"

Cindy sniffled and her stomach filled with the weight of a thousand dead butterflies. "He's the son of Mama's friend. They set us up and Mama made me go out with him and—"

"Made you." He shook his head.

"I didn't want to, but it would have upset Daddy and I didn't want him to—"

"Daddy? You were more worried about upsetting *him* than your boyfriend?" Mike pushed a hand through his hair. "Jesus, Cindy. You went on a date with someone else because of your *daddy*?"

Cindy clenched her fists. "If you'd just listen and quit interrupting me, I'll explain."

Mike glared at her. "This should be good. Let's hear your excuses. No, wait let me guess. Your mom is too scary, and you can't tell her no because she'll bake you into a cake. Or Elijah might get wasted if you don't go out with Tavis instead of me. Or maybe your little brothers will spontaneously explode if they find out you're dating a white boy."

"You're making a stupid scene." A girl nearby giggled and Cindy turned to her. "This isn't the freaking movies."

The girl grabbed her friend's arm and rushed away.

79

But Mike waved his hand. "See, you stand up to complete strangers because they piss you off, but you can't stand up to your parents to fight for me. I don't matter."

She narrowed her eyes. "That's not true."

"I don't see you sacrificing anything for this relationship. I'm the one who gives up everything so you can stay safe in your world, hiding away from the truth. And I don't even know why!"

Dammit. He was right, sort of. He had no reason to hide and only did it for her because God knew *she* had to. But there were things she gave up, too. Like her integrity and self-respect. Not to mention her happiness because she couldn't be with Mike like she wanted to.

She glanced in the direction of her parents, thankfully out of earshot. They'd made it to the other side of the track but with slow progress in the grass due to the wheelchair. All she needed was for Mama to turn around and see her arguing with Mike.

"Come here," she said, grabbing his hand. They had to get somewhere more private before all hell broke loose.

She pulled him away from the track and over a grassy hill filled with more spectators. Opening the door to the metal storage shed where they kept the track equipment, she stepped inside and turned to him with her hands on her hips.

"Mama surprised me yesterday by giving me permission to date. Then she said she'd set me up with Tavis and told me he'd be there soon. She gave me one hour's notice, and I didn't know what else to do."

"Do?" He held out his arms then pointed to himself. "How about saying no because you already have a boyfriend?"

"I couldn't. My dad—"

"This isn't about your dad. You cheated, went out with another guy. What am I supposed to do with that?"

"I didn't cheat." She reached for his arm and he pulled away. Her stomach fell to her knees. "It wasn't a real date."

"Really?" Mike scoffed. "So, I can take Jenny to dinner and you'd be okay with that?"

"That's different. Jenny likes you, so going out with her *would* be cheating."

"You went on a date with some random guy, but it isn't cheating because he doesn't *like you*?" He closed his eyes and rolled his head between his shoulders. "God, Cindy. Do you hear how pathetic that sounds?"

"It's not pathetic." She narrowed her eyes. "What's pathetic is that you don't trust me. And you won't let me explain what happened."

Mike crossed his arms, leaning a shoulder against the wall of the shed. "Fine. Tell me how it's okay for you to go on a date, keep it secret from me, let our friends know it happened, and blame me for not trusting you."

You hurt him, give him a chance to deal.

She blew out a deep breath. "I didn't want to go. But I didn't want to stress out my dad."

He opened his mouth, and she held up her hand. He snapped it shut again.

"When Mama told me to get ready, I didn't know what else to do. Then I thought maybe going out with Tavis would help *us* because my parents would get used to me dating. I argued with Mama and said I should pick who I dated, but then Daddy came in and he looked so happy because he thought *I* would be happy which is all he ever wants and…" her voice caught in her throat.

"What does your *dad* have to do with this?"

She'd hoped her dad would just get better so when she went to college with Mike, things would be ok. Cindy stared into Mike's eyes, her body shaking. Telling him would almost make her dad's illness more real.

"Well…" she said. "He's sick."

Mike lifted his hands and eyebrows. "And?"

"What do you mean?"

"Why does that matter? He didn't seem to share your mom's opinion. She's the one who doesn't want us dating."

"Yeah…Daddy is more agreeable, but Mama…"

"C'mon, Cindy. Help me out." Mike sighed and sank onto a stray hurdle behind him. "I still don't get it."

"My dad is… very sick. When he gets stressed out, he gets worse."

"And you think if you tell them, she'll get mad and it will upset your dad?"

"Which was why I couldn't get out of the date without telling them about you." Cindy took a step closer to him. "When Elijah got busted for stealing with that group of jerks last year, Daddy ended up in the hospital for a week. His heart almost stopped. They had him on drugs and straightened him out, but he grew weaker. He came home with the wheelchair."

"Damn. I think I understand now." Mike rubbed his eyes. "What's wrong with him."

Cindy hung her head. "He has Parkinson's and a really bad heart condition."

Mike reached for her hand. "I'm sorry. Aren't there treatments for him? Some way to help him get better?"

"Sure, and they keep making progress. So I know they're going to find a cure. He's going to get better. I know he will."

"Okay." Mike squeezed her hand and grabbed the other one, too, pulling her between his open legs.

Her chest tightened and she took a deep breath to loosen it.

"That's why I have to keep this from them. Daddy always wanted me to date and have fun, but Mama told him no. She said she didn't want me to get knocked up."

Mike snorted. "Really? She said that?"

"Stupid, I know. Last night, I didn't want to disappoint him, not when he'd finally talked Mama into allowing me to date." She shook her head, imagining how much he must have fought for her. "He'll get better faster if I can help him avoid stress. Anyway, I went. And I planned to sabotage it the whole time so I could tell them how terrible Tavis was to avoid having Mama set up a second date."

Mike muttered, "Was it terrible?"

"Yes." She laid her hands on his arms. He raised his gaze to hers, and her breath caught at the shimmer in his eyes. "Because it wasn't with you."

"What about Tavis?" he whispered. "What if he asks you out again?"

"He won't."

"Right."

"Honest you don't have to be jealous of him." She raised her hands to his shoulders.

"How can I not be?" He tightened his fingers on her waist. "When I think about someone else taking you out, holding your hand, looking into your eyes. Jealous is the *only* way to feel."

"Tavis doesn't like me and he won't be asking me out for a second date." Grinning, she leaned her face closer to Mike. "He's already seeing someone."

"What?" Mike asked.

She kneaded the tight muscles in his neck. "Tavis has a *boy*friend and doesn't want his parents to know."

"He's…" His eyes widened. "He's gay?"

"Mm-hmm." Their lips were so close, she could almost taste him. "He only went out with me to keep hiding from his parents. He said he hoped the date helps clear the way for you."

The muscles relaxed under her hands.

"Okay. But promise me something."

"Anything."

He brushed his lips against hers and her breath stuttered. "Please don't go on any more blind dates your mom sets up."

"I promise." She pressed her lips on his.

Mike stood and pulled her hips close. She leaned into him. This time, the quiver in her stomach had nothing to do with guilt. She moved her fingers to his hair, and he slid his hands around to her butt, pressing her to him. A small moan echoed in her chest.

"Does this mean you forgive me?" she asked.

"Maybe," he whispered, moving his lips to her neck.

She giggled. "Good, because I hate it when you're mad at me."

He pulled back. "Your mom could tell how I feel about you. That's why she mentioned Tavis in front of me."

Cindy raised her eyebrows. "You think?"

"Yes." He blushed. "She caught me staring at you."

"Oh." Her stomach tightened. "Mama's good at spotting things."

"She did it to warn me, to make me think you had someone interested in you so I would back off."

"Then the joke's on her, isn't it? I don't want you to back off. In fact, you need to come closer." Leaning on his chest again, she wrapped her arms around his waist.

He shook his head. "I've been a bad influence on you."

"Yes, you have." She kissed his cheek and rubbed the stubble with her lips. "Please don't get upset when we leave this shed and I stop touching you. If Mama suspects you like me, she'll watch you like a hawk."

He kissed the top of her head. "One question. How did Molly and Hayden know about Tavis?"

"Oh… uh…"

Mike held up a hand. "You and Molly are best friends. I guess they had more loyalty to you."

"That's not it." She sighed. "They saw me at the restaurant with Tavis and I begged them not to tell you. They only agreed because I said I would after the meet. I didn't want to ruin your first one."

"Tell Molly I'm not mad at her."

"What about Hayden?"

Mike smirked. "I'll talk to him myself."

"It's my fault. He probably wanted to tell you, but I begged Molly to tell him not to and you know how he is about her, he'd do anything she said, and I knew and that's why I asked her and—"

He touched her lips with his finger. "I'm not mad at him either. But guys have our own way of handling things."

"Don't hurt him. Molly would kill me."

"Don't worry, just a few throat punches. No big deal."

She glared at him. "You wouldn't."

He laughed. "No, but I'll think of something just as good."

"Guys are weird. If you could tell each other how you feel that would make life easier."

"Oh?" He pulled her back to him, sliding his hands behind her waist and back down to her butt. He pressed her against his hips and kissed her, his tongue slipping past her lips.

Her stomach did a flip and their heavy breaths echoed inside the little shed.

CHAPTER ELEVEN

MIKE

Mike stood in the shower on rubber legs, letting the warm water relax his muscles. As the leadoff runner in the four by one hundred, he'd tried to give the team an advantage by busting his ass on the track. He thought he was fast enough. He wasn't. Thankfully, Hayden was faster than the other team's anchors to give them the win.

After toweling off and dressing, he threw his uniform into his bag and rubbed a hand through his wet hair. Water droplets splattered his face, and he closed his eyes against the mini storm.

"Good race today." Hayden said. He sat on the bench next to Mike to remove his spikes.

"Sure." Mike shoved his shoes into his bag and shook his head. "I bobbled the handoff. And I wasn't fast enough."

"You handed off second by three-tenths of a second. You'll get faster." Hayden pulled out his street clothes and laid them on the bench by his shoes. Stripping off his uniform, he wrapped himself in the white locker room towel. "And we'll practice the handoffs. Don't worry about that."

"Yeah." Mike sat to put on his shoes.

"It's tradition to go eat after meets. We're going to Sammy's Subs."

"Okay." Mike stood and slammed his locker.

Hayden sighed. "Just say it."

"Really, man? You couldn't have *said* something?" The anger he'd pushed aside to focus on the race exploded. "You see my girlfriend with another dude, and you say *nothing*? What if that had been Molly? You would have wanted to know."

Hayden returned his glare with a nod. "Sorry."

"That's it?" Mike threw his bag on the bench. "Well, I guess I shouldn't have expected more from you I already know you don't follow the bro code. Your last best friend learned that."

Hayden stood, his face red. "If I thought she was cheating on you, I *would* have said something."

"For all you knew, she was. The only reason you didn't tell me was because Molly asked you not to and you can't tell her no." Mike flexed his fingers, but throat punching a guy wearing a towel wasn't cool.

"After we saw them at the restaurant, Molly told me how Cindy's mom set her up, and that she didn't know how to get out of it without upsetting her dad. She said Cindy would tell you and we didn't need to get involved." Hayden blew out a breath. "And yes, I kept quiet because Molly asked me to. But that's how relationships work. You trust each other. And sometimes you do things for them because it's what *they* need, even if it's not what you want for yourself."

Mike stared at Hayden, gritting his teeth. "You should have your own *Dear Abby* advice column in the paper."

With his weird old-man-in-a-teen-body ways, Hayden was right. But it still sucked. Mike sat back on the bench, leaning his elbows on his knees and rubbing his head. "She told me everything. And you're right, she wasn't cheating."

"I didn't think she would." He joined Mike on the bench. "You might not see this, but she's almost as crazy about you as I am about Molly."

"No one's that crazy, Hayden." Mike leaned his head back against the locker. "Besides, she said Tavis has a boyfriend so I'm not too worried about him moving in on her."

"Hmph. That makes things easier. Why the sudden approval to date?"

"I don't know. But Cindy said going out with Tavis was just a way to get her parents used to her dating so *we* could go out together." He turned his head toward Hayden. "I take back what I said. She does sound crazy."

Hayden chuckled.

Mike glanced around at the empty locker room. "Who knows, maybe she's right." He stood and shouldered his bag.

"So, we good?" Hayden asked.

Mike smirked. "Yeah. Cindy said I couldn't hit you because it was her fault you didn't tell me. She'll be glad to know I kept my word."

Hayden laughed. "Thanks. I've taken enough punches to the face this year. Tell Molly I'll be out in a minute. I wanna take a quick shower." He walked toward the stalls at the end of the locker room, whistling.

Mike turned to leave. Then he looked down at Hayden's pile of neatly folded clothes.

He understood why Hayden didn't tell him about Cindy and Tavis and talking to him about things had helped him chill out.

But, like he'd told Cindy, sometimes guys had to *do* something to show their feelings. Mike grabbed Hayden's clothes and track uniform and tucked them in his bag.

"Show don't tell," he said, and Hayden would definitely be showing. "*Now*, we're good." Mike left the locker room, smiling as Hayden whistled in the shower.

****

Cindy sat next to him in the booth at the diner. She took a bite of her turkey sub and checked her watch for the third time.

"Where are they? I thought you said Hayden left right after you did."

Mike nodded. "They'll be here." He lifted his sandwich to his mouth.

"They better hurry. It looks bad when the senior leaders blow off the team on the first meet meal."

"Meet meal? I didn't realize there was an official name for this." He set his food in his basket and held her by the waist, kissing her cheek. "Aren't I good enough company for you?"

She laughed and pushed him away. "Stop."

"Why? Can't I kiss my girlfriend in public?" He tried to kiss her lips, but she pulled away.

"Yes, but keep it PG." She tweaked his nose. "I don't know if you know this, but you have a reputation."

"Me? What reputation?" He took another bite.

"That you're a bit of a player. And you had quite a few… conquests. I don't want people to think I'm the next one."

"You aren't my next conquest." He laughed but stopped when she frowned. "What's wrong?"

"Nothing." She picked the edge of her bread, tossing the pieces on the wrapper.

"Something." He turned her face to his with his finger under her chin. "Come on, tell me."

"You don't deny the rumors?"

He gazed into her eyes, wishing he *could* deny it. "That depends. What did you hear?"

"Just that you, well, that you've," she shook her head. "Never mind. It's in the past. Doesn't matter." She took a bite of her sandwich.

"I can't change what I've done." He held her hand and kissed her fingers. "But you know how I feel about you. You're all that matters now."

She turned to face him in the seat. "I know that, but everyone else doesn't. What if they see us and think that you're just trying to," she stopped, looking down at their hands.

"Trying to what?"

"You know what I mean." Her cheeks darkened with her blush.

"I do." He leaned in and this time she let him kiss her. "But I know you don't want that right now. And that's okay. Besides, haven't we already decided we don't care what everyone else thinks?"

"Yeah, but that doesn't mean I want them to think we're doing it. If that rumor got back to my parents, we'd both be dead."

"It would be worth it." Mike's pulse quickened. He wouldn't hold her to anything. Still, if she offered, he wouldn't say no either. "I'm only joking, sort of."

"Eat your sandwich." She giggled and glanced at her watch again. "What on earth is taking them so long?"

"I think Hayden had to go home and get clothes."

"Clothes? Why? He had street clothes already."

"He did." Mike couldn't hold back his laughter. "Until I took them when he got in the shower."

"You took his clothes?" She wrinkled her forehead. "Why'd you do that?"

"Because you told me I couldn't hit him."

Cindy chewed her food slowly, staring at him. "So, you took his clothes because he didn't tell you about seeing me with Tavis."

"I told you, men need action to express our feelings."

"How would he get to his car with no clothes?" Cindy snickered.

"He had a towel," Mike said. "Besides, Molly might thank me for it. She's been trying to get him naked for months. Maybe that's why they're so late."

"Oh my god, Hayden is going to kill you." She laughed with him.

"Nah, he won't. It's a guy thing."

The bell above the door rang, and they looked toward the sound as Hayden and Molly entered. Hayden met Mike's smiling face and shook his head. He gave Mike a thumbs up, and Molly laughed.

"Told you." Mike patted her leg.

Cindy picked up her sandwich. "Guys are weird."

Molly and Hayden joined them after ordering their food, sliding into the opposite side of the booth.

"You're welcome," Mike said to Molly.

She blushed and Hayden said, "I'm just glad you left the towel." Which made Molly's face even redder.

After they ate, Mike leaned back into the corner of the booth. Cindy rested against him with her back on his chest.

"This should be a great season." Cindy played with Mike's hand as she talked, and he smiled. "Two wins today for the 4X1's. It's been a while since we began the season on top."

Hayden nodded. He put an arm around Molly, and she leaned her head on his shoulder. "It's promising."

"Well, what did you expect? That's what happens when you get a real athlete on the team." Cindy elbowed Mike in the stomach, and he groaned.

"You're so modest." She shook her head.

"You love it. My confidence turns you on, admit it." He tickled her sides.

"I admit to nothing." He tickled her harder, and she laughed even more.

"What the hell are you doing?"

Mike and Cindy looked up as Elijah towered over them. Jamal stood next to him, glowering.

"What's it look like we're doing?" Cindy glared at him. "We ate and now we're visiting with friends."

"I told you to keep your hands off my sister." Elijah pointed at Mike. Jamal crossed his arms on his chest.

"You did," Mike said. "And it still isn't your call."

"What do you want, Elijah?" Cindy asked. She squeezed Mike's knee.

"I want my sister to stay away from users." He narrowed his eyes. "You aren't doing to her what you do to other girls."

"I'm not *doing* anything." Mike twitched, but Cindy leaned back onto his chest, holding him in the seat.

"Elijah." Hayden glanced at Mike's face. "Hang out with us for a while."

Elijah sneered at Hayden. "I'm cool with you, Hayden, but stay out of this."

"You stay out of this, too," Cindy said. She stood, standing toe to toe with her twin, moving her head from side to side. "Like it or not, Mike is my boyfriend. And if I want to get naked and dance in the street with him, you don't have any say at all. So, butt out."

Elijah's eyes widened and his mouth hung open. The shock on his face was mirrored on Jamal's. Mike and Hayden chuckled, but Molly shook her head, frowning at Cindy.

Conversations died around them, a quiet settled as everyone watched the argument. They knew Cindy.

Elijah glanced at Mike then frowned at Cindy. "I told you I'd be watching."

"And I told you not to worry." Cindy took a deep breath and blew it out. "Everything is fine."

Elijah shook his head. The look he gave Mike would make Freddy Krueger run back into a nightmare to hide. Mike's stomach dropped.

"You remember what Mama said." He lowered his voice. "Her and Daddy don't want you knocked up. And that's all he's gonna do to you. Then he'll leave you to deal with it. Just like he did the last girl."

Mike's heart pounded in his ears drowning out the gasps in the room. He looked at Cindy, hoping she'd let him talk before she ran out the door.

CHAPTER TWELVE

CINDY

C old sweat broke out on her forehead and she met Mike's gaze. "Is... is that true?"

She couldn't believe it. He wouldn't do something like that and then not tell her. Right? Mike stood and tried to take her hand.

She yanked it away. "I said, is that true?"

"Let's not talk about this in here." He jerked his gaze to Jamal and Elijah.

"It is. Isn't it? That's why you wouldn't tell me who..." Her throat snapped shut and she covered her mouth with her hand.

He glared at Elijah. "I don't know where you heard that but you're wrong."

Pink cheeked, Mike continued to focus on Jamal's face, but Cindy couldn't look away from his.

Elijah smirked and pushed Mike's chest. "You're just mad your sorry ass got busted and now my sister sees who you really are."

Mike stepped toward Elijah and Hayden leapt off the seat, getting between them.

"Come on, don't do this." He glanced over his shoulder at Elijah. "That never happened."

Cindy watched them with her hands balled into fists at her side. Mike still hadn't looked at her. *Feeling guilty?* Her stomach churned and she finally looked away to glare at Hayden. "You're Mike's friend. Why should we believe you?"

"Cindy," Molly said. "Hayden wouldn't lie."

"Maybe not to you. Stay out of this."

Molly's face reddened, and she crossed her arms.

Cindy switched her gaze from Elijah to Mike and back again. Her brother returned her stare with a frown. She knew he'd never lie to her. Mike still watched Jamal.

"Come on, Elijah. Take me home." Cindy grabbed her purse from the seat and slung it over her shoulder.

"Cindy, wait. Talk to me."

Even Mike's pleas rang with guilt to her ears.

"No," she glanced around. "Y'all can go back to eating. Show's over."

The others looked away from her glare, whispering to each other, or taking quick bites and sips from their food and drinks.

She headed toward the door.

Mike followed and grabbed her arm. "Please, wait."

"Get your hands off her." Elijah shoved Mike backward. Mike righted himself and pushed Elijah, knocking him into the closed door.

Hayden groaned and grabbed Mike's arms from behind while a smirking Jamal put his hand on Elijah's shoulder.

"Save it for later," he said with a laugh.

The store owner came from behind the counter, his salt-and-pepper mustache quivered as he spoke. "You boys get out of here. I won't have fighting in here."

Mike shrugged out of Hayden's grasp. He looked again at Cindy.

She shook her head, her stomach churning. "Just… leave me alone."

Fighting tears, she turned from Mike and shoved open the door. Elijah and Jamal's footsteps followed her.

"I brought some security in case he got mouthy." Jamal pulled back his jacket and flashed the gun in his waistband. "But man, he might be the dumbest rich cracker I know. Thinking he could fight you, Lil EZ."

"Shut the hell up, Jamal." *That psycho has a freaking gun?* "And find your own ride home. I need to talk to my brother."

He raised his eyebrows. "What? Come on, baby. I could help ease your loneliness." He tugged on her braids.

She knocked his hand away. "Don't touch me. I wouldn't date you even if the Russians wiped everyone out and we were the only two left to re-populate the planet."

Elijah laughed but stepped between them. "Go on. I'll talk to you later."

Jamal held up his hands and walked toward the payphone in front of the building.

Cindy rubbed her temples with her fingers. The boiling anger was wearing off and the hurt would soon explode in a gush of tears. She wanted to get home where she could sob into her pillow in private.

She got in the car and Elijah joined her. She leaned her elbow on the window while he drove, covering her mouth with her hand and glaring at the houses blurring past outside.

"You okay?" Elijah asked.

"Hell no, I'm not okay."

Elijah nodded. "I'm sorry. You needed to know."

"Who told you?"

"The girl he did it to."

"Who was that?" She didn't want to believe it, but she trusted her brother to tell her the truth.

"Jenny."

The flare of anger and jealousy burned away her tears, replacing the desire to cry with the desire to kick Jenny's ass. Or maybe Mike's. She imagined them together until her tear ducts had seared shut. Maybe forever.

No wonder Mike had never told her who he had sex with. All the rumors were true. Jenny had gotten pregnant with Mike's baby. Vomit burned in the back of her throat. How could she be so stupid? She should never have dated him.

Elijah said, "What now? Think you could date that Tavis guy? He seemed nice."

"Too soon, idiot."

"Come on. Best cure for a broken heart, right? Move on fast."

"No," she snorted. "That won't happen."

"Why not? Because Mama set you up? Just give him a chance. Maybe you'll like him."

"Did Mama pay you to promote him?"

Elijah gave her a crooked grin. "No, I just want you to be happy."

"Thanks, but Tavis isn't for me." And she was happy, with Mike. The tears tingled in her eyes and she pressed her fingers against her eyelids to squish them back inside her head.

"But *why not*? He's a brother, in college, got a job…" He let the *duh* hang.

She shouldn't tell Tavis's secret, but Elijah wasn't going to let that possibility go. "He's taken already."

Elijah jerked the car a little as he turned his head to look at her. "What? He went on a date with you when he's dating someone?"

She smirked. "Yeah. He's got a boyfriend named Brett. He only went out with me because his parents don't know he's gay and he's trying to keep it that way. So don't tell Mama."

"He's gay?"

"Yeah." She rubbed her eyes again.

"Mama set you up with a gay boy."

"Yep. If you like him that much, you could date him. You're more his type than I am."

Elijah was silent for a moment, then his laughter filled the car. When tears streamed down his face, Cindy laughed with him. She wasn't quite sure when the hurt bled into her tears of laughter, and the sobs she repressed broke free.

****

Later that night, after her little brothers had gone to sleep and her parents retired to their bedroom for the night, Cindy tiptoed to the kitchen. She took the phone from its cradle on the kitchen wall and dialed the number, then sank to the floor, twisting the cord around her index finger.

"Hello?"

"Hey, it's me. Can you talk?" It wasn't the voice she wanted to hear, but she wasn't sure she'd ever hear that one on the phone again.

"Sure," Molly said. "I'm always here for you."

"I'm sorry I snapped at you earlier. That was wrong."

Molly's breath came through the phone. "Yes, you're an idiot. But you know I forgive you."

Cindy swallowed around the tightness in her throat, unable to speak.

"You okay?" Molly asked. "Have you talked to Mike?"

"No." His name broke the dam in her throat. "I've been doing homework, cleaning the house, plotting his murder. Too busy to call him."

Molly sighed again into the phone. "Hang up right now and call *him*. He's the one you need to talk to."

"Why? So he can lie?"

"He won't lie to you. Besides, you didn't even give him a chance to explain."

"What is there to explain?" Cindy raised her voice. Her dad's snores stuttered from the other room, and she whispered instead. "That he got a girl pregnant but didn't bother to help her? Or tell me? Everyone's heard the rumor about Jenny being pregnant her freshman year and that's when Mike claims they went on that *one* date."

"That's just it. How do you know that's true if you don't talk to him? You can't trust rumors, Cindy."

"But Elijah wouldn't lie to me." She gave a weak snort. "We have that twin bond you know."

"Maybe not, but that doesn't mean somebody wouldn't lie to *him*. Remember when you convinced me not to let Hayden explain the lies Trevor told me about him? If I hadn't finally let Hayden talk to me, we wouldn't have the wonderful 1940's relationship everyone makes fun of today."

Cindy smiled despite her pain. "You guys are a little ridiculous you know."

"That's beside the point. Call. Mike."

"This is different. You had your crazy manipulating ex-boyfriend lying to you. My *brother* told me this. And you saw Mike's face. He didn't deny it right away."

Molly groaned. "I know Elijah wouldn't lie about what he'd been told but think, Cindy. *Who told him?*"

Cindy wrinkled her nose. "The girl it happened to."

"Who was that?"

"Jenny."

There was a heartbeat of silence then Molly laughed. "If Jenny had hooked up with Mike, the whole school would have known. She's full of herself and loves the attention she would have spread the rumors herself."

Cindy stared at her slipper-clad feet, biting her thumbnail until it hurt.

"My point is," Molly continued, "when you need to learn the truth, you have to go to the source. Give him a chance."

"I guess you're right. But only about the chance. If he tells me it's true, that's it."

"If he tells you it's true, I'll help you hide the body."

"That's the nicest thing you've ever said to me."

"Like Dionne Warwick says, that's what friends are for."

Cindy laughed quietly. "Thanks for making me feel better. It sucks to be on the other end of the lies. I didn't do so well when you had your trouble with Hayden."

"Yeah, I think you threatened to call the cops a few times when he tried to talk to me."

"Hey, I was just looking out for you, girl." Cindy glanced around the dark kitchen.

"True. Now hang up and call him. I'm sure he's going crazy thinking about you. I'm surprised he hasn't busted down your door yet."

"He'd better not. I'm not sure who'd beat him first, my brother or Mama." They were both silent for a moment and then at the same time they answered.

"Mama."

Cindy breathed a quiet laugh.

"Call him now and end his torture," Molly said. "And yours."

"Okay." She smiled in the dark kitchen. "Thanks, Molly. See you tomorrow."

She stood to dial Mike's number into the buttons on the cradle, this time wrapping the cord around her whole hand. He answered in a rough voice and Cindy's chest tightened.

"Hello?"

"Mike?" Duh. Who else would it be answering his private number?"

"Cindy? Oh my god. I'm so sorry."

"Sorry for what? Lying to me?" The skin on her hand tingled, and she unraveled the cord, sinking back to the floor.

"No. I never lied to you about anything."

"Then what are you sorry for?"

"That this is happening," he whispered. "That you have to hurt for nothing when there's already so much going on in your life."

She leaned her head back against the wall waiting for him to talk, resisting the hope threatening to build.

"I love you, and you've got to trust me. I have never… gotten anyone pregnant."

"Jenny disagrees." Anger ripped through her again at the thought. She squeezed the phone, and it creaked under the pressure.

"*Jenny*? God, I would never do anything with her. I never *have* done anything with her." He sighed into the phone. "Why would she say that?"

Cindy cocked her head. "She hits on you all the time. Is it because you had history?"

"No, the only history we have is one date and a long list of times I told her no."

She listened to his breathing, imagining his lips next to her ear instead of the phone. God, she wanted to believe him.

"Don't you believe me?"

"I want to."

"What's stopping you?"

"You. You couldn't even look at me tonight after Elijah got there. Pretty sure not making eye contact is the sign of a liar."

Mike sighed. "I wasn't avoiding your eyes."

"Really? Could've fooled me."

Cindy twisted the cord faster.

"I wasn't. I —"

"You didn't look at me until I was walking out the door."

"I know, but I couldn't because—"

"Because you felt guilty?"

"No!" Mike sighed into the phone. "Because I was watching Elijah's friend."

"What?"

100

"He had a gun and I didn't want him to hurt you or anybody else."

Dammit, he was right. Cindy rubbed her throbbing temple.

"Is that why you don't believe me? Because I didn't look at you?"

"Only one reason." Her voice cracked, and she swallowed. "You never told me…"

"Never told you what?"

She drew a deep breath. "You never told me who you slept with, or how many so, what if it was Jenny?"

"Oh."

"Well? I think I deserve to know."

"You do, it's just—."

"Just what?"

"It's embarrassing."

She rolled her eyes in the dark. "I'm not asking for a detailed description, just a number. Make a ballpark estimate if you have to."

"Wow." His voice cracked again. "You have a low opinion of me."

"Prove me wrong." Grabbing the phone cord again, she twisted it around her hand but pictured wrapping it around Mike's neck.

"Okay. Then how does one sound? Is that rough enough for you?"

She raised one eyebrow and tucked her chin. "One?"

"Yes."

"Who?" she whispered.

"God, Cindy," he whispered back.

"I need to know." Did she? Would it help her to believe him, or would it add another body for her and Molly to hide?

"Why? She doesn't matter. It was a bad decision I made at a party."

"Was it Jenny?"

"No. But if I tell you, you'll hate me."

The quiver in his voice sent vibrations into her chest and down to her stomach. "If you don't want to tell me, how do I know I can trust you?"

"You're right."

He grew quiet and her stomach knotted like the phone cord.

He whispered the name. "Andrea."

She closed her eyes and wrinkled her nose. "Please tell me you're joking."

"I wish I was. It happened last year. We were both drunk, and I was stupid and…"

"And she was experienced." She envisioned track practice tomorrow. Practicing handoffs she was liable to hit Andrea over the head with the baton instead of passing it to her.

"At the time, I was kind of with a girl named Dana."

"You had a girlfriend? You cheated?"

"No. We weren't what you call official, I guess. We'd only gone on a couple dates." He breathed into the phone. "It wasn't like us, Cindy. She didn't even get mad. She hooked up with someone else at the same party."

"Jeez, Mike. How come you never told me this?"

"Because I didn't want you to see how stupid I was before we met."

She didn't have a reply for that.

"Why did you make me tell you?" His voice broke at the end. "You hate me, don't you?"

Her heart reacted to his pain with a resounding thump in her throat. She didn't hate him. But that might be because she craved his laugh, his stupid jokes, and his strong arms around her shoulders.

"Thank you for telling me."

"I want you to believe me. I've never slept with Jenny."

She hugged her knees to her chest. But she only had Mike's side of the story. "I want to believe you."

"How can I prove myself?"

Like Molly said, go to the source. "Tomorrow, you and I need to talk to Jenny. Ask her why she told my brother that."

If he refused, she would know he was lying and didn't want to get caught.

"Alright."

"Alright? Just like that?" Did he think she was bluffing?

"I'm telling the truth. I want to know why she's lying about me, too."

Cindy snorted. "If she's lying—"

"She is."

"—then the reason is obvious."

"What is it?"

"Uh, to get us to break up so she can make her move on you." For a *player,* he sure didn't understand the game.

"God, why do girls do stuff like that?"

A nervous chuckle escaped. "Only some girls."

"Yeah," he said. "Why can't you be like guys? Just punch each other in the face and move on with things."

"Or steal each other's clothes from the locker room while we're in the shower."

"There's that, too." He gave a soft laugh. "I wish I could see you right now. Too bad our phones don't have cameras like on The Jetsons."

His voice warmed her face. The more they talked the easier it was to forget to she was mad at him. "I have to go."

"I know. But I don't want you to."

"I'll see you tomorrow."

"Will you meet me in the parking lot?"

If she did, she'd give in and end up kissing him before they talked to Jenny. Already she wanted to forget what had happened and move on like Mike said. But she had to know the truth.

"No. Meet me by my locker and we'll find Jenny together."

"Okay," he answered, no hesitation in his voice. "I love you."

The words trembled on the edge of her tongue, but she forced herself not to say them.

"Goodnight, Mike."

She disconnected the call and walked back to her bedroom, craving the oblivion of sleep, but when it finally came, Jenny and Mike haunted her dreams.

CHAPTER THIRTEEN

MIKE

T he students milling around the hall ignored Mike for the most part. A few guys tried to high five him, but most of the girls gave him dirty looks. It seemed impossible to believe one lie had turned him into a social pariah so fast. Now he knew how Hayden had felt when everyone accused him of lying about sleeping with Molly last year.

Whatever, as long as Cindy believed him. He glanced around and found her over the heads of the crowd.

She appeared at the end of the hall, walking toward him, and his breath blew out like he'd been punched in the gut. He wanted to see her smile, not frown. Wanted to wrap her in a hug and kiss her soft lips, have her touch his hair and the skin on the back of his neck.

Instead, she walked up to him, hugging her books to her chest, looking at him just like everyone else did—like a liar.

"Hey," he breathed. He reached to touch her cheek, but she flinched away. The air left his chest again with this second blow.

"Hey," she replied. Her gaze darted from side to side at the gawkers. Voice raised she called out, "Anyone want to take notes so you can tell everyone our business?" Lockers closed and people hurried away.

Mike grinned. "You sure know how to clear a room."

"Nosey assholes." She looked at the floor. "Let's go find Jenny. We only have a few minutes before class. I want to get this over with."

Over with? His stomach dropped. She sounded like she already decided he was lying.

"Yes, let's go so you can see she's lying." He touched her arm, grimacing when she flinched again. "I think she has chemistry with Mrs. Shaw first hour."

They walked toward the stairs that led down to the science hall. Jenny stood outside her class talking to Gavin. She touched his chest and threw her head back, laughing at something he said.

Mike glanced at Cindy. Surely she knew what kind of person Jenny was and wouldn't believe her over him. That girl flirted with any guy stupid enough to look at her. And he'd heard more than enough stories to know not to touch her unless you wanted to catch trouble—or something else.

The muscles in Cindy's jaw rippled, and Mike could tell she was close to exploding. He hoped it wasn't on him.

Jenny met his gaze and her eyes narrowed. She pushed Gavin away, and he walked into the classroom, frowning. She reached out and held Cindy's hands.

"Hey, Cindy. I guess you heard the news." Jenny's face wore a mask of sympathy. "I'm sorry you had to find out this way, but it's better. You shouldn't have to go through what I did."

"Cut the bullshit, Jenny." His face filled with heat. "*I* didn't do anything to you."

Cindy shifted her books and glanced between them. "Tell me the truth, Jenny. And don't make shit up just because you're trying to break us up so you can get Mike to go out with you."

Jenny blinked and a tear rolled from under her thick black eyelashes. "What? No, I wouldn't do that to you. I don't want to go out with him. Once around the track is enough for me." She sneered at Mike. "Even if he wants me back, I wouldn't take him."

Mike scoffed, "We went out on one stupid date. We never had sex. And if you got pregnant, it wasn't from me."

Jenny's face turned red. "That's what you said when I told you. Get a new line."

"If you got pregnant, where's the baby?" Mike bit his tongue to keep from yelling. "That's not something you could hide."

"You know what happened." Jenny's eyes filled with tears. "H-how could you bring that up? If I hadn't miscarried, I'd be a mother and you'd be a... a deadbeat dad because you wouldn't take responsibility."

"That never happened."

"Right." Jenny rolled her eyes and wiped a tear from her cheek. "I forgot, we said we wouldn't talk about it because you didn't want anyone to know."

"Stop. You know you're lying."

Cindy sniffled and Mike's gaze flew to her.

"God, Cindy, you can't believe her."

Tears rolled down her cheeks and his throat closed.

"I... I gotta go." She spun and ran down the hall.

Mike watched her go and clenched his fists. He would never hit a girl, but right now, he wanted to tear Jenny apart. He swallowed hard before turning back to her.

"Why the hell are you doing this? You and I both know you're lying."

"Am I?" She put a hand on his chest and leaned in close. "Right now, it looks like you're the liar. Maybe you shouldn't have blown me off."

He knocked her hand away. "Maybe I blew you off because I don't want to go out with a white trash ho who can't keep her legs together."

Jenny gasped and Mike turned away, afraid to say any more. The way Jenny slept around she *would* end up pregnant. He stormed through the hall, his jaw clenched, glaring at the floor.

How could Cindy not trust him? He'd done everything for her, anything she asked for. Lied to his parents, lied to everyone at school when he pretended not to like her, lied to himself when he said someday she'd tell her parents the truth.

When it was his word against Jenny's, Cindy believed her instead of him. If she loved him why couldn't she trust him? The unfairness burned a hole in his stomach. Maybe she *didn't* love him. Maybe Tony was right, and she had used him.

Distracted by his pain, he didn't realize he'd left the school until he stood at his car in the student lot under a cloudless blue sky. He unlocked it and got in. He couldn't stay here, couldn't take the whispers and stares and laughter. He couldn't be near Cindy when he knew she hated him.

He floored the pedal, tires kicking up gravel as he raced from the lot, no destination in mind other than escape.

****

His escape led him all over town. He wandered, thinking about Cindy and how to make her believe him. Short of forcing Jenny to tell the truth, he didn't see a way.

Out of blind desperation, he found himself at the trail where he and Cindy spent their time hiding from the world. He just wanted to be with her, and this might be the closest he'd get.

When he pulled into the lot and saw Cindy's car, his hopes skyrocketed at the chance to talk to her alone, here where they had good memories to remind her how she felt about him. Maybe she'd skipped school too, trying to get away from their mess.

Instead, Elijah sat on a bench near the trailhead, smoking a joint.

Mike grinned. He needed someone to blame and a perfectly good candidate sat right in front of him. He got out of the car and walked toward Elijah.

"What the hell do you want?" A cloud of smoke encircled Elijah's head when he spoke.

"To talk to you," Mike lied.

"I got nothing to say to you." Elijah stood, grinding his blunt on the table to put it out. "Go on, get out of here before something bad happens."

"You already took care of that. Thanks to your lies, Cindy hates me."

Elijah smirked. "Good. She has better options."

Mike ignored his comment. "Jenny lied. And you told Cindy so she wouldn't want to be with me."

"You're partly right. I don't want my sister going out with you." He stood, tossing the burned out joint to the gravel at his feet. "I told you to leave."

Mike's pulse throbbed in his throat. Talking wasn't enough distraction anymore but physical pain might be. Elijah could provide that. He smirked and took a step closer. "It's a public place."

Elijah raised an eyebrow. "Back off."

"And you're wrong. I *never* had sex with Jenny. Why don't you want Cindy to go out with me?"

"Because," Elijah smirked. "She doesn't belong with a user. And looks like, she agrees."

Mike's fist connected with Elijah's left cheek. Elijah moved quickly, planting his fist in Mike's stomach. He followed it with a hit to Mike's eye.

Mike landed two solid punches on Elijah's chin and nose with a resounding crack, releasing a torrent of blood. He bounced backward a step and waited.

Elijah groaned and answered with a hit to Mike's face so hard he knew he'd see stars for a week. He spat the blood from his mouth, looking in time to see Elijah's huge body flying at him.

Elijah tackled him to the ground, and they rolled. Rocks stabbed his back and Mike grunted. Fighting for the top position, they wrestled, continuing to hit each other. Dust from the gravel stuck to the blood on their faces, powdering Elijah's dark skin in huge patches.

Mike's lungs burned, his face ached, and his stomach felt like he'd been hit repeatedly with a sledgehammer. But as much as he hurt physically, the pain from losing Cindy still overshadowed it. He threw punch after punch, took hit after hit not caring what happened. He just wanted the pain from the beating to erase the pain from losing her.

The blip of a police siren warned of company. Elijah struggled harder, trying to gain the advantage before their fight ended. Mike let him win. Elijah sat atop him, his fists delivering hit after hit to Mike's head, seeming intent on beating him into the unconsciousness Mike craved.

"Stop. Hands behind your heads. Now." The officer's voice boomed across the lot, but Mike and Elijah ignored him. He hit Elijah's nose again, sending a warm spray of blood across his own face and the gravel behind his head. Elijah answered with two more blows to Mike's face.

A burly officer pulled on Elijah. Breathing heavy, Mike scrambled toward them, intending to ram his shoulder into Elijah's gut. But another officer grabbed him from behind, restraining his arms.

"I said knock it off! Both of you. Or I'll have to arrest you."

Mike stopped struggling and glared at Elijah. "You couldn't just leave us alone. She was happy."

"If she was so happy why hadn't she told us? Why did she hide it?"

Mike spit a mouthful of blood on the ground.

"Shut up." The officer holding Mike shoved him toward the police cruiser. "You can both tell your story at the station."

Mike sneered at the officer's name badge. "I thought you weren't arresting us, Officer Byrne." He wiped blood from his busted lip.

The officer chuckled and opened the car door, pointing Mike inside. "No, but I am taking you in so I can call your parents. Shouldn't you boys be in school?"

"Whatever." Mike fell into the car, grunting with pain, wishing it was more.

"You cool off here while we talk to your friend. Then we're all going to play nice and take a ride downtown without fighting in the back seat." He shut the door and walked back to where Elijah sat on the bench, the other officer towering over him.

Elijah wore a look of belligerence. Covered with blood and dust, lumps on his face, he looked like shit. Mike was tempted to tell the cops to check his pockets for joints. But it would hurt Cindy to see her brother busted for drugs.

He winced and rubbed his throbbing jaw. Elijah should take up boxing. Or maybe professional wrestling.

"Idiot." Mike leaned his head on the seat. Everything hurt. And the fight didn't work anyway. His heart still hurt worse than his broken nose and busted lip.

After a few minutes, the door opened, and Elijah flopped into the seat next to Mike. He crossed his arms over his chest, grimacing. Mike smirked, glad for Elijah's pain. This mess was his fault to begin with.

"You two behave yourselves. We need to discuss things then we'll leave. If you start fighting again, we'll arrest you." Officer Byrne went to the front of the car and smiled, lighting a cigarette.

"You should've left." Elijah peered at Mike with his swollen right eye. Blood dripped from the corner of his mouth and his busted nose.

"Yeah." He looked at Elijah through his swollen left eye. "I guess I needed to blow off steam."

"By having me beat the hell out of you?"

"Better to hurt on the outside than on the inside." Mike looked away and leaned back on the seat again. "It didn't work though."

They watched the officers leaning on the car "discussing" their cigarettes. Mike shook his head. His parents were going to kill him. He'd be grounded for sure. Not that it mattered, he didn't want to do anything without Cindy. He leaned forward and held his head, exhaling a huge sigh. "Why don't you want us to date?"

The muffled laughs of the officers and the sound of Elijah's breathing filled the car. Elijah said, "She's my sister. I want what's best for her."

He met Elijah's angry stare and frowned. "You don't even know me. How do you know I'm *not* what's best for her?"

He shrugged. "You're a hothead who starts fights and got a girl pregnant. That's how."

"I didn't get anyone pregnant. And the fight wasn't with you."

"My bloody face and sore gut says it was."

"I just wanted to forget…" He didn't finish. He already sounded like a wuss. "Never mind."

Elijah uncrossed his arms and ran his hand over his head. Dust dislodged from his hair floated along a sunbeam coming through the window. "Why do you want to date her?"

Mike closed his eyes and let his head fall back against the seat again. He pictured her face, her smile, her laugh. The way she looked when she ran, the determined way she held herself while she waited for the gun. Her face when she played with Drew. Her loyalty to her friends.

The way she looked right before he kissed her, and after, when her cheeks flushed and her eyes burned, waiting for him to kiss her again.

He looked at her brother, not caring if he believed him or not. Not caring if Elijah thought he was the world's biggest pussy. He said the only thing that mattered whether Elijah wanted to laugh or hit him. "Because I love her."

Elijah frowned and looked out the window.

Mike closed his eyes again, trying not to think about Cindy, and failing. Elijah's chuckle cut into his thoughts and Mike lifted his head to look at him. "What?"

He shook his head, using his sleeve to wipe the blood from his lip. "You know, I've been in lots of fights."

"Yeah, I can tell." Mike pointed to his aching face.

"But I've never fought someone who *wanted* me to kick their ass."

"First time for everything I guess." He laid his head back again, frowning.

"It makes me wonder though, are you crazy, or do you like my sister so much you'd take an ass beating for her?" He squinted at Mike.

Mike shrugged, then wished he hadn't. "What does it matter? Like you said, she doesn't want me anymore. She believed Jenny's lies. And yours."

"Why would Jenny lie about something like that?"

"Because she's a bitch, and I told her I didn't want to go out with her. And she doesn't want me dating your sister either." Mike swallowed, the metallic taste of blood combining with the bitter taste of hate. "Maybe you two should hook up. Then she might leave me alone."

Elijah laughed, and Mike fought the urge to punch him in the face.

"Nah, she isn't my type." He glanced out the window.

Mike followed his gaze to the officers. They ground their cigarettes out in the gravel and walked toward the doors.

"Mine either. Which is why I never went out with her, and the reason she's spreading lies to make Cindy hate me." Mike glared at Elijah. "And you fell for it."

Elijah frowned. "I didn't fall for anything."

"Don't you think if I had gotten her pregnant, everyone would have known? Shit like that doesn't stay secret for long." He waved a hand. "Believe what you want. I'm done talking about this."

Elijah wrinkled his forehead, lips pressed together then turned his gaze back to the window.

The car shook as the front doors opened and the officers got in. Elijah's restrainer turned and spoke through the cage separating them. "You boys making up back there?"

Mike rubbed his forehead. "Can we just go?"

"Tsk, tsk. You need to learn some patience, boy. Don't you know good things come to those who wait?" The officers laughed, then the one driving put the car in gear and pulled from the lot.

Wait. Mike stared out the window. He'd done nothing but wait over the last few months. Wait for Cindy.

They drove toward the police station, the officers talking in the front, Elijah stewing beside him. Every bump sent vibrations of pain until Mike could tell exactly where Elijah's fists had connected with his body.

As they pulled off the road and into the parking lot at the station, the wheel on Mike's side hit a pothole and the car jolted. Mike groaned grabbing his side. He chuckled humorlessly to himself. Yeah, the only good thing his waiting had earned him was a good ass-kicking.

CHAPTER FOURTEEN

CINDY

Cindy wanted to throat punch every person who offered her condolences. It wasn't like someone died—yet. Her boyfriend lied and got another girl pregnant. They could save their words of reassurance for his family at his funeral after she killed him.

She entered biology and looked for him. Her body played Wheel of Emotion, like Vanna White stood flipping the tiles from concern to guilt to relief and finally spelling out anger. Mike wasn't there.

"Probably couldn't face me," she said to herself. She pulled out her notebook and waited for class to start. Tapping her foot against the leg of the desk, she doodled on the cover of her notebook, grimacing when she realized she'd written Mike's name. She blacked it out with her pen.

Molly slid into her seat next to Cindy. "Hey, girl."

She pitched a neatly folded note onto the desk. Cindy read her name in curly script on the outside of the triangle-shaped paper.

"Uhm, you see, notes are for classes when we won't see each other. That way we have something to read when the teacher is talking."

Molly smirked. "This isn't from me. Andrea asked me to give to you." She pulled out her notebook and laid it on the top of her shiny desk.

Glancing at the cover, Cindy laughed. Molly had written Hayden's name across the cover and outlined it with tiny hearts.

"Really?" She covered the black blob on her book with her fingers.

Molly blushed. "Shut up. Open the note. I want to know what it says."

"You didn't read it?" Cindy unfolded the paper.

"No. I knew you'd tell me what it said, and I thought you should read it first."

"Read it with me." She held the paper between them.

> *Cindy,*
>
> *You want to know the truth, and I know how to get it. Meet me in the girl's locker room at 3:15.*
>
> *Andrea*

Cindy frowned and re-read the note.

"What is this about?" Molly asked.

"Oh, you know, the truth about who shot J.R."

"Smartass."

Cindy narrowed her eyes. "How could Andrea know the truth about Mike and Jenny?" An image of Mike with Andrea flashed behind her eyes and she crumpled the note. "Whatever. I'm not going." She lifted the note and aimed for the nearby trash can.

"Wait." Molly grabbed her hand. "Maybe we should go."

"I don't see how Andrea can help. Or why she'd want to." Cindy narrowed her eyes. "She's the second to last person I'd trust with the 411 about Mike."

Molly nodded. "True, but she has been nicer lately."

Snorting, Cindy glanced at Mr. Miller as he waddled to the front of the class. "Okay. We'll go right after class. But if she jerks me around, I'll kick her ass again."

Molly rolled her eyes. "You sound like Elijah. Guess we finally know your twin superpowers."

After class ended, Cindy rushed with Molly to the locker room. They walked around the corner and into one of the u-shaped coves of orange painted lockers. Cindy wrinkled her nose at the smell of stale sweat and pine-scented cleaner, then checked the clock above the teacher's dark office.

"3:15. Where the hell is she? We've got practice in twenty minutes and this locker room is about to fill up with nosey teenaged girls." Cindy reached in her bag for her track clothes then threw her bag into a locker. She pulled off her Guess sweatshirt and jeans and pulled on her shorts.

Molly did the same. "Maybe she's late. Or was jerking you around."

They finished dressing and Cindy sighed in frustration. "She's not coming. Let's go outside and warm up."

The squeak of the door opening cut through the locker room, echoing off the metal and tile. Cindy put a finger to her lips, whispering, "That's got to be her."

Molly nodded, and they sat on the bench to wait.

Andrea came around the corner and froze, her shoes squeaking against the floor.

"Oh. I didn't know Molly would be here."

"Well, she is," Cindy quipped. "What do you want?"

Andrea sighed and sank onto the wooden bench beside Cindy. She dropped her chin to her chest and pulled a note from her pocket, folded into a triangle. The edges were dark like it had been folded and unfolded a hundred times. She turned it over and over in her hands.

"First I need to say something." Andrea raised her head to meet their eyes. "I'm not proud of what I'm about to show you. You'll both probably hate me more after you read it. But maybe… maybe it will make up for some of the stupid things I've done."

She held the note out to Cindy.

Cindy glanced at it and wrinkled her nose. "What is this?"

"The truth," Andrea said with a sigh. "Just read the first bit. Then see who signed it."

After a head nod from Molly, Cindy took the paper. Carefully unfolding it, she flattened it out on her thigh then held it so she and Molly could read together.

Andrea,

You are a total bitch! I can't believe you would do this to me, your best friend. You knew I liked Mike but that didn't stop you from screwing him, did it? Nope. Because you've always been jealous of me. You just threw yourself all over him at that party and took him away from me. God, I was so mad I couldn't think straight. Because of you, I was so upset I slept with stupid Trevor for comfort and now look what happened. I'm fucking pregnant. All because you couldn't keep your legs together and let me have the guy I really wanted.

I hate you. My life is ruined now. I could end up white trash like you. A pregnant teen. Thanks a lot. I hope this makes your pathetic life happier. If you—

Skimming the rest, Cindy flipped the page over to see the signature on the back.

From your ex-best friend,
Jenny

Cindy dropped her hands to her lap and stared at the lockers across from them.

Molly grabbed the note and waved it at Andrea. "Trevor got Jenny pregnant?"

"No." Andrea sniffled. "Jenny never got pregnant. It was a false test."

Scrunching her forehead, Cindy said, "Wait. Everyone talked about it. Who spread the rumor?"

With red cheeks, Andrea answered. "I did."

"Why?" Cindy asked. "Why would you do that to your best friend?"

"Did you *read* the note?" Andrea gave a short laugh. "Jenny doesn't have friends, she has minions. She was always mean, bossy, always telling us what to do and who to hang out with. Who to hate. And we did it. Anyone who got on her bad side had a fresh rumor about *themselves* going around the next day."

Cindy blew a breath out her nose. "Yeah, guess Jenny deserved it."

Molly laid her hand on Cindy's knee. "It wasn't Mike."

Refusing to let the hope take over, Cindy shook her head. "How do we know this isn't fake? What do you care?"

"Because Jenny is still Jenny. Doing the same mean stuff to people. When she started this, I tried to stay out of it. But seeing you so upset, and Mike…" Andrea shook her head. "I knew I was the only one who could help. And after everything I did to you and Molly… I thought I should. I kept this note in case Jenny lied about me, but I'm glad I did and that it showed you the truth."

"You bitch!"

All three of them jumped as the scream echoed off the metal lockers and cement walls.

Jenny stomped around the corner as they stood from the bench.

Andrea narrowed her eyes. "What's the matter, Jenny? Don't like getting busted?"

"So what." Jenny waved a hand at Cindy. "Now she knows. But how does she like knowing that you *did* have sex with her boyfriend?"

Jenny's words sent a bolt of heat through Cindy's chest. She ignored it though. Because Andrea was right, she'd totally busted Jenny. Mike didn't lie. He never got Jenny pregnant or even slept with her. Part of Cindy wanted to sing, but she gave in to the bigger part of her that wanted a piece of Jenny.

Pushing past Molly, Cindy stepped around Andrea. Fire filled her gut and she shoved Jenny in the shoulder.

"You're the bitch, Jenny. And the liar."

"I'm not afraid of you." Jenny shoved her back.

Molly grabbed Cindy's arm. "Don't do it, Cindy. She's not worth the trouble."

"No," she said, fighting against Molly's hold, "but Mike is."

Pulling free, she grabbed Jenny by the shirt and shoved her into the lockers. Jenny smashed into the metal and landed on the floor, rubbing her head.

Cindy fell on her, smashing a fist into her nose. Jenny cried out as Andrea and Molly each grabbed an arm and pulled Cindy to her feet.

"Stop!" Molly pleaded. "You'll get in trouble again. And your mom will kill you."

Andrea laughed. "As much as I would like to see you kick Jenny's ass, Molly's right."

Cindy quit struggling and they let go of her arms. "If you lie about him again, I'll give you worse than this." She panted, pointing at Jenny.

Jenny wiped her face. "Whatever. He's all yours. But you'll look like the pathetic loser who's dating the asshole. And when I tell Mr. Roberts you hit me because you're mad that I told everyone the truth, you'll get suspended again, and people will still believe me. She waved at Andrea and Molly. "Nobody will believe your friends. They'll just think they're

117

lying to help you. Trust me, the teachers here are idiots and I know how to handle them."

This made Andrea laugh even harder. Cindy and Molly glanced at her.

"Rookie mistake, Jenny. Always have a backup plan." She glanced behind them and grinned. "Not to mention back up."

Mrs. Richter walked around the corner of the teacher's darkened offices. Cindy opened her mouth in surprise. Crap, she was busted.

"See, I learned this last time when it was my word against Cindy's. The teachers here are smart and know a liar when they see one." She smiled at Mrs. Richter. "But sometimes it helps to show them."

Jenny curled her lip.

Mrs. Richter crossed her arms and nodded. "Well, girls. This was an enlightening show this afternoon. But I think it's time to end it. You girls better get ready for track."

Jenny huffed. "Aren't you going to punish her? Look what she did to me!" Blood covered Jenny's chin and spots dotted the front of her designer shirt. A bruise already formed under both of her angry blue eyes.

The relief from knowing Mike hadn't lied calmed her worry, but she didn't want to get busted for fighting again. Last time her dad had such a bad episode, he was in bed for two days. Dammit, why didn't she think of that?

Mrs. Richter tilted her head. "Actually, no." She looked between Jenny and Cindy. "This problem is over. Do I make myself clear?"

The corner of Cindy's mouth pulled up, and she nodded.

Jenny opened her mouth to protest but snapped it shut. She turned her back to them and stalked toward the bathroom.

Cindy exhaled with relief. "Thank you, Mrs. Richter. For not turning me in."

She winked at Cindy and Molly. "I don't condone fighting, but from what Andrea told me and what I heard Jenny say, she deserved it. But that's just between us. Now go, before those nosey girls you mentioned get here."

She patted Cindy on the back and left the locker room.

Cindy turned to Andrea.

With red cheeks, Andrea dropped her gaze to the floor. "Was I that bitchy to you and Hayden?"

Molly opened her mouth, but Cindy snorted. "Yes."

"No wonder you kicked my ass," Andrea said.

Molly grinned. "Well, you made up for that a little today."

Cindy wanted to be thankful, but the past had a way of ruining the present. Still, Andrea had shown her the truth. Cindy bit back her anger and leaned on the lockers. "Thanks, Andrea."

She shrugged. "I told you I could get the truth."

Cindy frowned. "Did you do it because you like Mike?"

Andrea shook her head. "I don't like him. At least, not like that. He's a nice guy." Her cheeks turned redder. "It's obvious how much he likes you. And that's why I did this. I caused hell for you and Hayden, Molly, and I know what it feels like to be lied to. I did date Trevor after you and he's the king of the bait and switch."

"Tell me about it," Molly groaned.

"Being with him made me realize I didn't want to be the girl who hurts people because she doesn't have any friends. Anyway, Cindy's been nice to me, helping me with track and stuff, despite what I did. I thought, well, I owed you both." She glanced at the floor again. "And I hoped we could start over."

Cindy shifted on her feet. Glancing from Andrea's red face to Molly's open mouth, she laughed. "I never expected this to turn into an episode of Oprah."

Andrea's blush increased and Cindy touched her shoulder. "Clean slate starts now."

"Really?" Andrea glanced at Molly.

"Yep," Molly agreed. "Grudges suck. Besides, you had to deal with Trevor, that's enough punishment."

Andrea laughed with Molly.

"Come on, let's get out of here before we start singing Kumbaya. Besides," Cindy pushed Andrea's shoulder. "You could use some practice with handoffs."

They stepped outside through the door, squinting in the sunshine.

"Yep," Andrea said. "But at least now you know, I can learn from my mistakes." She jogged off toward the track with Molly.

Cindy bent to tie her shoe, smiling. Her chest lighter now, she drew a deep, pain-free breath and got ready for her two favorite things, running and Mike. He hadn't been in classes, but she'd bet he'd come here to see her. Butterflies filled her stomach thinking about his reaction when she told him she knew the truth.

Anticipating his laughs— and kisses—she finished tying, then stood to join Molly and Andrea. Shock rooted her to the ground. Her mom waited by the fence. One look at Mama's face and Cindy knew the only thing she should anticipate—pain. And lots of it.

CHAPTER FIFTEEN

MIKE

There must have been a law passed that only allowed police stations to be furnished with out-of-date, uncomfortable furniture scented with the odor of twenty-year-old sweat and cigarette smoke. Also, the walls could only be painted from the rejects of a paint store that sold shades of brown, gray, and green.

Mike winced and shifted his weight on the chair underneath him, glancing across the row of mismatched metal desks to Elijah. At least he sat on a softer seat, a fake-leather padded chair. The padding, lumpy as it looked, would be more comfortable for injuries than the hard, wood chair Mike had.

He adjusted the position of the ice pack Officer Byrne had given him closer to his jaw. His head throbbed, his throat needed water an hour ago, and he had to pee. And Cindy hated him.

This was officially the worst day of his life and he just wanted to go home.

"I'm here for my brother, Mike Ryan."

Mike looked through the door to his left and saw Tony standing at the reception desk. From the look on his face, Mike could sense a great big slice of *I told you so* pie coming his way. He closed his eyes, wishing his parents weren't out of town. They would only yell at him. Tony would rub a pound of salt into Mike's wounds and laugh.

The sound of footsteps ended next to him. Mike opened his eyes and scowled. "Don't say anything. I'm not in the mood."

Tony raised an eyebrow. "You're lucky Mom and Dad aren't here. They'd leave you overnight." He laughed. "Want me to see if they have a room for you?"

Mike considered it. At least then he wouldn't have to listen to Tony gloat. "Shut up."

Tony pointed to the lump on Mike's cheek. "Don't tell me, the other guy looks worse."

Glancing at Elijah, Mike said, "You tell me."

Following his gaze, Tony's eyes widened. "Who's that?"

"Cindy's twin brother, Elijah."

He glanced over at the mention of his name and glared at Mike. Crossing his arms, he leaned back, balancing his chair on the back legs only.

Tony smirked. "I told—"

"I said don't say anything." Mike moved the ice pack to his right eye to work on the swelling.

Officer Byrne returned to the desk, his potbelly a step ahead of the rest of his body. He huffed and then eased into his worn swivel office chair which squealed in protest.

"I've tried calling your parents but the number you gave me is busy. You sure they're at a hotel? Those places usually have multiple lines." He glanced between Tony and Mike. "Your brother here was the only one I could get a hold of."

Mike shrugged. "Our parents are in Mexico. I don't know why their phones are busy."

"My parents left me in charge. I'll take him home."

The officer nodded. "Yes, but first we have to finish the paperwork." He pointed to another wooden chair at the next desk. "Pull up a seat. It will only take a few minutes." He shuffled the stack of papers on his desk as Tony moved the chair next to Mike.

"Damn. I left one in the copy room. I'll be right back. You stay here." He pointed at Mike, heaved himself out of his seat, and walked away.

Mike laid his head on the desk. He'd skipped school, missed practice, and got his ass beat. He pictured his bed and groaned until a commotion in the other room drew his attention.

"I'm here for my son. And you better give him a bodyguard to protect him."

Cindy's mom appeared in the doorway, pushing Cindy's dad in the wheelchair. They came into the room and Mike grimaced. Her dad looked awful. His hands shook along with his head. His skin had a pasty color to it, like he'd been bleached.

Mike's face burned, greasy guilt oozing in his stomach. Guilt for hurting Cindy's family, even if she didn't care about hurting him.

Her dad gazed around the room, starting when he saw Mike at the desk. He reached up to tap his wife with a shaky hand.

"What is it, babe?" she asked.

He pointed.

Her eyes went wide for a moment, then narrowed as she looked at Mike.

"Shit," he whispered under his breath.

Tony glanced at Cindy's parents and shook his head. "Yep, I told you so."

"Yeah, you're a genius. Shut up."

Cindy's mom turned her burning gaze on Elijah. "What happened?" She put a hand on her husband's shoulder.

Elijah glared at Mike. "Nothing, Mama. Just a fight."

"A fight?" Her voice was calm, and Mike suspected it was for her husband's benefit, not her son's.

"Yeah. Can we just go?" Elijah looked at his dad. "I'm sorry, Daddy. Everything's good."

It was hard to tell if the nodding of his dad's head was intentional or just from his disease.

Mike frowned. Cindy's dad shook so much the wheelchair wiggled with him. Why was he here? Seeing him like this, Mike understood what Cindy meant by stress being bad for him.

"I want to know why you two boys were fighting." Her mom glared at Mike and his dry throat closed.

Maybe Elijah didn't want to get Cindy in trouble, or he didn't want to further upset his dad. Whichever the case, he and Elijah stared at each other, mouths slightly open.

Cindy's mom tapped her foot. Tony smirked. Cindy's dad shook. Neither of them said anything. This was just like an episode of Jerry Springer.

Then someone walked into the room. Mike turned his head and all the pain from the fight faded, replaced by a ripping sensation in his chest, like the guy in *Aliens*. Only instead of a weird headed creature, his heart pushed its way out with a bloody squelch through his skin.

Cindy stood in the doorway, eyes wide, lips parted in surprise, her hands clenched in fists at her sides. She looked from him to Elijah and back to him again.

He wanted to run to her and wrap her in his arms like they did in the movies. Kiss her and ride off into the sunset. Then he remembered she hated him. She'd probably kick him in the nuts.

Her mom gasped, and everyone looked at her. She glared between Mike and Cindy. "I'll ask one more time, and I expect an honest answer."

She spoke through closed teeth, probably trying not to upset Cindy's dad. But it had the opposite effect on Mike. He tried to swallow, tried to breathe, anything. But he couldn't because, well, because she scared the shit out of him. Even Tony shrank a little in his seat.

"*What* were you boys fighting about?" She leveled her stare on Cindy.

Cindy closed her eyes. Then, she walked to her dad and knelt in front of him, holding his shaky hands. "They were fighting because of me." Her whisper floated through the silent room.

Her mom crossed her arms. "Why were they fighting because of you?"

This was not how he imagined the moment she would tell her parents about him. In his mind, it was happy and warm. Not cold and filled with tense fear.

Mike caught Cindy's eye and shook his head. She didn't have to do this, not if they weren't together. She didn't need to hurt her family any more than he already had. It would be different if she still *wanted* to be his girlfriend.

The corner of her lip pulled up into a sad smile. Then she looked up at her dad's face. "Because Elijah doesn't like that Mike is my boyfriend." She looked back to Mike and mouthed *I'm sorry.*

Chills covered his spine as his shoulders sagged and he sighed.

"Boyfriend?" Cindy's mom threw her hands in the air, her voice no longer calm, or quiet. "You are not allowed to have a boyfriend. Especially not someone like him."

Cindy stood, hands on her hips as she glared at her mom. "Why not? You told me I could date. Well, Mike is the one I choose to date."

"No." Her mom pinched the bridge of her nose. "Go get in the car. We'll discuss this at home. You were supposed to go watch your brothers."

"Molly's watching them, and I say we'll discuss this now." Cindy stood by Mike and laid her hand on his shoulder. "Tell me one good reason why I shouldn't date him."

"Cindy, you don't have to do this." Mike glanced at Tony. "Just go. I'll come home later."

"No. I'd like to hear her reasons too." Tony stood and faced Cindy's mom with an angry frown. "What's wrong with my brother?"

Elijah launched out of his seat. "Don't talk to my Mama like that. I'll tell you what's wrong with your brother. He knocked another girl up then moved onto Cindy. And I don't care if he says it ain't true. He's a liar."

"He did what?" Cindy's mom screeched. Without waiting for an answer, she yelled at Cindy. "That's reason enough right there. You are NOT dating this boy."

Tony narrowed his eyes and took a step toward Elijah.

Mike stood and grabbed Tony's arm. "Please, just go. I can handle this."

His brother's temper was worse than Elijah's, and it wouldn't be long before he blew. He glanced at Cindy's dad shaking harder in the chair than before.

"Mama, it's not true. Elijah's wrong."

Mike squinted at Cindy with his swollen eyes. "What did you say?"

"Jenny told me she lied." Her eyes filled with tears. "I'm so sorry I didn't believe you."

"She *told* you?" Despite the tense battle they were in, Mike heaved a sigh of relief. "God, Cindy. I..." He hugged her. She believed him. She believed him and that was the only thing that mattered.

Her mom grabbed her by the arm and yanked her away. "Go home. Now. And *you* keep your hands off my daughter."

Elijah moved next to his mom and pulled Cindy further away. She struggled, slapping his hands.

"Stop it, Elijah. I'm not leaving."

"Let her go." Mike ignored her mom— and his common sense— and made to go after Cindy. This time, Tony grabbed him.

"Forget it. We need to go before you get arrested."

Cindy's mom nodded, smirking at Tony. "I agree. You need to get away and stay away." She pointed at Mike.

He shook his head, gazing at Cindy. "I'm not going anywhere."

Elijah brushed past his mom, bumping Mike with his chest. "I kicked your ass once, and I'll do it again."

"What the *hell* is going on here?" Officer Byrne entered carrying his paperwork. He looked at Elijah and Mike. "I warned you boys to knock it off, or I'd have to arrest you."

Elijah smirked. "Arrest me then." He punched Mike in the face.

After the earlier beating, Mike's bruised skin couldn't take the pressure. His cheek split under Elijah's knuckles. A warm gush of blood ran down his neck and he fell back onto the desk, cursing.

Cindy screamed and her mom yelled but Elijah reached for Mike. Tony body-slammed him, and they fell to the floor.

Officers ran into the room, grabbing Tony and Elijah. Cindy sobbed and ran back to Mike.

"Are you okay?" She ripped off her track warm-up t-shirt and held it to his face to stop the blood.

"Cindy, what are you doing? Put your shirt..." Her mom stopped yelling and gasped. "Carl? Carl are you okay?"

Cindy whipped around to her dad. Mike did, too. He no longer shook. He sat unmoving, slumped over in his chair. His head lolled onto his right shoulder and his eyes were closed. His chest didn't move.

"Daddy!" Cindy ran to him as her mom held his head.

Elijah and Tony stopped struggling with the officers. Elijah ran to his dad. Tony sank into a seat and rubbed his head.

Officer Byrne yelled to the receptionist. "Gina, get the medics!"

He and the other officer laid Cindy's dad on the floor. Then he felt her dad's neck. "He has a pulse. Stand back and let the medics have room."

Mike pulled Cindy back and held her from behind. She leaned against him, shaking, with a hand over her mouth to stifle her sobs.

Her mom looked up at them, tears in her eyes, and her lip curled in a snarl. "See what you did?"

"Mama it's my fault," Elijah said. Tears on his cheeks, he glanced at Cindy.

"I'm sorry, Mama. I'm sorry." Her sobs took over, and she was unable to talk.

Her mom looked away then patted her husband's cheeks and kissed his forehead. "You'll be fine, Carl. You'll be fine."

Mike glared at Cindy's mom. What kind of mother blamed their kid for something like this? He hugged Cindy, whispering comfort in her ears. "It's okay. He'll be okay. This isn't your fault."

The paramedics rushed through the doors, two young men, one blond one brunette, barely older than Mike it seemed. Two minutes later, they'd assessed her dad and lifted him onto the gurney. The dark-headed medic glanced from face to face and spoke to the room.

"His pulse is weak because he's having a heart attack. Good thing we were so close. He'll be treated at the hospital." He looked at Cindy's mom. "You can ride with us."

She nodded, and they ran out the door, pushing Cindy's dad between them.

Glaring once more at Mike holding Cindy she whispered, "Don't bother coming to the hospital unless you change your mind about him."

Cindy gasped. "Mama."

Elijah came to stand by Cindy's side. Mike glanced at his injured face, his own throbbing from the new injury. This may not be Cindy's fault, but he damn well knew it was his.

Her mom lifted her chin and turned on her heel. She ran after the paramedics and left Cindy crying in Mike's arms.

B.B. Swann

CHAPTER SIXTEEN

CINDY

Unable to look at her brother, Cindy clung to Mike, burying her face in his shoulder. Her tears mixed with the blood on his shirt. Fitting, since her world had ended.

Mike squeezed her, and she pulled away, hiccupping. "What do I do?"

He kissed her forehead and nodded. "You need to get to the hospital."

"Mama said not to come." She sniffled, and Mike reached for a box of tissues on the desk behind him. She took one and wiped her nose.

Elijah touched her shoulder, and she looked at his bruised and bloody face. His right eye was almost swollen shut and the gash on his lip probably needed stitches.

"We need to go. It doesn't matter what Mama said."

"He's right," Mike said. "She's hurt, but she needs you there."

She took a clean tissue and held it to the new gash Elijah had given him moments ago. "Yeah, and you guys look like you need a doctor, too. Why were you fighting?"

Mike and Elijah glanced at each other.

Mike's officer said, "I don't know what is going on between the four of you, but I think I have a good idea." His brow wrinkled as his gaze fell on Mike and Cindy. He pointed to Elijah. "I told you that if you continued to fight, I'd have to arrest you. Didn't I?"

Cindy's heart dropped. "But, our daddy—"

The officer held up his palm. "I'm not arresting anyone." He smiled and his face transformed from crotchety old man to Santa. "The police do have compassion, you know. You all can go. But I don't want to see you in here again. Got it?"

After Mike and Elijah signed it, the officer picked up the paperwork and left the room.

Cindy asked Mike, "How are we going to get there? Molly dropped me off."

Mike and Elijah both groaned.

"Our cars are at the trail," Mike said, blushing under the bruises.

Tony held out a set of keys.

"Here, take my car. I'll catch a ride with someone and go get yours." He dropped his chin to his chest for a moment then looked at Cindy. "I hope your dad's okay."

Cindy raised an eyebrow. "Thanks."

Tony smirked at Mike, "Just be careful and don't wreck it."

"Same to you." Mike took the keyring and handed his to Tony. Turning to Cindy, he took off his sweatshirt and slipped it over her head. "Let's go."

They exited through the reception area, and onto the wide cement stairs in the front of the building. Earlier when she'd arrived, dark clouds gathered. Now the rain came down so hard she could barely see the trees across the street in the City Park.

She jumped at the flash of lightning and the immediate clap of thunder overhead.

"Could this day get any worse?" Elijah muttered.

Mike kissed Cindy on the cheek and her brother rolled his eyes.

"I wasn't asking you to *make* it worse."

Mike ignored him. "You guys stay here. I'll go get the car."

"We can walk too." She took a step and Mike pulled her back.

"I don't want you to be uncomfortable. Just wait here." He took off running through the rain, down the stairs, and left toward the parking lot at the end of the building.

Cindy shook her head. Elijah shifted, and she glanced at him. "What?"

"Nothing," he said. But he pursed his lips and followed Mike with his gaze.

Cindy tapped her foot on the steps until Mike disappeared around the end of the building. She glanced at her brother's wounded face.

"Why did you start a fight with him?" She lifted her hand and gently touched his puffy eye. "You both look like crap."

He winced and pulled his head back. "I didn't start it. He did."

"Whatever." She crossed her arms, turning toward the oncoming lights of Tony's car. Like Mike's, it was red. She didn't know much about cars, but she could tell it was expensive. Elijah grunted, but she wasn't sure if it was in admiration.

They ran down the steps. Elijah jumped into the back and she sat in the front passenger seat. She was wet, but one look at Mike and she felt toasty dry and warm. The only way he could be wetter would be if he jumped into a swimming pool. His spiked blond hair looked about the same, but water dripped from it and every inch of his long-sleeved shirt and jeans. She looked down at the puddle on the floor at his feet.

"Well, at least the rain washed some of the blood off your face." She reached up and touched his puffy eye like she did her brother's. Mike didn't flinch. He held her hand and kissed it.

Her chest ached for this moment to be a happy reunion and not a fear-filled dash to the hospital.

Elijah heaved a breath. "Can we please go?"

Mike let go of her hand and glanced in the rearview mirror. "Right." He shifted the car into gear.

Cindy buckled her seatbelt and leaned her head back on the seat. Mama's angry accusation came back to her like someone kept rewinding a part in a video. Hot tears mixed with the cold rain on her cheeks.

Mike tapped something on her hand. "Here."

She opened her eyes to the box of tissues from the station. Mouth open in confusion, she glanced at Mike.

"Sorry, they got a little wet when I ran to the car. The ones on the bottom should be drier."

"Why do you have these?" she asked.

"I stuck them under my shirt." He raised his eyebrows.

Cindy held the tissues, fighting a grin. "You stole tissues from the police?"

"Well, it's not really stealing. Our parents pay taxes. So technically, they contributed to buying them." His lips twitched. "Right? Besides, you needed them."

Cindy chuckled. "Uhm, thanks." She dug to the dry tissues underneath. She pulled one out and dabbed her eyes. Using another, she wiped away the water trickling from Mike's hair into his eyes.

"Thanks," he whispered, glancing into the mirror again.

But Elijah remained quiet. When she turned, he only shook his head, his face more pensive than mad.

She laid her head on the seat again and watched Mike as he drove, replaying the events of the day in her mind. Jenny's lie, her stupidity for believing it, missing him, and finding out the truth.

And her daddy. White-hot guilt seared her stomach, and she grimaced. Her daddy could die, and it was all her fault. A sob escaped her, and she tried to cover it with a cough.

Mike reached over and touched her knee, driving with the other hand. "I'm sure he's okay. The paramedics got to him quickly."

"Yeah." She squeezed the hand on her knee, and he flipped it over. Lifting it to her face, she kissed his busted knuckles.

They reached the hospital, and Mike pulled under the canopy. "I'll park. You guys go inside."

Elijah shoved the door open, hopped out, and slammed the door.

Cindy shook her head. "I'll walk with you."

"I'm already soaked, you're still mostly dry. Go on, Elijah's waiting." He pointed to his face. "I don't want him mad at me. He hit hard enough when *I* started the fight."

She opened her eyes wide. "You started it? Why?"

"Long story." He touched her cheek. "You need to get inside and see your dad. We can talk later."

Her stomach clenched, and she nodded. "Hurry up." She leaned over and kissed him, then joined Elijah under the canopy.

She hugged him. "I'm sorry I accused you of starting the fight."

He wrapped his arms around her, too. "He told you?"

"Yes, and I didn't even ask. I know you don't like him." She sniffled and wiped her eyes. "But can't you give him a chance?"

Elijah squeezed her then let go. "Later. Let's go see about daddy."

"Yeah. Okay." The double glass doors swished open, and they stepped into the hospital.

Cindy expected chaos and noise, like on *St. Elsewhere* every week, where they solved the world's problems in an hour minus commercials.

Instead, the three groups of people in the room sat quietly in the molded plastic seats, either watching the tiny TV hanging in the corner above the row of pay phones on the wall or sleeping in awkward positions. The simple décor, pine-scented air, and clean white tiled floors soothed her frazzled nerves.

They rushed past a magazine rack to the desk across from the main door. A woman with curly red hair piled high in a bun on top of her head sat behind a desk. Her fingers flew across the keyboard of her word processor, long red nails clicking away on the keys.

She smiled as they approached but it fell when she looked at Elijah's face. "Oh honey, you need some help. Here, I've got some forms for you to fill out." She reached for a clipboard from the pile on the counter behind her desk.

"No, ma'am. We aren't here for him," Cindy said. "Our dad was brought here, in an ambulance. His name's Carl Wilson." Her voice cracked and Elijah put his hand on her shoulder.

"Oh, yes, he just came in." She picked up her phone and made a quick call, then patted Cindy's hand on the desk. "Someone will be here in a minute to show you back. Was your mom with him?"

Not trusting her voice, Cindy pressed her lips together and nodded. A set of doors to their right opened and an older woman with short, permed white hair stepped out.

The receptionist said, "Gladys, can you show these two to the ICU?"

Bile rose to Cindy's throat, and she covered her mouth. "Oh, God. The ICU?"

Elijah held her hand. His trembled and she gripped it tighter, trying to draw strength from their connection, and return it.

"Yes, honey. It's okay, all the ambulance patients start in the ICU." Gladys' smile was kind. "Come on, I'll take you back."

"Wait, my boyfriend is still coming." Cindy glanced back at the door, but Mike wasn't there yet.

Gladys shook her head. "Sorry, only family." She waved at the receptionist. "Debby will let him know where you are. What's his name?"

"His name's Mike." She glanced at Elijah. "His face will look a lot like my brother's."

Gladys punched in a code on the keypad by the door. The doors hummed, swinging inward, and Cindy and Elijah followed her into the hall.

Squinting against the bright fluorescent lights, Cindy tried not to look around at the curtained cubicles on either side. She had enough problems of her own, she didn't need to add to her pain by watching someone else suffer.

Gladys paused outside the fifth cubicle on the left. The plastic turquoise curtain was closed, so she knocked on the wall next to it.

"Hello? Mrs. Wilson?"

"Come in."

Cindy cringed. Mama's voice sounded rough, like she'd been crying. Elijah held her hand tighter as Gladys pulled the curtain back for them to enter.

The air left Cindy's lungs. The bed was empty.

"Where's Daddy?" Elijah asked.

Their mom sat on a small padded chair beside the empty bed. She rose in silence, lips pressed together. She stared at Cindy. Shifting her gaze to Elijah she answered. "They took him for a few tests."

Able to breathe again, Cindy panted. "What's wrong?"

"He had a heart attack which caused a stroke." She still spoke to Elijah. "The doctors said they were able to help him before too much damage was done. But because of his… condition, they aren't sure what long-term effects he'll have."

Elijah let go of Cindy and hugged their mom. "He'll be okay, Mama."

She returned the hug and patted him on the back. "I hope so, baby. He looked terrible when they took him. But he was talking and awake."

Cindy sighed. "When can we see him?"

"Elijah, I need you to go home and watch your brothers. They are probably worried sick."

Elijah dropped his chin and gazed at the floor. "Okay, Mama. But can I see him first?"

She shook her head. "He won't be back for a while. And your brothers need you."

"Don't worry, Mama. We'll take care of them," Cindy said. Her stomach churned while she waited for her mom to smile, and thank her for being responsible, for helping. Anything.

Her mom finally looked at her. The coldness in her eyes sent chills racing along the skin on Cindy's trembling arms.

"Are you finished with that boy?" her mom whispered.

Cindy's eyes filled with tears. "Mama, please."

"No." Her mom's forehead wrinkled, and she shook her head. "I'm *not* your mama."

Cindy's heart stopped. "W-what are you saying?"

"Mama," Elijah said, "You don't mean that. You can't disown her. This isn't Cindy's fau—"

"I'm not disowning her." Their mom narrowed her eyes. "I was never your mama."

Cindy looked at Elijah's confused face, but he stared at their mom with his mouth open slightly.

"For real?" he asked.

"Your daddy didn't want you to know. But considering what happened…" She narrowed her eyes at Cindy. "It's time you know the truth."

Cindy grabbed Elijah's hand and her tremors joined his. This couldn't be happening.

"When I met your dad, he already had you. You were only two months old." Their mom crossed her arms. "Your mother was a no-good tramp who liked dating more than she loved your daddy. After she had you two, she left you with him and took off."

Cindy clutched her brother's hand as her world was jolted off its axis. Her brain scrambled to keep up with the words she heard while her body reacted on instinct. Her pulse skyrocketed, pounding in her throat and ears but her lungs refused to expand to let in enough air.

Her mind rejected the idea that this wasn't her mama. The woman who raised her. The woman who took care of her and loved her and taught her what it meant to be strong. But the pieces slowly slid in place—the rule against dating, keeping her away from the chance of a boy getting her pregnant, not letting her choose who to date. It all made perfect sense with this new information.

"I tried to stop you from being like her. Tried to help you do better. But it didn't work. You've been running around behind our backs with that boy, just like she did. So, if you want to be *her* daughter, then you can't be mine. You can go home and pack."

The hospital noise faded as the blood rushed to Cindy's ears. "What?" she whispered. Glancing at Elijah's horrified face she blinked, and the tears fell hot and fast.

"That boy is the reason I might lose your daddy tonight. You make a choice." Her next words were the quietest whisper, but they echoed like a gunshot in Cindy's ears. "You come home alone, or you don't come home."

The slow heat building in her gut returned the strength to her legs. Cindy clenched her teeth and stood straighter.

"This isn't her fault," Elijah said. "I'm the one who got in a fight. I'm the one who upset Daddy."

Still staring at Cindy, she said, "But it was because of *her* lying about him."

She had to choose between her family and Mike? Head spinning, Cindy bit the side of her cheek to be sure this was real. Even then, it felt surreal. The only reality she could count on was Mike.

"You wanted me to find a good man. A good man like Daddy." She ignored the pain that flashed across her mom's face. "Well, I did. And his name is Mike." Cindy turned to the curtained doorway.

"Cindy, stop." Elijah pleaded. "Mama, you can't send her away."

Their mom sat in the chair, ignoring them, staring at the empty bed.

Cindy met Elijah's tearful gaze. "Come on. Mike and I can give you a ride home." She glanced at the side of her mom's face. "I have to pack."

Her mom flinched but otherwise ignored her.

Cindy turned and walked out of the room, leaving only the soft click of the door behind her.

****

While Mike drove them to their house, Cindy explained about her mom with a detached voice. Mike didn't interrupt—not that he probably even knew what to say. After she finished, Cindy stared out the window and chewed on her bottom lip. Elijah sat in the back seat, leaning forward with his hand on his forehead.

They reached her house and Mike followed her to her room, sitting on her bed as she randomly threw clothes into her suitcase.

How could her mom be so unfair? All her life, Mama had taught her to be respectful. Responsible. To treat others with kindness. Why couldn't her mom do that for Mike?

Cindy's stomach swooped. But Mama wasn't Mama. She shook her head, unable to wrap her mind around this new reality. Did it matter? She didn't have a clue who this other woman was, and she didn't want one either. If that woman didn't want her, then Cindy didn't *want* to know her.

She grabbed her pajamas from the bed and jammed them into the case.

Elijah watched her from the doorway, fists hanging at his sides, while their little brothers watched TV in the other room. "Just stay here. Once Daddy is ok, she'll apologize."

"No, she won't. And I wouldn't accept it if she did."

Mike sighed from his seat on her bed. "He's right. She doesn't want you to leave. It's just the pain talking."

Cindy threw her practice clothes into the case and flipped the lid closed. She latched the buckles, turning to face them. "Pain or not, she meant it." Her mom didn't own the rights to all the pain. "I'm ready. Let's go."

Mike glanced at Elijah.

"Where are you going?" Elijah asked. "Not to his house."

Cindy scowled. "Of course not. I'm going to Molly's."

Elijah hugged her. "Don't plan on staying there. I'll talk to… her. She'll get over this and you come home."

Cindy raised a hand to Elijah's cheek and gazed into his eyes, eyes like hers—filled with pain and confusion. In her selfishness, she hadn't even considered his feelings. "I know you're reeling from this like I am but... she's Mama. That other woman she talked about is just a stranger. I don't care what she says. Okay?"

Elijah sighed then wrapped her in his arms. "I agree, but I thought you might not."

"We can talk about this later." Cindy stepped away. "When I'm not so angry at her for kicking me out. I'll see you at school."

She looked around her room then her gaze fell on Mike. Her chest tight with pain, she reached for his hand.

He stood, grabbing her bag and taking the hand she offered. His face turned red, and he nodded to Elijah. "Don't worry, she'll be back."

Elijah grimaced. "Yeah."

Cindy and Mike left the house, sneaking out the back door before her little brothers saw them. With all the drama today, she didn't have the strength for that goodbye.

They drove in silence to Molly's house. Cindy should've called, but she knew Molly wouldn't turn her away.

Mike parked in the gravel driveway and cut the engine of his brother's car. "Cindy are you sure this is the right thing?" he asked, whispering in the dark.

Cindy reached for him and wrapped her arms around his neck. "Where else am I supposed to go?"

"Home," he said, rubbing her back.

She leaned back, trying to smile. "Mama gave me a choice, and I made mine."

He held her by the shoulders. "You *don't* have to choose between me and your family."

"I love *you*." She kissed him, careful not to hurt his injured lip. "If she can't accept us, then that's her choice. But I want to be with you."

Mike shook his head. "I love you, too. But I don't want to be the reason you leave your family. They need you right now."

"Yes, but *I* need *you*." She touched his leg, jeans still soaked from the rain. "I'm sorry about not believing you. Andrea was the one who busted Jenny."

"Andrea? How? Why?"

Cindy explained the scene in the locker room.

"Trying to turn over a new leaf, I guess. But I'm glad she showed me how stupid I was to believe Jenny. I should've trusted you."

"You are not stupid." He kissed her lips and grinned. "But can I say I told you so?"

Cindy chuckled. "Sure, as long as you keep kissing me like that."

"No problem." He returned his lips to hers.

The sweetness of his kiss mended some of the cracks in her aching heart. But she pulled away when the tears crept back in. "How am I going to find out about my dad?"

"We can go there tomorrow. I'll take you to see him."

"Mama will probably have a guard stationed at the door."

"You need to talk to her."

Cindy gritted her teeth. "No, she's the one who has to apologize."

"Okay." Mike wrinkled his brow. "Call Elijah, ask him to let you know when she's not there and we'll go then."

"Good plan," she said. The porch light on the house lit up and the curtain on the window moved as Molly peered outside. Cindy nodded her head toward the movement. "I better get inside before Molly calls the police. She's probably wondering who's sitting in her driveway kissing in their car."

He chuckled and kissed her again. "Sure you don't want to stay at my house? My parents wouldn't mind."

"Right." She breathed in to calm the quiver in her stomach. "I think it's safer if I sleep away from you, not with you. That's kind of the issue that started this disaster."

"True," he whispered. "Now that you're not stupid anymore, will you meet me in the morning?"

"Aren't you going to pick me up? Cat's out of the bag now."

"Yes, and it's about time. I'll be here bright and early."

They climbed out and Mike carried her bag to the porch where a surprised Molly greeted them.

"I can tell by the looks on your faces that this will be a long story with an unhappy ending." She hugged Cindy. "Come in, you look like you need some ice cream."

Cindy laughed, but it turned into a sob. "I hope you have a gallon. It's been a long rough day."

Molly patted her back. "I'm on it. See you inside."

Mike hugged Cindy, kissing her head. "I'll see you in the morning. Try not to worry, okay? Get some sleep. Things will be better tomorrow."

"Right. They can't get a whole lot worse, that's for sure."

"At least the rain stopped," he said. "Maybe I'll finally get dry."

She touched his cheek. "You know you didn't have to do any of this. Elijah and I wouldn't melt if we got wet."

"No. But a wise man once told me, when you love someone, you do things for them because it's what they need even if it means ignoring yourself."

Cindy squint-eyed him, then laughed. "Hayden said that, didn't he?"

"Yep."

"Then thank you. Now go home and take care of yourself. Get some medicine on those cuts."

"Alright. Later then."

She kissed him and he hopped down the stairs. She entered Molly's house and headed for ice cream oblivion.

CHAPTER SEVENTEEN

MIKE

Turning the corner onto his street with a warm shower and aspirin on his mind, Mike groaned. His parent's black Buick sat in the driveway in front of the three-car garage. Great. Cindy was wrong—things were worse.

He parked next to them and went into the house. They waited for him in the living room, sitting on the couch like statues.

"Hey," he said. No use in pretending he didn't know why they were home early from their trip.

"Hey? That's all you have to say?" By all rights, his mom should have had icicles dripping from her nostrils.

Swallowing, he glanced at his dad, expecting his more reasonable side. But even he looked at Mike like he wanted to tie him up and lock him in his room.

"Sit. You need to tell us what happened before we ground you for life." His dad pointed to the chair across from them.

Mike sat, wincing when his shoulder hit the back of the chair. "I'm sorry. I didn't mean to ruin your trip."

"The trip doesn't matter." Fire replaced Mom's ice. "Mike, you could have been killed. What were you thinking? Skipping school and then getting jumped by someone at a remote trail." Her voice wavered at the end, and his dad patted her knee.

"Mom, I didn't get jumped. I started the fight, okay?" Heat spread from his neck to his cheeks. "I just lost control."

"Who were you fighting with?" his dad asked.

Mike's stomach fell. "Cindy's brother."

His parents slumped back into the couch. His mom rubbed her eyes and his dad exhaled a forceful sigh.

"I knew she would be trouble for you," his mom muttered.

Mike jumped to his feet. "Why, because she's different? Because she's black and I'm not?" He paced to the window and stared out at the dark.

"No," his mom continued. "Because you think you're ready for a relationship like that, but you aren't. And this fight proves it."

"Mike," his dad said in a calmer voice. "We like Cindy. She's a nice girl. But your mom's right. If you have an unconventional relationship, you need to have the maturity to handle opposition. You can't start fights because someone else doesn't like what you're doing."

"That's not why we were fighting." He turned to glare at them. "I guess I blamed him for Cindy breaking up with me. And hurting on the outside is easier to take, so I threw the first punch just so he would throw the next one."

Mike fell back into his chair, and his parents exchanged a glance.

"She broke up with you?" his dad asked.

"Yes, but don't get your hopes up because we worked it out." The dull throb in his head turned into a full-blown migraine. God, he needed an aspirin.

"So... you fought just so you could get hurt?" His mom squinted at his dad.

"I'll explain later." He patted her leg again and frowned at Mike. "Tell us everything. If your story makes sense, maybe you'll only be grounded for the rest of the school year."

Mike explained about Jenny, the fight, and the events at the police station. He left out the part about Cindy's two moms. That wasn't his story to tell. When he told them about Cindy's mom kicking her out if she didn't leave him, his mom's eyes filled with tears.

"She made her leave? How could she do that to her daughter?"

Mike remembered having the same thought, but it wasn't fair.

"Mom, she's hurting. She didn't mean it. Cindy went to Molly's for the night. I'm sure they'll talk tomorrow." Doubt filled his mind though.

Cindy was stubborn. It might take an outside force to bring them back together.

His dad shook his head. "Maybe she needs to focus on her family first. It sounds like her dad is pretty sick."

"What do you want me to do? Walk away from her and tell her to come back when she fixes everything?" Mike stood again. "I may not be *mature*, but even I know you don't walk away from someone when things get tough."

"No," his dad said soothingly. "But you can support her without getting overly involved. Give her some space but be there to help if she needs it."

Give her space. Mike narrowed his eyes. "That sounds an awful lot like what I just described. And that's a bullshit answer."

"Mike, listen to your father. What if the next time, you're faced with a problem because of your relationship with Cindy, something worse happens? You need to be patient. Tackle one issue at a time when it's appropriate and related to you."

He snorted. "Everything about her relates to me."

"No, her family issues are hers to deal with." His mom came and touched his wounded face. "This was the result of a lie at school. What will it be like next time when it's about her and her problem with her mom, or her dad's illness? What if her brother decides he wants you gone, and he starts the fight?"

Mike brushed her hand away. "That won't happen."

"You don't know that," she countered.

"No, but I know this. I'm not leaving her. So, unless you want to give me an ultimatum like her mom did, you'll have to accept that Cindy is a part of my life now. And I'm not letting her deal with *anything* alone. Because when you love someone, you should be there for them, no matter what."

"There is no ultimatum. But I want you to be careful." She caressed his head and smiled sadly. "Take things slow, and think before you act, even if the other person doesn't."

He gazed at his mom, not used to her affection. She was just looking out for him, so he bit back the angry retort he wanted to give her. "I will."

She drew a deep breath and walked to look out the window. Mike glanced at his dad. "I'm going to shower. Am I grounded for life or just the year?"

His dad smirked and walked over to lay his hand on his mom's shoulder. "I think we'll just say you're on probation."

"Fine. Then I should probably ask first." He glanced at the floor. "I need to run out for a little while. I have to get my homework from Hayden."

His dad lifted a shoulder. "That sounds innocent enough. Just be home by ten."

"Okay." Mike left before his parents could see the lie on his face. He ran to his room and stripped off his damp clothes. After a quick stinging shower, some Neosporin, and a huge glass of water with two painkillers, Mike picked up the phone.

Hayden answered on the second ring. "Hello?"

"Hey, it's me. Don't ask why, but I told my parents I was coming to your house to get my homework."

"Let me guess, you're not."

"No, but I didn't want you to call when I was gone."

Hayden breathed into the phone. "Okay, so where are you really going and what the hell happened today? I heard you were at the police station."

Damn, news traveled fast. "Who told you that?" Mike jumped from foot to foot as he pulled up his jeans.

"My dad. He was there working on a case and saw you there. The officers told him you fought with Elijah."

"Jeez, your dad didn't tell anyone else, did he?"

"No, he only told me. I haven't said anything."

"Have you talked to Molly?" Mike sat on the edge of his bed to put on his shoes.

"No, why?"

He held the phone with his shoulder while he tied then stood to grab his jacket. "Long story. Call her in about an hour. Her and Cindy will have finished the gallon of ice cream by then."

"A gallon of what? What's going on?"

"I've got to go. I'll see you tomorrow."

"Wait, Mike, where are you going?"

Somewhere he could ease his mom's concern and maybe fix one of Cindy's family issues.

"I'm going to see Elijah."

****

Light shone through the blue curtains in the front room picture window when Mike pulled up to Cindy's house. He sucked in a breath as he parked by the curb and got out of his car. He walked up the front sidewalk and knocked.

The door opened and Elijah greeted him with a frown. "What are you doing here? Is Cindy okay?"

"Yeah, she's at Molly's keeping Ben and Jerry's in business. Can we talk?"

Looking around the street behind Mike, Elijah gave a nod and stepped back.

Mike stepped inside. "How's the face?"

"Fine. How's yours?"

Mike grunted. "It hurts like hell."

Elijah pressed his lips together. "Is that what you came to talk about?"

"No."

Three little boys tore into the room. The first carried a raggedy teddy bear above his head.

"Here, Gabe. Catch!" He threw the bear to the second boy and laughed.

"I got it, Josh."

The littlest one ran from brother to brother and reached for it, his tears shining on his chubby cheeks. "Give it back!"

Groaning, Elijah grabbed it. "Man, I told you guys to leave him alone." He handed the bear to the little one and picked him up. "Benny, I told you. You can't let them see you cry."

Mike raised his eyebrows. Cindy would have a different opinion about that.

"But they took Mr. Boo Boo." Benny sniffled.

"Then you come get me and I'll take care of it." He set Benny down and grabbed the other two boys as they tried to run away, holding one under each arm he growled. "What did I tell you I would do if you took Mr. Boo Boo?"

Mike frowned, torn between laughing at Elijah for using the name, and stepping in to protect the boys from their big brother. "Hey, they were just playing."

Elijah ignored him and carried the boys to the couch. "Alright. Who's first?"

The boys screamed.

Mike flinched, prepared to grab the boys away from him.

But Elijah laughed and tickled Josh on his sides. Josh laughed and Gabe came to his rescue, tickling Elijah. Benny threw Mr. Boo Boo on the floor and joined the fray.

Mike relaxed his shoulders, smiling at them. "For a minute, I thought I would have to call DCFS."

Elijah looked up from the floor where his little brothers piled on top of him. "A little help?"

He reached for the nearest torturer to lift him from Elijah.

Benny turned his shiny face to Mike and grabbed him instead, his tiny hands tickling Mike on his stomach. "I got you," he yelled.

Mike laughed and tickled him back. "How's about I give you a knuckle sandwich? My little brother likes those." He held Benny by the shoulder with one hand and rubbed his head with his bruised knuckles.

Benny laughed and jumped away, grabbing his toy and running into the hallway. After pushing Elijah back to the floor, Gabe and Josh followed their little brother.

"You better hide him good this time," Josh yelled.

After they left, Mike sat on the black leather couch, shaking his head. "Yeah, wasn't expecting that."

Elijah pushed off the floor and sat in a beige colored recliner that faced the couch. He put the footrest up with a pull on the wooden handle on the side. He didn't smile but at least he wasn't glaring at Mike either.

"So. Talk."

Mike opened his mouth, and the phone rang.

Elijah leaned across the arm of the chair to grab the cordless handset. "Hello? Oh, hi, Mama. How's Daddy?"

Mike gazed around at the oversized furniture and a multitude of framed photos. The room was small, not a lot bigger than his bedroom, but tons of frames filled with smiling faces made him relax into the soft sofa. At his house, the pictures were only shared in the basement family room where he and his brothers hung out, not where other people could see them.

Elijah scowled as he listened to his mom. Mike's stomach tightened.

"No, she's at Molly's." Waiting. "Well, that's what you told her." More scowling. "I guess that's up to you." Elijah glanced at Mike. "I don't know, Mama. I'm sure he's not there with her. Molly's mom wouldn't allow that."

Mike raised an eyebrow.

"Okay. Don't worry, I'll take care of them. Goodnight, Mama." He hung up the phone. "You better talk before something else butts in."

Mike said, "Cindy."

Elijah waited. "That's it?" he asked.

"She's all that matters." Mike leaned forward, resting his elbows on his knees. "I want you to know how I feel about her so that you know I'm not using her."

Elijah pursed his lips. "What about Jenny?"

"What about her? I never did anything with her. Cindy heard it from Jenny today that she lied." Mike rubbed his hand through his hair. "You can ask her about that, but it's not a problem for me and Cindy anymore."

"Yeah, she told me earlier." He looked at the floor. "Look, I know she likes you, and after today… well, I see how much you like her. But man, this isn't a good idea. Dating you is too much for her to handle."

"Why?" Elijah's argument sounded like the one his own mom had.

"She isn't ready for something like this. I don't want her to get hurt."

Mike met his eyes. "I told you I wouldn't hurt her."

"There are other ignorant fools who will."

Mike leaned back. "You can't not live life because you *might* get hurt."

"No, but if I can protect my sister from it, I will."

"Elijah, I'm not here to ask for permission to date your sister. I'm not here to ask for your blessing either."

He crossed his arms over his chest. "Then why are you here?"

Mike glanced around the room. Cindy's face peered from almost every single frame. He looked back at Elijah.

"Cindy loves your family and doesn't want to hurt any of you, and neither do I. Your parents, my parents, people at school, strangers on the street; they all have opinions on whether this relationship is a good idea or not."

Elijah put down the footrest, his forehead wrinkled as he listened.

Mike continued. "The only people who need to like this is me and Cindy. And we do. But, if everyone keeps fighting it, your family's going to lose her. And that would hurt her the most. It's not fair to her to make her choose between two things she loves."

The sounds of laughter floated from the boys playing back in their bedroom. Mike lifted his hand toward the noise. "You and I can't keep fighting because that's going to tear her apart. There's enough stress in life, and I guess I'm here to ask you to do what's best for Cindy. Because you love her, too."

With heat in his face and neck, holding his breath, Mike waited for Elijah to consider his words. Part of him laughed because he sounded like Hayden, some sentimental old man. The other part tensed, waiting to run out the door if Elijah decided to start swinging.

Elijah gazed at the plush brown carpet, his fingers steepled under his chin. "So, you're asking me to be friends?"

"Not friends, just friendly." Mike shrugged. "But friends would be fine, too. Just don't ask me to sleep over or anything. I don't think your parents would go for that."

"I can see one thing my sister likes about you." Elijah jerked back in his seat. Then he laughed. "You're a real smartass."

"Can't argue with you there." Mike stood and walked to the door. "Think about it."

Elijah followed him, the laughter fading as he folded his eyebrows to a deep V. "If my sister wants to date you that should be up to her. It took a lot of guts for you to come here and talk to me. Especially the same day you punched the hell out of my face."

Mike glanced at the bruises and cuts covering Elijah's dark skin. "Sorry, but I think you did more of a number on me."

"True." He grinned. "But that's what you wanted, right? Or you would have fought harder."

"Hey, I fought hard."

"Right. I told you, I've been in lots of fights." He pulled his chin back and raised his eyebrows. "What color belt do you have?"

Mike bit back a laugh. "I don't know what you're talking about."

"You're a terrible liar." Elijah shook his head. "I can't believe we thought Jenny was the one telling the truth."

Mike wiggled his eyebrows and pushed open the screen door. He stepped outside into the night, hopping off the porch without using the stairs.

Elijah stood at the open door watching him, hands on his hips, just like Cindy did when he messed with her.

"Hey, find out when your mom will be at the hospital. Cindy wants to go see your dad, and she wants to go when your mom won't be there."

Elijah lifted his chin.

Laughing, Mike waved. "And by the way, it's black. But only by one degree."

Elijah shook his head. Mike could still hear his laughter when he closed the car door. Inside his car, he turned on the radio, glad the first part of his plan was complete. He should pat himself on the back for the *mature* way he'd handled the problem with Elijah. Better than fighting anyway.

Next stop, school tomorrow. Given what his mom said earlier that would be a different battle altogether. Because if there was one thing Mike knew, high school was no place to expect maturity.

CHAPTER EIGHTEEN

CINDY

The smell of coffee woke Cindy. She rolled over on the couch in Molly's living room, squinting into the light spilling from the nearby kitchen.

"Sorry, I didn't mean to wake you this early." Molly's mom, Lisa, sat at the table holding her coffee cup between her hands. She took a sip and gave an apologetic smile.

"It's okay." Cindy sat up on the couch and pulled the extra blanket she'd used closer to ward off the chill. "Thanks for letting me stay here, Lisa."

"You're welcome anytime, you know that." She sipped again.

Cindy stretched and yawned. She walked to the kitchen, wrapping herself in the blanket as she sat at the shabby wooden table. The cold from the metal folding chair seeped through the fabric and Cindy shivered.

"Do you want coffee?" Lisa asked. "It always warms me up in the morning.

"No thanks. I'll stick with orange juice." Leaving the blanket, Cindy stepped around Lisa and grabbed a cup from one of the cheery yellow cabinets, and poured a cup of orange juice from the fridge. Cup in hand, she went back to the table and pulled the blanket around her shoulders.

"I don't know what's happening, but is there anything I can help you with, Cindy?" Lisa asked.

She stared at the steam rising from Lisa's coffee cup. "I don't know."

Her mind felt like a pinball machine, thoughts bouncing around, crashing into each other, and veering off in different directions. She didn't know what to do to get everything back on track.

Lisa patted her hand. "I'm here if you need me."

"It's just, I'm worried about my dad. And my mom kicked me out because I like Mike and..." She leaned her elbows on the table and held her head. "I don't know how to fix this, Lisa."

"You have a lot to deal with." Lisa set down her cup and took Cindy's hands into hers. "Your mom loves you. This isn't a permanent thing. Right now she's upset and hurt because of your dad, but she'll come around."

Cindy shook her head. "I don't know. She blames me and Mike for what happened, and she's right but—"

"No." Lisa squeezed her hands. "This is not your fault, Cindy. Your dad is ill. This could have happened anytime. You did not cause this."

"But he was upset because Mike and Elijah fought, and I lied to them about Mike and the strain was too much for him." The sting of tears burned her eyes.

Lisa moved her chair closer and put an arm around Cindy. "Your mom knows it's not your fault. Dealing with your dad's illness takes a huge toll. But she's hurting and needed something else to blame. Stress does funny things to people. It makes even the most rational person go a little crazy sometimes."

Cindy sniffled. "But I caused the stress."

"Life is filled with stress. We can't escape it or prevent it. And your dad's health isn't something you can control."

"No, but I can control what happens around him."

"Not always." Lisa squeezed her shoulders. "You've helped Molly countless times, you watch out for Elijah, you take care of your little brothers. It's time you realize, you can't take care of everybody, and not everything will go the way you plan. Including your dad. Sometimes, you just need to let go."

No. She couldn't let go of helping her dad. But she couldn't let go of Mike either. She wanted to have them both, but the two desires seemed incompatible. "What do I do?"

Lisa smiled. "Go talk to your mom. She probably needed the night to adjust, and I'll bet she's more reasonable today." She squeezed Cindy's shoulders one last time, then stood and took her coffee cup to the sink. "And remember to add yourself to the list of people to take care of. Your needs are just as important."

Cindy nodded. "I'll try. Thanks, Lisa."

"I have to get to work." She grabbed her purse and stepped to the door then turned back to Cindy. "It may not be my place to tell you this, but I like Mike. He's a great kid with a good head on his shoulders."

Cindy grinned. "Thanks, I like him, too."

Lisa pressed her lips together and frowned. "I know you do. And I know first time love can feel incredible, unstoppable. But yours is different because you both are, too. I guess what I'm saying is make sure you're fighting for the right thing."

"I'm not sure I understand," Cindy said.

"Are you fighting for this relationship because you love him, or are you fighting for the idea of the relationship? Because the second option isn't worth the things you stand to lose."

Cindy chewed on her lip for a moment. She pictured Mike's face, his laugh, the way he helped her last night when she'd lost everything and walked away from her family. Without him, she'd have her family, but that wasn't enough anymore. Lisa was right. It was time to think about what she needed.

She lifted her chin and met Lisa's concerned gaze with certainty. "I'm fighting for us because that's what *I* want. I want him, Lisa, and he's worth the fight."

Lisa winked. "Love gives you the motivation, but don't forget to use your common sense. Lean on each other, and your family. That's what love is for." Her lips pulled up in a smile and she left through the front door.

Cindy sipped her juice until a bleary-eyed Molly entered the kitchen wrapped in her blanket.

"It's always so cold in here in the mornings." She yawned and grabbed another cup from the cabinet. "I heard voices. Did you see my mom?" She poured some juice and sat in her mom's chair.

"Yes, she and I had a chat about the bogus day I had yesterday."

"Did she give you any advice?" Molly looked at Cindy over her cup.

Cindy laughed. "Yes, all good of course. Girl, your mom should open a clinic for troubled youth."

Molly blushed. "I know. Sometimes I forget she's old. She knows how to relate to teens. You'd think she'd have forgotten by her age."

Cindy snorted. "Your mom isn't old. She had you when she was like ten, didn't she?"

"Twenty. She just looks young." Molly stood and got two cereal bowls and a box from the pantry. "So, what's the plan? Is Mike picking you up or are Hayden and I taking you to school?"

"Mike's coming." Cindy checked the clock on the stove. "He said bright and early. I don't know what that means, so I better get ready."

"Eat first. I'm sure he's not even up yet. He is a dude. They like to sleep more. At least Hayden does."

Cindy raised her eyebrow. "Oh, how do you know how Hayden likes to sleep?" The blush on Molly's face intensified until she was tomato red.

"I don't. I mean... he's napped here before when we watch TV and..." She put her hands on her hips. "You know what I meant." She handed Cindy the box and milk.

Cindy poured a bowl and giggled. "Uh-huh. Sure, that's what I was talking about." She took a bite, laughing as Molly squirmed in her chair.

"You know *that* hasn't happened." Molly chewed on her cereal. "What about you and Mike? All those times alone in the woods?"

Heat prickled Cindy's face, too. "No, but not for his lack of trying." She giggled again. "He'd like to corrupt me almost as bad as you want to do to Hayden."

Molly's napkin hit her in the face and Cindy laughed.

"You are so mean." But she laughed, too. "Go ahead and take the shower first. Hayden won't be here for another forty-five minutes. I'm sure Mike is eager to see you."

Cindy emptied her bowl and put it in the sink. "You're probably right, thanks. I'll hurry." She hugged her friend, then walked to the bathroom to get ready.

****

School lasted an eternity and track practice took even longer. She and Mike were finally riding in his car to go see her dad. "Hurry up. Elijah said Mama would be gone for about an hour while she went to work to talk to her boss." Cindy bit her fingernails, good thing she never painted them.

Mike reached and took her hand in his. "Stop worrying. You'll have plenty of time to visit."

Pulling up to a stop sign, he waited as another car also came to a stop. Mike waved the car ahead of him.

She glanced at him from the corner of her eye. "Are you doing this on purpose?"

"What?" he asked a little too innocently.

She groaned. "You are. You're driving slow because you want me to have to face her." She pulled her hand away from his.

"The rain makes it hard to drive." He smiled. "I have precious cargo I need to take care of."

"You've hung out with Hayden too much."

She looked out the window at the rain-soaked town. Huge puddles dotted the grassy areas and a strong wind blew, making little waves on the tiny brown lakes. The late afternoon sky, dark as night, increased her anxiety about being late. "But you're right This rain totally sucks. Sorry, I'm just a little tense."

"It's okay." He squeezed her hand on his leg, then returned his hand to the wheel. Pulling into the parking lot, Mike headed toward the canopy.

Cindy shook her head. "No, go park. I came prepared this time." She held up a black umbrella.

He pulled into a spot about fifty feet from the door. "I think you need this, too." He leaned in and kissed her, soft and sweet, then took the umbrella out of her hand. "Wait there, I'll come around."

They ran through the rain and entered the hospital through the sliding doors. Cindy grimaced at her rain-soaked Nikes and jeans. Shaking out the umbrella, Mike bound it as they walked to the desk.

Debby was working again tonight, and Cindy smiled at her. "Hi. I'd like to see my dad, please. Carl Wilson."

Looking up from her paperwork, Debby's gaze widened when she saw Cindy and Mike. "Oh, of course." She looked down at her desk again, flipping through a chart. "He was moved to a regular room. Third floor, room 309."

Debby glanced again from her to Mike with wide eyes.

Cindy's face grew warm. She mumbled, "Thanks."

In the elevator, Cindy reached for Mike's hand and bounced her knees against the metal wall. "We should have taken the stairs. It would have been faster."

Mike kissed the top of her head. "Relax. If they moved your dad to a regular room that means he's doing better."

"Yeah, you're right." She exhaled and leaned into his side. Not the leaning Lisa meant, but touching him gave Cindy strength.

The doors swished open, and they walked the long bright hallway to her dad's room. She paused outside the closed door.

"Cindy?" Mike asked.

She raised her chin and pushed the door open. This was her daddy, nothing to be afraid of. But when she stepped into the room and saw him lying in the bed, fear took her breath away.

Fluorescent lights above his bed illuminated his frail form. The skin on his face looked almost as gray as his hair. The blanket covering his left arm jerked as he twitched underneath. His head rocked a little from side to side, and his mouth hung open as he stared out the window awash with the rain.

Cindy froze inside the doorway, unable to move.

Mike followed her into the room and squeezed her shoulder. "Go on. He's waiting for you," he whispered.

Swallowing the fear, she walked to her dad's right side and stood by the bed.

"Daddy?"

She touched his still right hand through the blanket. He turned his head to her, recognition flashing in his eyes. Only the left side of his face smiled. His right eye drooped and that side of his mouth remained slack.

She held back the tears that would upset him. "Hi, Daddy." She kissed his cheek.

"Hey, baby girl." He reached with his left hand to touch her cheek. "How are you?"

She pressed her lips and swallowed again. "I'm fine, Daddy. How are you? When do you get to go home?"

He chuckled but then it turned into a cough. He closed his left eye and covered his mouth with his left fist. Cindy glanced at Mike, desperate to help her dad, but needing him closer for strength. He took a slow step toward her. She nodded, and he joined her at her father's side. She clutched his hand as he stood beside her.

Her dad glanced between them with his watery left eye. His coughing had subsided, and he twitched in the bed. Then, a smile lit the left half of his face and he gazed at Mike. "So, I didn't scare you away, eh?"

Cindy glanced at Mike.

"No, sir. I don't scare easily." He returned Cindy's gaze, and his voice dropped to a husky whisper. "I'm not going anywhere."

The tears were impossible to hold back after that. She wiped her eyes and laid a hand on her dad. "I love you, Daddy."

She didn't know what to do or say. Remembering Lisa's advice, she let go of trying to fix her dad and did the only thing that mattered. She gave him her love because that was all she could control.

He patted her hand with his, tears leaking from his eyes into his sideburns. "I love you too, baby. Everything is going to be fine." He glanced again at Mike. "And I don't want you blaming yourselves for any of this because it's not your fault."

The tears fell hot and steady now, and she grabbed a tissue from the bedside table. She looked at all the wires and monitors hooked to her dad. "I'm sorry, Daddy. Sorry that I lied to you." She met Mike's gaze, and he nodded.

"Don't you worry about that. What's done is done." His eye closed then he chuckled again. "I understand why you did it. Your mama can be scary."

Cindy half laughed half sobbed. "Yeah, she can."

He opened his eye again. "But she loves you, baby. Don't ever doubt that."

"I don't, Daddy. I don't."

"When I'm gone, she's gonna need you. All of you."

Pain hit her stomach like a sledgehammer. "Don't say that, Daddy. You're not leaving." Her body shook, and Mike wrapped his arm around her shoulders, pulling her close.

Her dad smiled at Mike, pointing his chin at Cindy. "And she's gonna need you, too."

Mike swallowed and bobbed his head. "I'll be there, sir."

Cindy sobbed, leaning into Mike's side, trying to breathe under the crushing weight of her dad's words. When the door opened, Cindy glanced up from Mike's shoulder. Her mom stood in the doorway, frowning.

The words her mom had said rushed into her mind. The hateful name-calling, her shocking confession, the ultimatum. But when she walked to the bed, Cindy left Mike and went into her mom's open arms.

"I'm sorry, Mama. I'm sorry." She repeated the phrase, not even sure what she was sorry for.

Her mom held her, stroking her braids. "It's okay, baby. It's okay. I'm sorry, too."

"No matter what you say," Cindy whispered in her ear, "*you're* my mama."

"Yes. Yes, I am."

Her tears made Cindy cry even more.

After a few moments, Cindy pulled away and Mike handed her a tissue. She took it, chuckling through the tears. "You always know what I need."

"That's my job," he said with a smile.

She wiped her eyes and reached for his hand. Facing her mom, she took a deep shaky breath.

"I should have done this months ago, but I was too afraid of this happening." She waved a hand to the room in general. "But now I know all I did was waste time." She met her mom's eyes. "Mama, this is Mike, my boyfriend. And I know you don't want me to date, but I can't keep waiting, or avoiding life to prepare for my future."

Her mom looked at Mike, her forehead wrinkled. She glanced at her husband lying in the bed.

He chuckled, a wet rattle in his chest. "Go on, babe. You remember when I met your mama? I was scared to death, and she wasn't half as scary as you are."

Cindy laughed, and so did her mom.

"I'm not that bad." She glanced at Mike. "Am I?"

His cheeks turned pink as he glanced at them. "Uhm, why do I feel like this is a trick question?"

"It's not. And if you want to date my daughter, you'll need to learn how to answer my questions."

Mike stuck out his bottom lip. "Okay, then my answer is yes. You're scarier than Freddy Krueger."

Cindy bit back a laugh and glanced at her dad.

Her mom crossed her arms and raised her chin. "Good. Just remember that when you and Cindy go on your dates."

Mike swallowed and dipped his head. "Yes, ma'am."

Cindy caught his eye, and he winked at her.

Her dad coughed again, and Mama leaned over him. "Do you need something, honey?" She rubbed his forehead with her fingers and smiled.

He continued to cough, his body jerking under the thin white blanket.

Cindy watched them with tears forming again. When her dad pulled his hand away, blood dripped from his lip. Mama wiped it away with a tissue.

Mike brought a chair from near the door and placed it by the bed for her mom.

She glanced at Cindy and raised her eyebrows. "Thank you," she told Mike, sitting.

"You're welcome."

Her dad drew a rattling breath, and Cindy joined her mom at his side. He reached for her, and she held his jerking hand. She used to hate his trembling but now it reminded her he was still alive, still her daddy.

"You're my girls. Be good to each other." He grimaced like he was in pain and a sob escaped her mom.

Cindy put her other arm around her mom's shoulders and answered for them both. "We will, Daddy." Her mom leaned her head on Cindy's side.

The door opened, and a nurse came in. "I'm sorry, visiting hours are over now. The kids will have to leave." She smiled in apology and closed the door.

Cindy opened her mouth to protest—she didn't want to leave—but her mom nudged her.

"It's okay. I'll stay here with Daddy." She rose and hugged Cindy. "You go home and help Elijah. I'll bet your little brothers miss you, too."

Cindy knew this was her mom's way of saying she accepted that Mike was here to stay. She hugged her mom back like she used to when she was a little girl, squeezing tight and rocking back and forth.

"Thank you, Mama," she said. She leaned to her dad and kissed his cheek. "I'll see you tomorrow, Daddy. I love you."

He squinted, breathing hard. "I love you, too, baby girl. Be good." He looked at Mike. "Take care of her for me, Mike."

"Don't worry about her. She's tough." He patted her dad on the shoulder. "Thank you for trusting me."

"Be sure to earn it." He closed his eye again and relaxed into the pillow.

Cindy and Mike walked to the door, and she turned around for one last look. Mama gazed at Daddy the same way Mike looked at her. She glanced up at his face and Cindy knew, she'd found a future she would love forever.

CHAPTER NINETEEN

MIKE

On Friday afternoon, the locker room buzzed with noise. The cement floors and walls, like amplifiers at a concert, intensified the sounds until the twenty-four guys sounded like a hundred. Pre-meet excitement, pep talks, and razzing surrounded Mike. He ignored it all, dressing quick, in a hurry to go outside.

Hayden sat across from him, tying his shoes. He smirked at Mike rushing to get ready. "You know field events don't start for half an hour."

"Yeah, I know."

"Then what's the rush?"

"If I tell you, you'll laugh, then I'd have to punch you to make up for what you'd say about me."

Hayden laughed. "Oh, so you're rushing to see Cindy."

Smirking, Mike threw a shoe at Hayden. "Smartass."

"Where was she earlier today? She and Elijah weren't in our Sociology class." Hayden stood and stuffed his bag into the locker.

"She left for a while to go see her dad." Mike stood, stretching his arms above his head. "They took their little brothers to see him."

He frowned thinking about Josh, Gabe, and Benny. It might be one of the last times they ever got to see their dad.

"How come you didn't go?" Hayden asked.

"I offered, but she said she thought it might be better if it was just them today. For the little guys. Less confusing."

"She's probably right," Hayden said.

Mike closed his locker. "Let's go."

They left the locker room and stepped out into the warm spring sunshine. After the rain from the last few days, the grass had turned a bright green. Mike sucked in a gulp of the fresh air, squinting in the sun as he scanned the crowded area for Cindy.

She waved from near the fence where she and Molly stood talking to Elijah and her little brothers. He waved back and tapped Hayden on the shoulder. "There they are."

They approached the group. Mike closed the gap and hugged Cindy. "Hey, how's your dad today?"

"He's good." She pulled back and smiled. "I think he looked a little better than last night." She squatted down to tie Benny's shoe.

He glanced at her brother, wincing when Elijah shook his head. Still in denial. "Should we go back tonight after the meet?" Mike asked.

Cindy stood. "Mama wants me and Elijah to take the boys someplace fun." She smiled at Benny as he followed Josh and Gabe, running around in the grass outside the fence. A muscle flexed in her jaw and she wrapped her arms around her middle.

"I have an idea," Molly said. "Let's take them to The Pizza Palace. We can play games with them."

Mike agreed. "I'll bring Drew and they can play together. I think he and Josh are the same age."

Cindy glanced at Elijah. "That sound good to you?"

He shrugged. "Whatever. As long as we eat."

"Well," Hayden said. "I don't know about the eating part. Their pizza is kinda gross."

"It's about the kids having fun at a place like that," Molly said.

Cindy snorted. "And about their parents spending money on games to win tickets."

Mike hugged her around the waist, ignoring the way Elijah watched them. He needed to get used to their affection. "Maybe I'll win you a prize."

"Oh great, will you spend ten dollars to win a fifteen-cent rubber bracelet?" she asked, laying her head on his chest.

He held her for a second then whispered, "Track uniform."

She pushed him away and he laughed.

"I better take these guys to find something to do for a while." Elijah raised his eyebrows at Mike and Cindy. "Besides watching you two."

"Are you staying to watch the meet?" Mike asked him.

"It depends on them." He jerked his thumb toward the boys. "If they don't get bored."

Mike watched the boys playing tag. "Since this is a fun-run meet, we only have the one relay to do. Let's take off early."

"Sounds good to me," Cindy said.

They made plans to meet near the locker room after the relays, then Mike and Cindy walked toward the shot-put ring for his event.

"How's your dad, really?" Mike asked. Even he knew her dad was saying good-bye last night though he might not know exactly when he'd leave.

"I told you. He's good." She gazed around the field area.

Mike didn't push it. He kissed her cheek, ignoring the stares from the other school's athletes. A thrower from a visiting city school glared at him, reminding him of Elijah during their fight. Mike looked the other way.

Cindy noticed and glared back, opening her mouth to say something Mike probably would have loved to hear. But he put a hand on her cheek to stop her.

"It's not worth the breath." He tapped her nose. "Right?"

She pressed her lips together and glared at the boy. Then she looked at Mike and nodded. "Right. But lets at least show him we don't care what he thinks." She grabbed his face and kissed him on the lips.

Mike laughed. The guy turned and walked toward the line for throwers.

Cindy said, "Now kick his ass in this event please."

"I'll do my best." Mike went to warm up while Cindy watched. He did the stretches he learned from the coach and prepared for his turn, then joined the others in the event line, right next to their grumpy admirer.

"Leave the sisters alone."

Mike gritted his teeth. "Mind your own business." He glanced at Cindy. Her narrowed eyes focused on him and the speaker.

"I know who you are," the guy continued.

Mike finally looked at him with a raised brow. "Is that supposed to impress me? What are you psychic?"

"My cousin Jamal knows her brother." He tilted his head, posturing with his hands. "And they don't like you messin' with her either."

"Great. Tell your cousin to mind his own business, too." Mike shook his head. He wanted to be *mature* but if this guy didn't shut up soon, he'd deck him in his freaking mouth.

The shot-put judge called out the first name. "Devon Lewis, Lincoln High. Sixty seconds."

Grumpy stepped forward to throw. Before he left, Devon muttered, "Better watch your back." He shouldered Mike as he passed, and Mike chuckled.

"Hey, do they have a handbook for ignorant assholes at your school?"

Devon turned back around, his lip curled.

Mike smirked. "Tick-tock, tick-tock."

He glared at Mike and went to the ring. His first throw landed thirty feet out. Devon kicked the toe board and left the circle.

"Mike Ryan from Elkwood. Sixty seconds."

He grinned as Devon passed him. Glancing at Cindy's scowling face, he stepped into the ring. Positioning the shot, he focused on the throw, tuning everything out in case Devon blew a raspberry or something stupid like that.

He took a deep breath, spun, and released the shot, blowing the breath out with it. His throw sailed through the air and landed in the dirt past Devon's first mark.

"49 feet 11 and 3/4 inches."

Mike glanced at Cindy and she smiled, thumb in the air. It wasn't his best throw, but he'd done what she wanted.

Walking back to wait for his next turn, Mike met Devon's angry gaze. "Looks like you need to focus on your throwing instead of my girlfriend."

"Fuck off," Devon said.

He laughed. Maybe Mike hadn't acted very maturely, but he didn't care. After all, this was high school.

****

"Pizza! Pizza! Pizza!" The chant grew louder and louder until Elijah finally yelled.

"Alright, if I hear it again, you guys are eating PB and j at home."

Mike, riding shotgun in the Wilson's van, turned to look at Cindy and her little brothers behind him. Drew sat next to Cindy in the captain's seats while Gabe, Josh, and Benny had the last row.

He winked at Cindy, and she wrinkled her nose. Then she chanted, "Pizza! Pizza!" and the whole thing started anew, louder than before. Mike laughed and Elijah groaned, shaking his head.

"You put her up to that," Elijah accused over the yelling.

"Yes. Yes, I did." He slapped Elijah on the arm. "But it's fun, right? That's what your mom wanted for them."

Elijah's lips twitched. "Yeah, I guess so."

They finally pulled into the parking lot and everyone piled out the sliding door.

"I want to play Skee Ball!" Drew yelled.

Josh hopped next to him. "Me, too."

"No, let's do the basketball game first." Gabe mimicked shooting a jump shot and fell to the ground.

Cindy picked him up. "How about we sit down and order our food first, then we go play games?"

A chorus of groans answered her, and Mike laughed. He hugged her to his side. "I think it's a great idea."

Elijah snorted, propping Benny on his hip and carrying him through the parking lot. "That's because you worship my sister."

Mike glanced at him. "Always agree with your woman, Elijah. That's relationship 101."

Cindy slapped them both. "Here's another lesson. Don't talk about the girl when she's within striking distance."

Opening the door, Mike said, "Lesson learned."

"Good, but you can worship me all you want." She danced out of reach when he tried to tickle her.

The hostess greeted them, her tired eyes moving from head to head. "Seven?"

Cindy shook her head. "No, we have two more coming."

The girl stared blankly back.

"That makes nine," Cindy said.

"Yeah, I got it." The hostess grabbed a handful of menus. "Follow me please."

Cindy widened her eyes at Mike, and he smothered a laugh. "Maybe she's tired," he whispered.

They followed the hostess past rows of games with flashing lights, beeps, and whistles. Skee Ball machines, PacMan, Donkey Kong, Tetris, and other eye-catching technological wonders. Her little brothers gawked, trying to pull away and get to the games like a pack of starving raccoons after a trash truck.

The hostess stopped by a group of yellow-topped tables with red, pleather covered metal chairs. She laid the menus on the table and walked away.

Cindy adopted her mom's stance—hands on hips, eyebrows raised, chin tucked—and huffed. "It's a good thing she doesn't work for tips."

Mike grabbed her hands. "Can you blame her for being crabby? Look around, this place is nuts."

He waved at the kids running everywhere, screaming, jumping, racing around with long streamers of tickets flowing behind them like paper tails. Their parents either followed with a sort of dazed look in their eye or were nowhere to be found.

"That's why Mama and Daddy never bring them here. The noise makes Daddy's head hurt." Cindy smiled sadly at her brother's excited faces.

"Then I'm glad we brought them," Mike said. "Come on, let's sit and order so they can go play."

After a rowdy edition of who-got-to-sit-by-who, Molly and Hayden walked in. They played musical chairs again because Benny, Josh, and Gabe all wanted to sit by Mike and Hayden.

Elijah threw his hands up. "Jeez guys, you're only gonna sit while you eat. That's five minutes then you'll be playing games. Just sit already."

Cindy patted his shoulder. "Jealous that they don't want to sit by their big grumpy brother?"

He nudged her and grinned. "Shut up."

Mike smiled along with them.

The waitress came to take their order and it was go-time. Hayden nodded to Molly, and she pulled a huge bag of quarters from her purse. "Who needs some change?"

The kids yelled and ran to Molly. She gave each a handful and helped them to put it in their pockets.

"When you need more come find me." She winked at Elijah. "Sorry, sometimes you have to buy their affection. We girls need that to compete with you cool older boys."

"Molly, you didn't have to do that." Cindy frowned. "Mama gave me money for the boys."

Hayden laughed. "I brought the quarters. Molly just confiscated them for bribery purposes."

Laughing, Mike grabbed a handful. "Well, I didn't bring any. So thanks."

Benny pulled Elijah away, heading for the Skee Ball machines. Mike waved to Cindy as Josh pulled on his hand. "You gonna play with us?"

She shook her head. "Not yet, I'll find you in a minute. I need water before I play."

Josh pulled harder and Mike went with him and Drew. He played Skee with Josh, Frogger with Gabe, and had an epic battle on Rampage with Josh and Drew where he lost spectacularly when his monster was defeated by the national guard. Wanting to play with Benny, Mike looked everywhere but couldn't find him and Elijah.

He, Josh, and Gabe returned to the table where Cindy and Molly ate pizza.

"How's the pizza?" He fell into the seat next to Cindy and grabbed her wrist, directing her pizza into his mouth as she held it.

She giggled and wiped sauce from his chin with her napkin. "It's pretty bad, but I'm starving."

Molly handed a slice to each of the boys and they ate quickly.

As they finished, Molly stood, pushing the bag of quarters near Cindy. "I'm going to look for Hayden and play some games. You can be the quarter keeper for a while." She grabbed a handful.

"Wait for us!" Josh and Gabe ran after her, quickly shoving the last of their pizza into their mouths.

Mike chewed the rubbery crust and grimaced. "You're right. This is bad." He swallowed and Cindy handed him water. He took a sip and then kissed her. "Thanks, Mom."

"You don't kiss your mom like that, do you?" She snickered and put her arms around his neck.

"That is disgusting." He squeezed her side, and she laughed. "Now you have to kiss me again and wipe that image from my mind."

"If you insist." She pressed her lips to his.

It didn't take long until his heart raced, and his breath sped along with it. "Good thing we're not at track." She always heated him from the bottom up.

"Yep," she said and kissed him once more. "Was this why you came back to the table?"

"No, but I'm glad I did." He glanced around at the families eating at the tables near them. "They might appreciate it if we saved this for later. Kids watching you know."

Not to mention he would rather do this in private where it could last longer.

"True. So why did you come back?" She took a bite of pizza.

"I was looking for Elijah and Benny. Have you seen them?"

"No, did you try the bathroom? Benny always thinks he has to go. He likes to play with the hand dryers."

Mike bit into his pizza and nodded. "I'll try there. Be right back."

When he didn't find them in there, Mike's stomach tightened. "Where the hell are they?" He went back to the game room and Benny ran past with Gabe and Drew. They stopped by Hayden and Molly at the Skee Ball game. Mike followed them over.

"Have you seen Elijah?" he asked Hayden.

Hayden looked up from where he slid quarters into the machine. He pulled the release and the wooden balls rolled down the track, ready for rolling.

"You're up Benny." He shook his head. "No, Benny came out of the bathroom with Gabe and they've been with me."

Mike frowned. He glanced around the room. "Watch the boys. I'll go see if I can find him."

"We got them," Molly said. "Let us know when you find him." She and Hayden exchanged a worried glance.

Mike walked around the busy room and back into the main dining area away from the games. No Elijah. He checked outside the front door.

Elijah stood with another guy who looked vaguely familiar. Mike observed for a minute, then remembered the other night when Elijah accused him of Jenny's lie. This guy was there, too. Mike prepared to go back inside until the other guy pushed Elijah in the chest.

Mike clenched his teeth and strode toward them.

"And I told you not to let her date that cracker."

As Mike got closer, the guy glared at him and backed away from Elijah.

"What's the problem, Elijah?" Mike asked.

"Nothing I can't handle. Go back inside with the boys." He continued to stare at the punk.

"I don't mind the fresh air. Smells like kids and bad pizza in there." He studied Elijah's visitor. "You're Jamal, aren't you?"

Devon had said his cousin knew Elijah, and this guy had the same cocky smile.

"That's right. You got a problem with me?" He stepped toward Mike, moving his hands out to the sides.

Mike stood his ground. "Only if you don't stay out of my business."

"Aww, sorry 'bout that, bro. But you made it my business when you started datin' his sister."

Mike moved closer, getting into Jamal's space. "I don't care what you think."

"Come on, let's go back in." Elijah grabbed his arm, leading Mike back toward the door. "Stay away from him, he's fucking crazy." They glanced back when Jamal called out.

"See ya later, Lil EZ. We gonna hang out real soon." Jamal laughed and walked backward. "Bring your cracker friend, too."

Back inside the restaurant, Mike turned to Elijah. "What the hell was that all about? Who was that?"

He stared out the window for a moment. "A friend of mine."

"Friend?" Mike cocked his eyebrow. "Time for a new one."

"No shit. You shouldn't have stayed out there. You're the one he came to see." Elijah frowned. "And Jamal's always packin'."

"Yeah, I noticed that day at the meet meal." Mike rubbed his forehead. "Why can't people just leave us alone? What's the big deal that I'm with Cindy?"

"Well," Elijah said with a smirk. "The blond hair and blue eyes have something to do with it."

Mike shook his head. "Come on, let's get back. I left Molly and Hayden with all the boys. They're probably going crazy. I didn't tell Cindy because I didn't want to worry her."

"Fine by me. She'd get pissed at me anyway."

Back in the room, the kids were at the table eating pizza with Hayden, Cindy, and Molly. When he walked in, Cindy glanced at Mike, worry plain on her face.

"Where were you guys?" Cindy asked.

Mike sat next to her and grabbed a slice of sausage. "We went outside to get away from the smell for a minute."

Elijah bit into his pizza without answering. Guess he wanted Mike to do all the lying—for now anyway.

Cindy touched his leg and leaned in. "Is everything okay?"

His stomach twisted. "Yeah, everything is great. We were just talking. We're good." It wasn't a complete lie.

"Okay," she said.

The tourniquet on his gut tightened, but she had enough to deal with. He promised himself it was better she didn't know Elijah's crazy friend wanted to meet Mike in a dark alley with no exit someday. He wished he didn't either.

CHAPTER TWENTY

CINDY

Cindy smiled as she watched the little boys sleeping in the van after they left Pizza Palace. The twenty-minute ride was just long enough for them to nod off, their sauce stained hands clutching bags of plastic toy soldiers, bouncy balls, and cheap suckers from the ticket prizes.

Elijah pulled into the driveway and cut the engine.

"The next time Molly suggests we go to that place we're sending her by herself with all the kids." Elijah leaned his head back on the seat. "My ears are still ringing. Man, horror movies have less screams."

Mike chuckled. "Yeah, even Michael Myers would run from that place holding his head."

"Quit being babies," Cindy said. "The boys had a great time, that's what counts. Let's get them inside."

Mike left Drew in his seat. "I'll come back out for him."

He picked up Josh and Elijah lifted Gabe.

Cindy carried Benny who snuggled into her shoulder, wrapping his arms around her neck. She kissed his cheek and whispered, "We're home, Benny."

He moaned but his eyes stayed shut. They carried the boys to their bunk beds and laid them under the covers.

"Should we have them brush and use the bathroom?" Elijah asked.

"No, they can brush tomorrow. And they'll wake up if they need to pee, they always do."

Mike patted Elijah's shoulder. "See ya later. Thanks for the great time."

Elijah grinned. "Yeah, we'll go again sometime."

They both looked at Cindy and laughed.

"Not," they said together.

"You guys are brats." She pushed them both in the chest then took Mike's hand. "Let's get Drew in your car."

"Alright. Bye, Elijah."

"Later," Elijah grunted, heading for the bathroom.

She and Mike walked back to the van. He lifted Drew, transferring him to the car, without waking him.

"Wow, did they put sleeping pills in the pizza?" She pointed to Drew passed out in the front seat of Mike's car.

"Maybe that's a courtesy they throw in for the parents who have to suffer through the experience. That way they can relax once they get home."

"You're probably on to something there."

He closed the door and leaned against the car, pulling her to his chest. "I had fun tonight. I'm just kidding about all the other stuff."

She leaned into his body and almost purred. "It was fun. I think it's just what they needed."

"Was it what you needed?" He rubbed his hands on her back.

"Yes, I had a great time." She tilted her head back to look at him. "But tomorrow, it's just us."

"What do you want to do?"

Her stomach tingled. She knew what she *wanted* to do. "I don't know, surprise me. As long as we're alone."

He moved his face toward hers. "That just what *I* need."

His kiss was warm and strong. It could last all night and never be enough. The porch light came on flooding them with its glow.

She giggled. "I think that's a signal."

He narrowed his eyes at the light. "That's a gutsy move. Just when I thought we were getting along." He kissed her again, quick.

"That reminds me," she said. "What happened tonight? When you and my brother went outside."

"I told you, we talked." He blinked, dropping his gaze to her lips.

"About what?"

Mike winced. "I just wanted tonight to be fun."

The warm glow surrounding her dimmed. "What happened? Did you and Elijah argue?"

"No." He closed his eyes for a second and shook his head. "But Jamal and I did."

She ground her teeth. "What? Why was he there?"

Mike told her about Devon at the meet and what he said, and about searching for Elijah at the restaurant. Her face grew more and more heated as he talked.

"God, I hate that guy. He's bothered me ever since the first time I met him when I went to get Elijah from one of their stupid parties."

"Forget about him." He kissed her again and her anger melted away. "How long do you think I could kiss you before Elijah comes out here with a baseball bat?"

"With the mood he's in after that crazy place? I'm surprised he isn't out here already." She pulled him back to her for one last kiss, then stepped away. "You better get Drew home."

"Right. My mom's probably wondering where we are." He rubbed a hand down her arm. "I'll see you tomorrow."

"Good night." She waited for him to open the door. "I love you."

He walked back to her and hugged her. "I love you, too."

The porch light flashed, and they both laughed.

"I'll pick you up around ten." Mike waved toward the house and got into his car.

She waved as he drove away then went inside.

Elijah sat at the table in the kitchen, drinking a glass of milk. He smirked when she walked in. "Oh, back so soon?"

"Funny." She joined him. "Tell me what Jamal wanted."

He raised his eyebrows. "Jamal?"

"Yes, Jamal. Mike said he was there when you went outside."

Elijah narrowed his eyes. "Man, that boy tells you everything."

"Why shouldn't he? You were the one who didn't want him to lie to me."

"Yeah, I guess." He shrugged. "He came there looking for Mike."

She cocked an eyebrow. "He came there to fight him, didn't he?"

He nodded. "Maybe. Jamal found me first and I tried to keep him away. Told him Mike wasn't there."

She leaned back in her chair and rubbed her eyes. "Then Mike came out to find you and Jamal knew you lied." She swallowed to wet her throat. "Elijah, I told you not to hang out with him. He thought you were a punk like him and now..." she didn't finish.

"Yeah, now they won't trust me again." He put his glass in the sink. "Don't worry about it. I'm not hanging out with them anymore. You should be happy."

"Happy that they want to beat you both up now? That's how they work."

"They're all talk. You could take Jamal, he's a wimp. Last year he got in a fight with a dude, took one punch, and got knocked out."

"So, maybe that guy got lucky." She pictured Mike's face bruised from Elijah. "Can Mike even fight?"

Elijah raised his eyebrows. "Don't you know he has a black belt in karate?"

"He does? Then how did you beat him up so bad?"

"Your confidence is overwhelming, sis." His head bobbed from side to side. "I know how to fight."

"You know how to street fight. When's the last time you fought Chuck Norris?"

"Damn, fine," Elijah grumbled. "He let me beat him. He said he hurt so bad on the inside from you leaving him, he wanted to hurt more on the outside to forget about it."

"That is seriously sick." Tears prickled in her eyes. "But awesomely freaking sweet at the same time."

"Oh God, do NOT tell him I told you that. This is already like *General Hospital*." He threw his arms up. "Who am I kidding, you two can't keep anything a secret. You'll tell him everything I said. I'm going to bed. Good night."

He walked away and Cindy followed, laughing, glad the day was over and happy she could end it with a smile instead of tears.

****

Eggs sizzled in the pan and the toaster popped, the smell of toasted bread and bacon filled the kitchen. Cindy flipped the eggs, trying to keep the yolks from breaking.

Her mom shuffled in. "Hey, baby."

Cindy put the spatula on the counter and hugged her mom.

"Hey, Mama." She touched the bags under her mom's eyes. "When did you come home?"

Her mom grabbed a cup and poured the coffee, sitting at the table and drinking it black. "Your daddy kicked me out around two. He made me come home to sleep."

Cindy glanced at the clock. "You should go back to bed. It's only eight."

She sipped and shook her head. "I need to get back up there." Tears spilled down her cheeks. "I don't have much time left with him and I don't want to waste it sleeping."

Cindy's breath caught in her throat.

"Don't say that, Mama. Daddy's going to get better." She sat in the chair next to her mom.

Her mom reached out and held her hand. "No, he's not. You need to come to terms with that, Cindy."

Hot tears fell and Cindy shook her head.

"I need you to be strong, you'll need to help your brothers." Her mom squeezed her hand tight and Cindy met her gaze. "Please, can you do that for me?"

She couldn't accept her daddy dying. "Mama, I can't. He's *got* to get better."

Mama's face scrunched and Cindy looked away. She returned to the eggs and slid them onto a plate. "Here, I made breakfast for everyone. Eat something before you go back." She handed her a plate filled with food.

"Thank you." Her mom picked up her fork and pushed the eggs around her plate.

Elijah came in carrying a bleary-eyed Benny. They both rubbed their eyes and sniffed.

"Thanks, Mama. You didn't have to make breakfast." Elijah sat Benny in a chair and hugged her.

"I didn't." She gestured to Cindy with her fork. "Cindy did. I'm just here for a few minutes then I'm going back to the hospital."

Elijah and Cindy shared a glance. "Thanks," he said.

"No problem." She bit into a slice of toast. "Are the other two up yet?"

"Yeah, they're in the bathroom." Elijah fixed a plate for Benny and then himself.

Mama sighed. "I need to go. Can you guys watch the boys today?"

"Well," Cindy glanced at Elijah. "Uhm, Mike and I kind of have plans. If that's okay, Mama." Her stomach squirmed, she didn't want to dump the kids on Elijah, but she wanted to spend time with Mike.

Elijah chewed his eggs, shaking his head. "How about we split the day? You can take care of them this afternoon."

Cindy nodded.

Mama glanced at her. "What are you and Mike doing?"

"I don't know. Just hanging out." She turned to clean up the counter so her mom couldn't see her blush.

"Well, you better hang out someplace public, or at least not alone." She chuckled. "Just because I gave this the okay doesn't mean I won't keep an eye on you."

Cindy said, "Don't worry, Mama. Elijah is doing that for you."

He grunted. "I got this, Mama."

"Good, Daddy will be glad to hear that you're looking out for your sister." Her lip quivered and tears gathered in her eyes.

Benny looked at Mama, his eyes wide.

Cindy knelt next to him and smiled. "Hey, why don't you go get Gabe and Josh and tell them to hurry up?"

"Okay, save my eggs." He hopped off his seat and ran to the back of the house yelling, "Breakfast is ready, hurry up or I'll eat all the bacon!"

Cindy hugged Mama, patting her back.

Mama wiped her eyes and exhaled a shuddering breath. "Sorry, I shouldn't cry in front of them."

"It's okay," Elijah said. "Don't worry about them."

"Don't cry, Mama. Daddy will be okay."

"No." Her mom pushed her back, holding her by the shoulders with a glare on her face. "Your Daddy is *dying*. He isn't going to get better, and he isn't going to be okay. I need you to understand that."

Elijah stared wide-eyed between them.

Cindy glanced at his face. "You believe that, too?"

Tears pooled in his eyes and he nodded.

"Well, you're both wrong." Cindy jumped out of her seat. "He's going to get better and everything will be back to normal."

She ran to her room and slammed the door. Sitting on the edge of her bed, she held her head.

"Please, daddy. You have to get better."

She changed her clothes and put on her running shoes. Craving an escape, she bolted through the hall and out the front door. If the rhythm of her feet on the pavement wasn't enough to erase her anger, she knew who would—Mike. And as the sweat mixed with her tears, his face entered her mind and she could finally breathe.

CHAPTER TWENTY-ONE

MIKE

Parking in Cindy's driveway, Mike stared at the house, lost for a moment in the surreal new reality. They'd not only told her parents about their relationship, but they'd been given the green light by her family to date.

Though his wish came true, the pain they had to face because of it totally sucked, for Cindy most of all. Her denial about her dad's condition would make the end harder for her, too.

He walked up the sidewalk toward the front door and knocked. The door opened, but instead of Cindy, Elijah greeted him with a frown.

"Hey." He stepped out on the porch, pointing to the bench. "We need to talk."

Mike sat. "What's wrong? Is it your dad?"

"Sort of." He sat next to Mike and leaned back. "It's crazy, knowing he's gonna die. Not wanting it to happen but wishing it would just be over with."

Damn. What should he say to that?

"I'm sorry."

"Yeah." Elijah met Mike's gaze, his eyebrows bunching up. "But Cindy is the one who needs help. She won't accept that it's happening. She's gonna blow when it does."

Mike rubbed his eyes. "I know. I've tried to get her to talk, but she just keeps saying he'll be okay."

"The stroke caused a lot of damage to his heart. He's really weak. Mama said the doctors told her it could happen anytime." He caught his breath and pressed his lips together.

Mike waited, shifting his gaze to the cars passing on the street to give Elijah time to compose himself.

"I don't want Cindy to lose it," Elijah said. "But she won't listen to us."

Mike's stomach tightened. "You want me to try talking to her again?"

"She'll listen to you," he said.

Mike pretended not to notice when Elijah wiped his eyes. He pursed his lips. "I don't want to hurt her but you're right. She needs to be ready." He'd hurt her, no doubt about that.

"Thanks." Elijah stood and opened the door.

Inside, Josh, Gabe, and Benny looked up from the floor where they lay watching Saturday morning cartoons. With squeals, they ran to him.

"Hi, Mike!" Josh punched him in the stomach. As Mike bent over, fake moaning, Gabe jumped on his back, and Benny hugged his neck.

"You guys got me." He fell to the floor, and they piled on top, tickling his neck and armpits. He laughed, tickling them back while Elijah smirked.

"If you let them get started, they'll go like that all day."

"Good thing we're leaving then," Cindy said, arms crossed as she watched her brothers tackle Mike.

He gazed at her, freezing in place as Benny belly-flopped on his stomach. His throat went dry, and he had to remember how to close his mouth.

Cindy wore a tight pair of acid-washed jeans that hugged each of her curves, and a pink and gray striped sweater that hung off one shoulder, leaving her smooth skin exposed and his heart exploding in his chest. His gaze traveled down, ending on her little black shoes, then back up again, past the skin and up to her long braids, spilling around her face and on that bare shoulder he couldn't stop looking at.

Trying to swallow again, he stood, shaking off the boys. He sucked in a breath. "Hey," was all he got out.

"I'm ready if you're done playing." She waved to the door. "Can we go?"

He glanced at Elijah who stood smirking at his sister. "Girl, remember what Mama said."

Mike looked back in time to see Cindy blush. She met his gaze. "We need to be in public. I'm not allowed to be alone with you."

Heat spread from his face to his toes. At times like this, his coloring was a pain in the ass, announcing his embarrassment like a freaking red spotlight. Ignoring Elijah, he reached for Cindy's hand. "No problem, let's go."

"Bye, boys," Cindy said. "I'll be back later. Be good for Elijah."

Josh and Gabe waved to her, settling back in to watch He-Man. But Benny ran to her and hugged her legs.

"Where are you going?"

Cindy picked him up and looked at Mike. "Where are we going?"

An image of his bed flashed through his mind and his face got hotter. He glanced at Elijah's crossed arms and swallowed. "I'll go anywhere you want."

Elijah shook his head. "Man, dude."

Mike laughed. "Sorry, she's the boss you know."

Cindy chuckled and kissed Benny's cheek. "Go watch cartoons. I'll be back then later we can make some cookies."

Benny's eyes grew wide. "Chocolate chip?"

"If that's what you want." She tweaked his nose, and he giggled, then joined his brothers on the floor in front of the TV. Cindy patted Elijah's shoulder. "Have fun. I'll see you later." She walked to the open door.

Elijah looked at Mike, eyebrows raised. Mike nodded. He knew he needed to talk to Cindy about her dad, but then he looked at her again and his mind drifted someplace else. A place where talking wasn't important.

He followed her out the door, reminding himself to think about what she needed. But when she got into his car, winked at him, and laid her hand on his leg, he knew he was in trouble.

"So where should we go?" His voice cracked and he cleared his throat. "How about the mall, that's public?" He backed out of her driveway, ignoring her hand still resting on his leg. Or trying to.

"I guess." She swirled her fingers and his pulse skyrocketed.

He grabbed her hand and kissed it, trying to control his breathing. "Is there something else you'd rather do?"

She shook her head, her lips pulling up at the corners. "No, the mall is fine."

He put her hand on her leg and returned his to the wheel. "Okay, we can eat in the food court if you want. I'm starving." His eye was drawn to her bare shoulder and he almost swerved off the road. He corrected his direction. At this rate, his face would be permanently red.

Giggling she leaned over and kissed his cheek. He almost groaned when she laid her hand back on his leg.

"Don't crash. We finally get to have a real date without hiding. A trip to the hospital would totally ruin it." She patted his leg and then reached for the radio. "How about a little top forty to set the mood?"

"Okay, but I have *Licensed to Ill* if you want to listen to it."

"Nah," she said. "I'm not that into rap."

He chuckled, and she slapped his knee. "Shut up. Don't stereotype, or I'll find Spandau Ballet for you."

"Oh god, please don't."

"Then be nice." She flipped through the stations while he drove, trying not to think about that sweater. He didn't realize she'd stopped until a high falsetto voice sang out, *"Big girls don't cry!"*

"I'm being nice. Why did you stop on this?" He turned to tease her. The tears on her cheeks chilled the fire in his chest. "What's wrong?"

She shook her head and wiped her eyes. "Nothing."

He pulled to a stop at the light and held her hand. "Why are you crying?"

"It's stupid." She tried to laugh, but it came out as a sob. The light turned green and the car behind them honked.

"Dammit," Mike muttered. He pressed on the gas and pulled into the parking lot in front of a grocery store, parking at the end of the row away from the building. "Come on, tell me what's wrong."

He held her while she cried.

"My dad used to sing me that song whenever I got hurt. I told you it's stupid. It just reminded me of him and…"

She sniffled, and he reached into his back seat to grab the box of tissues he'd bought. "Here."

She grabbed one, laughing through the tears. "I hope you bought stock in Kleenex. They're making a killing off me right now. I can't wait until he's better and I can stop crying so much."

"Buying tissues is the easy part." He chewed on his cheek while she dabbed at her eyes, Elijah's request battering at the back of his mind. "Cindy, we need to talk."

She blinked at him. "What about?"

"Your dad." Hurt flashed across her face, and he felt like the world's biggest ass. He pushed through the guilt squirming in his stomach. "I know how much you love him and want him to get better."

She glared at him. "Don't say it."

"We need to talk about this," he pleaded. "I'm worried about you."

She closed her eyes and more tears leaked down her cheeks. "Elijah asked you to do this, didn't he?"

"Yes, and he's right. You need to prepare yourself." He wiped her cheeks with his thumbs, and she opened her eyes, miles deep with pain that threatened to drown them both.

"He has to get better," she breathed. "He won't leave us. He can't."

"He wouldn't want you to lie to yourself."

"I'm not. The doctors could be wrong. He could get better."

Her tears were a river, but he pressed on. "If you keep lying to yourself, you'll miss your chance to say goodbye, and have to live with that forever."

Her face crumpled, and he pulled her to his chest. His tears falling now as her pain became his.

"I don't want him to die. I don't want him to die." Her voice was thick with angry tears.

"I know. It's okay."

She repeated her mantra, and he listened, rocking her in his arms and soothing her the best he could. After a while, she stopped talking and just cried. He knew he'd done the right thing for her, but it sucked. He held her tighter to make up for the hurt he'd forced her to confront.

When her sobs quieted, she took a deep shuddering breath and let him go. He held out the tissues, and she took the box.

"I didn't want to hurt you, and I didn't mean to make you cry."

She blew her nose, throwing the tissues on the floor by her feet. Giving a tearful laugh, she said, "You and my brother need to go back to not talking to each other."

He smiled a closed-lip smile and rubbed her knee. "Sorry."

She set down the box and held his hands. "I won't say thank you. I hate knowing this truth."

"I hate it for you." He lifted her chin with his finger. "But you needed to learn it."

She sighed. "I love you."

"And I love you." He put his hand behind her neck and kissed her, leaning his forehead on hers.

"Now that this is done, can we go on our date?" She touched his lips, her fingers warm and soft.

"Anything for you." He turned the key and pulled away from the grocery store.

"Watch out. Elijah will tear your man card if he hears that."

"I don't care." He reached for her hand. "If you like it, that's all I need."

She laughed, and he drove toward the mall, man enough to know he didn't need a stupid man card as long as he had her.

****

"Thanks for the new cassette. I love Madonna." She tossed the bag into the back seat and fastened her seatbelt.

"You're welcome. She's cool, I guess. But she's no Mike D."

"Thank God." She rolled her eyes. "If you love the Beastie Boys so much why don't you marry them?"

"What are you, like five? No thanks." He poked her side, and she flinched, laughing. "Do you want me to come help you with the boys?"

"I don't need help, but yes, I want you to come home with me."

"Okay, I have to stop at home and feed Bonkers. My parents went with Drew to a birthday party in Chicago. They won't be back until late, so I have cat duty."

"Of course, you need to take care of your baby."

She patted his leg for the hundredth time.

For the hundredth time, his body reacted. Stealthily he shifted in his seat and adjusted himself, fighting the growing urges. What the hell? She always touched him, and he'd always controlled himself. But today even a brisk breeze might send him over the edge.

He drew a deep breath and shook his head. He knew the reason. After the cry-fest tension eased, the bare shoulder tension went back into effect, playing on his emotions. Well, one certain emotion. The one he tried to repress because he wanted to respect her—and not have her mom kill him.

He pulled into his driveway. "Wait here. It'll only take a minute."

"I'll come in," she said. "A little kitty snuggle time will be good."

"Okay, come on."

They crossed the driveway and went in through the garage. In the kitchen, he grabbed the cat food and poured it in the bowl. Bonkers didn't come.

"Bonkers," Mike called. Still no cat. "Maybe he got stuck in the room downstairs. Sometimes Drew shuts the playroom door and traps him in there." Mike walked to the basement door and down the stairs. Cindy followed calling Bonkers' name.

They heard him meowing behind the closed playroom door.

"Ugh, told ya. One of these days Drew is going to have a mess in here that might teach him to check the room before he closes the door." Mike smirked. "The litter box is out here."

"Eww," she said.

Mike opened the door and Bonkers ran out, running for the back room where the litter box was kept. "See? I'll bet there's a pile of—"

He turned and the joke he planned froze on his tongue. Cindy stood in the middle of the room under the recessed light in the ceiling. Like a spotlight, the glow illuminated her hair and that damned skin on her bare shoulder. He groaned.

She raised her eyebrows. "What?"

Stepping closer, he raised his fingers to the spot where the skin of her arm met the sweater, then leaned in to kiss her from the tip of her shoulder to behind her ear, surprised when his heated breath made goosebumps on her skin.

"Sorry," he breathed, taking a stumbling step backward. "I've been wanting to do that since you walked out of your room."

"You're lucky I don't mind then." She closed the distance and kissed his lips.

He allowed one more touch on her shoulder, but made himself let go, while his hand would still follow directions.

Cindy rubbed her hands in his hair, her breath uneven. Then she slid them to his shoulders. "I think it's time, Mike."

He nodded, checking his watch. "Yeah, we should get back before—"

"No," Cindy said, looking at the floor. She raised her gaze to his, caressing his neck with trembling fingers. "I don't mean... time to leave."

"Oh. Y-you mean... we..." he gulped, then sucked in a breath. "Are you... ar... are you sure?"

"Yes," she breathed. "I love you, and I just want to think about us right now."

"I want that, too. But you don't have to... if ... you... don't want to."

"If I didn't want to, I wouldn't have suggested it."

She pulled at his shirt and he let her lift it over his head, shuddering with excitement—and fear—as her fingers lightly rubbed the skin on his stomach.

"I don't really know how..." He leaned his forehead on hers. "I'm not... not an expert at this you know."

God, he wanted this, he wanted *her*. But he didn't want to hurt her with his inexperience.

"That's o-okay," she said, sliding her hands up to his shoulders. "I'm sure we can figure it out."

"Yeah," he chuckled nervously. "You're... probably right."

"So," Cindy's gaze darted around the basement and back to his chest. "Are we gonna stay here or..."

"What? Oh...no. We uh. We can go to my room." He stepped toward the stairs and bumped his leg on the couch.

Smooth move ex-lax!

"Ok... sure."

Mike squeezed Cindy's hand as they walked up the stairs and to his room. His head spun from the blood rushing through his body. He pushed the door open and waited for her to go inside. Her eyes darted to his briefly then she pulled him in behind her, turning her head as she glanced around his room.

"Nice," she said, waving a hand at the blue-covered bed and gray walls. "At least you aren't like Elijah. I don't even see one pair of underwear or dirty jeans on the floor."

"Yeah," he said, rubbing the back of his neck with his hand. "I uh, I try."

In truth, the house cleaner had come today, but the fact they had someone else to clean would only make Cindy uncomfortable. Their different lifestyles didn't matter to him, but he knew she thought about it.

She giggled and he followed her gaze to the Heather Locklear poster on the inside of his open closet door.

"Oh, sorry." He released her hand and rushed to close the door. *Total dweeb.*

"It's fine. Though if that's your crush, I'm not gonna compare."

He walked back and took her hands in his. "You don't. You're so much better."

"Nice save." Her smile grew and she tapped the end of his nose with her fingertip. Then she trailed her finger down his chin and onto the skin of his chest, continuing to the muscles on his abs.

He closed his eyes for a moment, imagining her hand going lower. But she stopped, and he opened his eyes to watch her walk to his bed.

His stomach quivered like a five-year-old waiting for a shot. What if he hurt her? What if she hated it?

Oh God, what if I don't have a rubber?

Remembering his brother's teasing in the basement the other day, he blew out a breath.

Thanks, Tony.

Cindy sat and kicked off her shoes. "Do you have a...you know... for ... protection?"

He followed her movements, his gaze roving over the bare skin on her shoulder. Then he nodded, ducking away to his nightstand so she didn't see his boiling face. He slid the drawer open and grabbed the condom he'd thrown inside. Holding the square of foil, he sank next to her on the mattress and turned to face her.

She smiled and grabbed the bottom of her sweater.

Mike held his breath.

Slowly, she lifted her top over her head, dropping her sweater to the floor in a pink and gray puddle. Her eyes skimmed his for a moment then darted to the bed as she reached back and unhooked her strapless bra.

Seeing her perfection for the first time, Mike exhaled, releasing his insecurities, his fear. She was so beautiful, and *she* loved *him*. He didn't' care what she looked like—it was just a bonus—but her physical beauty excited him, too.

The rest of their clothes joined her sweater on the floor, and she slid under his covers. Mike swallowed and turned away to open the package. The crinkling of the foil from his shaking fingers sounded as loud as the ocean in his silent bedroom. After three tries, the stubborn thing refused to tear. Mike looked down at his slowly deflating body and silently cursed himself.

Dammit, idiot. You're not gonna need this if you don't hurry up.

Using his teeth, he finally got it open. Her fingers on his back and a quick glance behind him at Cindy's perfect legs under the clinging blue sheets was enough to remind his body to cooperate. He rolled the condom on and joined her under the covers.

Reaching out, he touched her gently and his fingers stuttered along her collar bone. "If I hurt you—"

"You won't." Cindy kissed him, pressing her bare chest against his.

He wrapped his arms around her, sighing as he slid his hands over her smooth back. This was right. So right. He pushed her back until they both laid with their heads on his pillow. He met her melted-chocolate gaze. "I love you."

"I know." She smirked. "Otherwise we wouldn't be here right now. C'mon. Talky-time is over."

Mike chuckled and pulled her back to him.

A hundred emotions had touched them that day. Excruciating sadness, heartbreak, happiness, humor. But afterward, as they laid together in his bed, echoes of her sighs still floating around his bedroom, Mike had one undeniable thought; their love was the most important thing in his life. Their lives. And it would see them through the rest, no matter what they might face.

****

He drove toward her house, one hand on her leg and the other on the wheel.

Cindy smiled at him—again. Every time her lips curved up, his followed.

"If you keep looking at me like that, Elijah's gonna bust us." He rubbed her leg, his pulse speeding when he remembered how it felt without the jeans.

"Good thing you have a black belt then." She laid her hand on top and twisted her fingers with his.

Mike eyed her. "How do you know that?"

"Elijah told me." She snorted. "By the way, *letting* yourself get beat up is really stupid. Don't ever do that again."

"Don't ever leave me again and I won't have to."

"And that does it for your man card, but deal." She sealed it with a kiss on his cheek.

They parked in her driveway and before they could even get out of the car, Elijah ran out of the house, a deep frown on his face.

"Gotta go, bout time you got here." He jumped in the Escort, fired it up, and left.

Mike watched him go then turned to Cindy. "Well, that was easy." He opened his car door.

"Yeah," she said, staring after Elijah with a frown. "I wonder where he's going."

"You can't watch over him all the time." But he frowned at the Escort's fading taillights, too.

"Let's get inside. I told the boys we can make cookies and they'll hold me to it."

They went inside and after the usual wrestling welcome, they settled in at the kitchen table to make the chocolate chip cookies. Cindy opened the refrigerator. "Darn it."

"What is it?" Mike asked.

"No eggs." She grimaced. "Sorry guys. Can't make cookies without eggs."

All three boys groaned at the same time. Mike bit back a smile and kissed Cindy. "I'll go get some. Is a dozen enough?"

"Yay, Mike!" Benny yelled, clapping his hands. His brothers clapped, too.

"Yes, a dozen would be great." She slapped his butt when he turned to leave.

"I hope they don't tell your mom." But the boys were busy, playing with the bowls, using them as drums.

"Hurry back. I don't know how much of this I can take." She waved at the impromptu jam session.

He ran out to his car and drove to the nearby convenience store. Parking near the door, he jumped out and jogged forward to open it. Andrea walked out, holding a full bag of groceries in front of her face. She ran into him and the bag fell to the ground. They both knelt to pick up the contents.

"Oh, excuse me. I didn't see…" She looked up at Mike and her face turned red. "Hey." She stuffed a box of powdered donuts into the bag.

"Hi, Andrea." He handed her a bottle of ketchup. He waved to the items on the ground. "Sorry."

"It's okay. I wasn't watching where I was going."

They put the rest of her items in the bag and stood. He glanced at her still red face, remembering what she'd done for him and Cindy.

"Thanks, for what you did. Telling Cindy the truth about Jenny." He swallowed, looking at the ground. "I owe you one."

She shook her head. "Don't worry about it."

"I'm serious. You helped Cindy see the truth, to see I didn't sleep around and…" His cheeks burned. "I mean, well, you know what I mean. And I'm sorry about you and me, that night. I shouldn't have, you know."

Her laugh rang out and Mike's face burned even hotter.

"I do know." Her smile faded. "You're a good person, Mike. Don't worry about hurting my feelings. That night was an accident. We're good."

"No, you don't get it," he insisted. "Without your help, Cindy might not have ever heard the truth. And we wouldn't be together. I *owe* you."

A wrinkle formed between her eyes. "Just be nice to her. She's done that for me, and she deserves the same."

Mike was about to answer when he heard a weird muffled sound like someone hit a punching bag over and over. Loud laughter followed. "What's that?"

He stood and walked to the corner of the building. Andrea trailed behind him.

When Mike turned the corner, he saw a group of guys kicking at something on the ground. The something was Elijah.

"Hey!" He yelled, and one of them turned around. Jamal. His lip curled and he glared at Mike. The snarl on his face reflected on those of the guys he was with, Devon and three other guys Mike had never seen.

He clenched his fists. "Andrea, go inside and call the cops, now."

She hesitated, then turned and ran toward the building.

"Leave him alone." Mike ran toward Elijah, who was moaning on the ground.

Jamal smirked. "Sure thing, cracker." He turned and kicked Elijah in the gut. He coughed and blood dribbled on his chin.

Mike dove, slamming his shoulder into Jamal's stomach. They rolled on the ground and Mike punched him in the jaw, knocking him out cold. He stood to face the other four, knowing damn well this wouldn't end in his favor, but also knowing he had to help Elijah.

Black belt or not, he'd never fought street thugs, and that's what they were. He expected dirty fighting, and that's what they gave him. Devon rushed him first.

While he side-kicked Devon, another guy came up behind him, punching the back of his head. He wobbled, stars floating in his vision, and spun, landing a punch on the offender's jaw. The guy doubled over, spitting blood on the ground at Mike's feet.

Mike blinked hard, but his vision stayed blurry. He spun again, looking for the next opponent. Then, one of the guys, a dead ringer for

Mr. T, punched him in the stomach with a fist like a sledgehammer. Mike gasped for breath, falling to his knees in the dirt. Devon pulled Mike up and held his right arm and someone else took the left. Then Mr. T used Mike's body for a punching bag.

Jamal still lay on the ground unconscious. Elijah moaned, covered with blood. Sirens rang in the distance, and Mike pictured the arcade games he'd played with the boys. But if this was a video game, he'd used up his lives *and* ran out of quarters.

The guys holding him let go of his arms and Mike fell to the ground. Feet replaced the fists. Mike struggled to breathe and to lift his arms to protect his head. Just after his ribs cracked and before he passed out, he thought of Cindy, hoping she wouldn't get mad when he left like her dad.

CHAPTER TWENTY-TWO

CINDY

Cindy pulled the flour from the cabinet and set it on the table. She pulled out the cookie sheets and a large mixing bowl to get ready for when Mike came back with the eggs. Elijah nagged at the back of her mind.

She looked at the oldest of the little boys as he sat at the table watching her get ready. "Josh, did Elijah say anything about where he was going?"

"No," Josh said. "He just answered the phone. I was playing."

She frowned. "Did you hear him say who he was talking to?"

Josh scrunched his face for a moment and nodded. "Some guy with a funny name."

"Funny name?" She pursed her lips. "Was it, Jamal?"

Josh's face lit up. "Yes. What kind of name is that?" He ran off to the bedroom with Gabe. "Let's get our lightsabers!"

Gabe followed and screamed, "I get the red one!"

Cindy's stomach clenched. Why would Elijah go see Jamal? She stared out the window and considered putting the boys in the van to go look for Elijah. Maybe when Mike got back, they could go together. The phone rang, and she jumped, knocking into the table.

Crossing the kitchen to the wall where it hung, she lifted the handset from the cradle. "Hello?"

"Cindy?" Mama's voice sounded strained.

"Hey, Mama. Is everything alright?"

A painful second of silence fell.

191

"You need to come to the hospital. Now."

Her stomach dropped to her feet. "I have the boys and…"

"Bring them, too. It's time to… to say goodbye."

Cindy blinked, sliding her back on the wall and sinking to the floor. This was it. The moment she'd been ignoring, avoiding—denying. Remembering Mike's love today, she didn't argue with Mama. "Okay. We'll be there soon."

"Get here quick." The dial tone replaced Mama's voice.

Cindy sat on the floor, staring for a moment at nothing. Then, she stood. Mama was counting on her and she wouldn't let her down.

"Boys!" Cindy yelled. "Come here, we need to leave."

They ran from the bedroom and slid onto the kitchen tile on their stocking feet like Tom Cruise in *Risky Business*. Despite the pain, she grinned. Daddy loved when they did that.

"Get your shoes on. We need to go see Daddy."

"Yay!" Benny said. "Daddy! Daddy!"

"What about the cookies?" Josh asked.

"We'll make them later. We have to go now." Cindy stifled the tears. She grabbed a piece of paper and wrote a quick note for Mike. *At hospital. Come now.* She left it next to the door under the empty flowerpot.

The boys climbed into the van and buckled. She got in and turned the key. "Let's go guys."

They backed out and headed toward Daddy. As she drove, Cindy looked for the Escort, but never saw it. Mike's Camaro sat at the little corner store, but she didn't have time to stop and get him. He'd see her note. She continued to the hospital, deep breathing to keep from losing control and bawling like a baby. She parked in the lot and took her brothers inside.

Familiarity with the hospital wasn't something she wanted, but when she entered with the boys through the same sliding doors into the same beautiful waiting room and Debby sat at the desk, she experienced déjà vu. Or as her friends said, same shit different day.

Debby looked up when they entered, her usual smile replaced with a sad frown. She jumped up and walked to the door leading to Cindy's daddy. Without a word, she punched a code in the keypad on the wall to let them in.

Cindy waved her thanks, afraid to speak and release the tears she desperately tried to keep in check for her brothers. Walking through the stark lemon-scented hallway, she led them to the elevator.

"I get to push the button," Josh said.

Gabe pushed his hand away. "You did it last time."

Cindy pushed it herself. "Sorry, guys. There isn't time for this." The door slid open, and they stepped in. Cindy pushed the button for the third floor and the doors swished closed.

She looked at her brothers, swallowing the lump in her throat. "Guys, I need to tell you something. This is important, so listen to me."

Three sets of dark brown eyes stared at her.

"When we get there, Daddy might look... tired. So, will Mama. But remember, it's just Mama and Daddy. And there is nothing to be afraid of, okay?"

Josh and Gabe exchanged a glance and Benny's bottom lip trembled. Cindy knelt and hugged them all. "Really, it's okay. Just tell Mama and Daddy you love them. That's all they need to hear."

They returned her hug, and she stood. Josh sniffled, then punched Gabe in the arm when he sniffled too.

"You aren't supposed to cry, baby."

Gabe punched him back. "I'm not, you are."

"Stop," Cindy said. "There's nothing wrong with crying when you're hurting. But, right now, Daddy needs to see your smiles. And so does Mama."

They nodded as the doors slid open. Cindy placed Benny on her hip and walked toward Daddy's room. Josh and Gabe followed her.

Inside the room, Mama sat in the chair next to Daddy's bed. She held his hand to her chin. It didn't shake.

She looked up when they entered. "Hey guys, come say hi to Daddy."

Josh and Gabe clung to Cindy's legs. She gazed down at their upturned faces and pointed with her chin. Josh moved first, Gabe followed, and they walked to Mama's side.

She opened her arms, and they went to her, hiding their faces in her side. "Oh, come now. Daddy wants to see you."

Cindy walked closer, holding Benny to her side. He stared with wide, teary eyes. His little body trembled as he looked from Mama to Daddy, and Cindy hugged him tight.

"Smile, Benny," she whispered in his ear. "It's Daddy."

He nodded and at least stopped his lips from quivering.

"Carl, Carl, the boys are here."

Cindy scrunched her eyes. She moved Benny closer and stood behind Mama.

He blinked a few times, his once brown irises a milky white. Benny flinched, and she squeezed his leg.

"Hey, boys." Daddy's voice sounded thick and wet.

Cindy pressed her lips together and squeezed her eyes, determined not to cry yet. Once the boys left, that would be a different story.

"Hi, Daddy." Josh was the first to speak. Mama put a hand on his shoulder, and he seemed to draw strength from the contact, his next statement louder. "I love you, Daddy."

Gabe went next. He put his hand on Daddy's and said, "I love you, too, Daddy. When are you coming home?"

Cindy looked up at the ceiling, biting her tongue until she tasted blood.

"I'll see you real soon." Daddy smiled. "You have to promise to be good until then, okay?" He coughed, hunching his chin onto his chest and black blood leaked from the corner of his mouth. Mama wiped it with a tissue.

Gabe drew his hand back, cringing into Mama's side again. Benny cried.

Cindy hugged him, rocking him like Mike had done for her. "It's okay, Benny."

Mama glanced at her. "Where's Elijah?"

"He left when I got home and didn't say where he was going."

She nodded, then gazed at Daddy again. The love on her face made Cindy think of Mike.

The door opened. Cindy looked, hoping to see Elijah's face, but Gladys came in. "Hey, little guys. I have a room full of toys. Would you like me to take you there so your mommy and sister can visit with Dad?"

Josh looked at Mama. "Can we go?"

She pressed her lips together and nodded. "Give Daddy a hug and tell him good-bye first."

The promise of toys erased their fear. Josh hugged Daddy. "Bye Daddy. I love you. I'll see you later." He squeezed Daddy's arm and ran to Gladys.

Gabe, still nervous, spoke quietly. "I love you, Daddy." He kissed Daddy's cheek.

Daddy smiled, a tear rolling from one milky eye.

As Gabe joined Josh, Cindy held Benny closer to Daddy's ear. Benny kissed him, patting his face. "Don't be sad, Daddy."

"I won't," Daddy said. "And I don't want you to be sad either. I love you guys."

"I love you, Daddy."

Cindy set Benny on the floor and he ran to Gladys, hugging her leg.

She smiled at Mama, then Cindy. "I'll take these little men to the playroom down the hall. You come and get them when you're ready." She led the boys out and closed the door behind her.

Mama looked back to Daddy, caressing his head with steady hands. Cindy had a sudden surge of pride for her strength.

"Cindy," Daddy's thick voice interrupted her thoughts.

She scooted closer and bent near his face. "Hey, Daddy. I'm here. I love you." She kissed his cheek, tears gathering now that the boys were gone. But she held them back, this time for Mama.

He smiled, gazing at her with his unfocused, milky eyes. He tried to lift his hand, but it twitched and flopped back to his chest.

Cindy held it to her cheek and a single tear slipped out. She scrubbed it away with her other fist.

"You be good to yourself. I want you to be happy. Do good things." His breath increased, and he panted, squinting his eyes.

Mama clicked a button and the machine next to Daddy beeped, numbers flashing on the screen. After a moment, he relaxed and opened his eyes again.

Cindy clutched his hand like she used to when she was little. Like when they watched the Wizard of Oz and the monkeys came. Or when Scooby and Shaggy ran into the monster who always ended up as an imposter in a costume.

But this time she couldn't escape into her daddy's arms, because daddy's arms held the monster.

Daddy focused on her again. "Tell Elijah, I love him. And... to be good, too. He needs..." Daddy coughed and scrunched his face. "He needs... to take care of you and... Mama."

"I will, Daddy. Elijah loves you, too. He's coming. But he loves you."

Daddy smiled, but it looked more like a skeleton at Halloween than her Daddy. "I want you to let Mike take care of you, too. He's a good man, baby girl. He loves you," his eyes turned to Mama, and his tears fell, "almost as much as I love Mama."

Mama covered her mouth with a shaky hand, the pain finally showing as she kissed Daddy, tears streaming on her face.

Cindy tried to cry quietly. "I will, Daddy. I love you." And that was it. She gave in and sobbed.

Mama did, too then Daddy smiled once more and closed his eyes. His chest moved in spurts, no rhythm to the movements.

The door opened and a young doctor walked in. His face was kind, his blond hair cut short like Mike's, which made Cindy sob even harder.

Mama hugged her, keeping a hand on Daddy's chest.

"Mrs. Wilson. I'm sorry to intrude. But your son is here." The doctor's soft voice carried over the slow beeping of Daddy's heart monitor.

Mama sat up. "Send him in here, quickly. He needs to say goodbye."

The doctor shook his head. "I'm sorry. But he can't come in. That's why I'm here."

Mama stared at him. "I... I don't understand."

The doctor met her eyes and Cindy's heart, already broken, cracked completely. "Where is my brother?" she demanded.

"He came in five minutes ago, in an ambulance with his friend. They were attacked in an alley by a store and beaten pretty badly."

Mama gasped and Cindy jumped from her seat. "Is he okay?"

"He will be. He has a few broken ribs, a concussion, and a broken arm. We had to sedate him to set the arm. But he'll be okay."

Cindy glanced in the hall and the hairs on her neck raised. She'd been here long enough for him to come. She turned her gaze back to the doctor, her body shaking. "Who was the friend?"

He looked down at his chart, flipping the pages. "Uh, Mike Ryan."

Cindy fell into her chair, staring blankly. Mama squeezed her shoulders and took over the questions. "How is he?" she demanded.

The doctor shifted on his feet. "Sorry, I can't give you that information. His parents are on their way. But I will say, that if he hadn't shown up when he did, your son wouldn't have made it to the hospital. Whoever did this was very angry, and I don't think they intended to hold back. Mr. Ryan stopped them but paid a heavy price."

Cindy tried to slow her breathing, but the air came too fast. A high-pitched wheeze reached her ears, and she realized it was coming from her. The doctor cupped his hands around her mouth.

"Try to breathe slow. You're hyperventilating. Slow and easy now. You'll be okay." He looked at her mom. "Boyfriend?"

Mama nodded.

Mike. Mike. Mike. She wanted to scream but she couldn't even breathe, let alone talk. She met her mom's loving gaze.

"Go to him, baby girl. I'll stay with Daddy." She put her hand back on Daddy's slow-moving chest. "He's mine. You go to yours."

Cindy looked at Daddy and her eyes filled with tears. She kissed him on the cheek, but he didn't even flinch. He was already leaving, but Mike was waiting for her. She hugged Mama and walked with the doctor to the door. She turned for one last glimpse of her parents together.

Mama looked at Daddy like Mike looked at her. Mama kissed him on the lips one last time. That was a love worth living for. Turning, she followed the doctor to where her love waited.

****

The doctor led her to the ICU waiting room. She stepped through the door, scanning the room for Mike's parents.

Renee saw her first and ran to her, hugging her close. "Oh, Cindy. Thank God you came."

"Yes," Greg said, "Mike would want you here."

She hugged Renee, glancing at Greg. "I was here already. My daddy is… upstairs."

Renee's eyes opened wide. "Oh, I didn't know. Is he alright?"

Cindy swallowed, shaking her head. She glanced at Tony and Drew, sitting in the chairs.

Tony met her gaze and frowned. Standing, he walked toward her, the frown deepening. "I'm sorry about your dad."

"Thanks." She knelt to talk to Drew, his face deathly pale and hands shaking. "Hey. You okay?"

He nodded but his bottom lip quivered. Cindy glanced around and saw a volunteer sitting at a desk. By the looks of it, she and Gladys were either sisters or had the same hairdresser.

She walked over and spoke quietly. "My little brothers are in the third-floor playroom. Could you show Drew where they are? He knows them, and they would probably like to play together." She glanced at Renee and Greg. "If that's okay with you?"

Rene nodded. "Sure."

Drew hugged Cindy. "Gabe and Josh are there?"

"Yes. Would you like to go see them?"

He glanced at his parents. They nodded, and he said, "Yes." He walked out the door with Gladys' look-a-like.

With Drew gone, Cindy's fear exploded. She looked at Renee and Greg, her body shaking. "What's wrong with Mike?"

"He's in bad shape," Greg answered. "Broken ribs on both sides, right arm, left leg, concussion, his spleen ruptured. They're removing it now." His voice faltered, and he bit his right knuckle.

Renee put her hand on his shoulder. "Mike's a fighter, though."

Cindy glanced at them, but they wouldn't meet her eyes. She looked at Tony. "What else?"

Tony glared at the floor. "He also has a cracked skull. The bastards that beat him, used a pipe they found lying in the alley." He lifted his gaze to Cindy. "They hit him with it and ran, right before the police came."

Her hurt, her sadness, her desperate desire to see him whole and healthy, were all consumed by the burning bitter taste of hate.

"Did they catch the guys?" she asked.

Tony nodded. "One of them. He's here, too."

Cindy nodded. Elijah would know who the rest were, and he would give the police their names. She looked at Renee. "When will we be able to see him?"

"They said surgery could take a while. When he's in recovery we can go in." She wiped her eyes.

"Thank you." Cindy looked at the floor. "I know that sounds weird. My dad is dying. My mom's with him now."

Renee and Greg gasped, exchanging a glance.

Cindy drew a deep breath. "If Mike hadn't stepped in, my brother would have died tonight, too. The doctor told us that. I love Mike. And I just want you to know that… if I… could take his place I would."

For the third time that day, Cindy broke down. She fell to the floor, tears hot and thick on her face, shoulders aching with the force of her sobs.

Tony lifted her from the floor and held her, his arms like Mike's but not the same. She sobbed on his shoulder. Her dad was dying, and Mike could, too. It was too much. As the blackness came closer, Cindy walked willingly into the arms of oblivion.

CHAPTER TWENTY-THREE

MIKE

Y ou don't wanna go……. she still says no.

Cindy's voice called to him, and he tried to wade through the muck holding him down to get to her. He knew he should answer, but his body wouldn't work right. Cotton filled his head and his mouth. He peeled his tongue off his fuzzy teeth and tried to open his eyes, too. They weren't as sticky as his tongue, but he still had to blink a few times before the crust on his eyelashes gave way.

When it did, his eyes opened to the most beautiful sight in the world. Cindy's face, smiling. The tears on her cheeks marred the picture, but relief flooded his chest, so fast and full, he gasped and tried to reach for her.

That's when the pain hit.

"Uhhh." he groaned. Then he realized he couldn't reach for her anyway. His right arm was in a cast, pinned to his side. The left one tingled like it had been asleep for months. He glanced past his chest, to his left leg, suspended from the ceiling with a system of ropes and pulleys. The right one lay under a blanket, but he couldn't feel it.

A series of beeps near his head grew louder and faster. He opened his eyes to find her face again and the beeping slowed.

He tried out his voice with his most favorite word. "Cindy." It was rough and dry and crackled, but it worked. And she smiled, so it was worth the strain and hurt.

"Shhh. Don't talk." She brushed the hair from his forehead.

"Cindy," he said again. She gave him a kiss and even in his muddled and broken state, he knew that was better than a smile.

"I said don't talk." She blinked, and the tears wet her cheeks again.

"He's too stubborn to listen to you."

This voice didn't make his heart beat faster, but it still made him feel happy, even if he didn't know why. He closed his eyes to see if it helped his brain connect the pieces.

"Shut up, Elijah. He's just waking up. He's confused."

Elijah, Cindy's brother. He knew that meant something. "Elijah?" His name wasn't as easy to say, but even it made her smile.

"Yeah, I'm here. Thanks to you."

Huh. Weird thing to say. Mike closed his eyes again. Maybe he was dreaming. Or needed more sleep. But when her lips touched his again, he didn't want to sleep. "Cindy?"

"Yes, I'm here. I love you."

There was a softer beep, and then a warm sensation crawled up his arm and into his chest. The cotton grew thicker in his brain and he struggled to open his eyes and see her again. "Cindy." This time the word went unanswered, and he fell back into the soft and white.

****

Haven't seen a smile that pretty in a while... Oh no, it could not be... it's such a sight to see.

Her voice again. He wanted it, to touch it, to feel it. His mind fought against the ropes holding him down. They were strong, but her voice was stronger. It called to him. He couldn't remember why, but he knew he needed to reach it. He pushed with his mind, pushed to get what he wanted.

The voice. The words.

Cindy.

Yes, that was what he wanted. *Who* he wanted. She was the one he struggled to get to. Once he remembered, the ropes lost their strength, and he broke free. He blinked his eyes open again, and this time, they obeyed better. He drew a breath, still painful but easier than last time.

She was there again, those lips. He stared, soaking in the warmth of her face. He drew another breath and used it for good this time. "Cindy."

"Mike." She laughed.

He soaked in the sound for a moment then said, "I love you."

Had she ever smiled at him like that before? He couldn't remember, but it didn't matter. She did now.

"I love you, too." She kissed him then, his cheeks, his nose, his forehead, and finally his lips. She laughed again when the beeps increased.

"Where am I?" A window to the left, doors to the right. His left leg still rested in a bed of ropes, and his right arm still sported a cast. His left arm no longer tingled, but his right leg did. At least he could move it. He bent his knee and Cindy gasped, her eyes filling with tears again.

"You're in the hospital. You were hurt, but you're going to be fine." She held his left hand and raised it to her perfect lips.

"What happened? How did I get here?"

"Do you remember anything?" she asked.

He closed his eyes and remembered parts of things, but it was all jumbled up like someone cut apart his life and put the pieces into a blender on high speed. Some of them stuck to the side and he could see them.

"You run track." Yes, he remembered that part.

Her eyes twinkled. "Yes, so do you."

"I do?"

"Mm-hmm. Very well."

Okay. He looked for another piece. This one was huge, demanding attention. "You're my girlfriend."

"Yes," she whispered. "I am."

Good. He liked her face. And her voice. The next piece was big, too, but he wasn't sure why. "Your dad."

For some reason, this piece hurt. Her face scrunched, and she nodded. He wanted to wipe away her tears. His hand followed directions, and he lifted it to wipe her cheek.

She finished the piece of that memory. "He died the day you came to the hospital."

He didn't like that piece from the blender. "I'm sorry."

"Me, too."

He searched for something good. Something that would make her smile again. And he found it. "We made love."

Red bled through the darkness of her beautiful face. She bit her lip and nodded, looking to her right. He followed her gaze to another face, a face like hers.

He knew this face too. "Elijah." His lips formed the word before his brain could remember. Or maybe it was the other way around.

Elijah laughed. "Hey, Mike." He glanced at Cindy then back to him. "I'll ignore that last part."

"My head hurts." Mike sighed and closed his eyes. Searching through a blender was hard. "I'm tired."

Cindy kissed him. "Go to sleep. I'll be here when you wake up."

She clicked a button and cold seeped into his arm. It reached his head though, like melted honey on toast. He struggled to open his eyes, but he did, to see her.

"I love you, Cindy."

"I love you, too."

He took one last look before the warmth covered his eyes.

****

The third time he woke up things were different. He remembered where he was, his eyes and mouth worked the way they should, and he had to go to the bathroom.

He opened his eyes, and she was there. The cottony fog still hung heavy on his brain, but more like high wispy clouds, not the thunderheads from before. He could sift through it and remember things.

Cindy's eyes were closed as she slept curled up in the chair next to his bed. He used the time to remember her face—the shape of her eyes, the feel of her cheeks, the taste of her lips. She sat to his left this time, and he took advantage of that, too.

Ignoring the IV taped to it, he lifted his left hand and touched her sweet face.

She blinked, then jumped. "Mike?"

"Hey, sleepyhead." His voice was still rough from disuse but worked just like he wanted it to. "I thought only the patients were supposed to sleep in the hospital."

She laughed, then kissed his cheek. "Hold on." She ran out the door, but came right back in, pulling someone with her. Mike smiled at his mom and dad.

"Oh, thank God." His mom burst into tears. She held his face, crying and kissing his forehead over and over.

"My turn." His dad didn't kiss him, instead, he leaned in and gave Mike a tight hug around the neck.

"Dad, that kind of hurts," he said. But he laughed anyway.

"Sorry," his dad said, wiping his eye. "It's just good to see your eyes and hear your voice."

Mike blinked and focused on Cindy standing behind his parents. Her face was the most important. "How long have I been in the hospital?"

Cindy said, "The doctors said it could upset you."

"Give me a ballpark estimate if it's too much." He winked, and she laughed.

"It's more than one day." She came closer, standing next to his mom to hold his hand. "You've been here for two weeks. You've woken up three times, counting now.

The heart monitor beeped faster for two beeps. "Two weeks?" He looked at the ceiling for a moment.

"We've been waiting for you to wake up," his dad said. "They weren't sure how long it would take."

"The doctors said it would take time for your brain to heal." His mom rubbed her fingers through his hair. He winced when she touched the top of his head.

"Sorry," she said, drawing her hand back.

He squinted as the pain faded. "What happened? Why does that hurt so much?"

"Don't you remember?" His mom's tears fell again.

He shook his head, glancing at Cindy.

She pressed her lips together. "Do you remember the fight?"

He closed his eyes and images of Jamal and Elijah filled his mind. "Yes. Sort of."

"You found Jamal and his friends beating Elijah and you jumped in to stop them."

Mike nodded. "Sounds like me."

"Someone hit you with an old pipe right before the cops got there." Cindy sniffled and her voice shook. "You have a small skull fracture. That's why you wouldn't wake up."

The news should have upset him, but he wanted to know something more important. He looked at Cindy. "How's Elijah? Is he okay?"

"He's fine, better than you are." She squeezed his hands and tears filled her eyes. "Thanks to you."

He sighed, but his throat tightened seeing her tears. He pulled her closer with his good hand and squeezed her arm. His dad handed her a tissue and she wiped her eyes.

"I think Cindy is the one who helped you the most," his dad said, patting Cindy's shoulder.

Mike raised his eyebrow. "What did you do?"

She gave him a shaky smile.

"Well, I read somewhere that patients with traumatic brain injuries respond and heal quicker when they hear a familiar voice talking to them and saying familiar words. So, I read to you."

Something stirred in his memory. The words. The words that called him back to her. He remembered some of them, repeating them in his head.

Then he laughed. "You read me the lyrics to the Beastie Boys songs."

She rolled her eyes. "I did because I know how much you loved that stupid album."

"Now I know you love me."

"You knew that already." She glanced at his parents who smiled at her. "But I'm glad I don't have to read those dumb words anymore. You know, I hate rap music."

He reached up and touched her cheek. "Thank you." He wanted her to kiss him, but his parents were there, and he didn't want to embarrass her.

"I'd do it all over again if I needed to."

"Even if you had to read Vanilla Ice?"

She wrinkled her nose. "Well, I have to draw the line somewhere."

"Okay. I don't like him anyway." He stared at her lips and the stupid monitor beeped faster.

His dad cleared his throat. "I think I need some coffee to celebrate." He winked at Mike and put his arm around Renee. "Let's go to the cafeteria for a cup."

"Sure." She bent over and gave Mike's forehead another kiss. "I love you, honey. Thanks for coming back."

His cheeks prickled and he glanced at his mom. "I love you, too, Mom."

She smiled and bobbed her head, wiping more tears from her cheeks. Mike grinned. It only took a pipe over the head to make his mom get affectionate. Better late than never.

As they left, Cindy sat in the chair next to his bed, pulling it close so she could lean her elbows on the mattress next to him.

Mike rubbed his finger along her bottom lip. "I could use a kiss if you don't mind."

"Okay, but I warn you there isn't a lot of privacy here."

She leaned in and kissed him, bringing on the fastest round of beeping yet.

Cindy pulled back. "See, I told you."

"I don't care." He traced her cheek with his fingertip. "Nobody knows what we're doing."

"Thanks to you, Elijah does."

"Elijah does what?"

Leaning in close she whispered, "The last time you woke up, you told him we made love."

"I did?" Mike frowned. "Why would I do that?"

"You were remembering things, pulling memories out of the blue and that was one you shared." She laughed and ran her fingers through the hair above his ear.

He closed his eyes for a moment, enjoying her touch. "How did Elijah take it?"

"Well, considering you saved his life, *and* you love me, I think he's giving you a free pass."

Memories of their time together flooded his mind, but they brought with them other memories far less happy. His thoughts jumbled together in the blender for a moment. Pictures from the fight emerged along with questions.

"Why was he there? At the store?"

"Jamal had called looking for you. He told Elijah he was coming to our house to find you." She narrowed her eyes. "Elijah went to meet him and keep him away. He thought Jamal would be alone."

"So, he went to protect me, and then I showed up and gave them what they wanted. A chance to beat on me, too."

"You didn't do *anything* wrong." She cupped her hand around his cheek.

"Yes, I did." He leaned into it and whispered. "I wasn't there for you when you needed me. I'm sorry about your dad."

A wrinkle formed between her eyes, tears flowing down her cheeks. "It's okay. You were a little busy healing after saving my brother."

"But I should have been by your side."

He shook his head, the monitor beeping his anxiety. He took a deep breath to slow the blips, but it didn't help. He'd failed her during the hardest time of her life.

"You needed me, and I wasn't there." He turned his head so she wouldn't see his tears.

"No," she held his chin, turning his face back to hers. "You *were* there, for Elijah. If you hadn't stopped them, they would have killed him and we would have buried him, too. You were there when he needed you, and that's what I needed."

Mike blinked away his tears, nodding. She wiped them away with her thumbs and kissed him again.

She drew a deep breath and leaned back in the chair. "The worst is behind us. Now we can focus on you getting better."

"Okay." He blinked and his eyelids almost refused to open. "I can't believe I'm still tired."

Cindy stood. "I'll go so you can sleep."

His monitor beeped and he caught her hand. "No, I'd sleep better if you lay next to me."

"Uhm, are you kidding?" She glanced at the door as a nurse passed by in the hall. "I don't think that's allowed."

"Please?" He patted the bed next to him. "I'm disoriented and confused. If anyone says anything, you can blame it on that."

She giggled. "Okay, but keep your *hand* to yourself."

"No promises," he teased.

She laid on the covers to his left and rested her head on his shoulder. "Does that hurt?" she asked.

"No, it feels incredible." He kissed her cheek and closed his eyes. "Please don't get up until you're sure I'm asleep. I want to hold you for as long as I can."

"Then it's your lucky day. I don't have to go anywhere. I can stay here forever."

"Hmm. Good."

The fear was behind them now, and the only mar on the scene was her dad's death. But as Mike drifted off, with Cindy's breath on his neck and her fingers on his chest, he smiled. Forever sounded like the perfect amount of time. The future called, their future. Together. And it was time to start living it.

The End

Stay tuned for book 3
Coming September 2020
PREORDER TODAY!

Breaking the Cycle
(Sneak Peek!)

CHAPTER ONE

Some assholes shouldn't be allowed to have kids.

Andrea slammed the door of the kitchen cabinet. Tiny chips from the peeling paint spiraled in the sunbeam coming through the small, dirty window of the trailer home she lived in with her dad.

"Knock it off, smart ass," her dad yelled from the couch. He shifted and the already sagging piece of furniture threatened to dump him on the floor. "And hurry up with that grub. I'm hungry."

Andrea glared at the top of her dad's head. His greasy red hair, peppered with gray, stuck out in clumps against the arm of the couch. She tightened her grip on the wooden spoon in her hand for a moment, then turned to the stove and dipped it back into the macaroni and cheese boiling in the pot.

At least one of us is smart.

She tapped the spoon on the edge of the pot and laid it on the counter with a sigh. Same shit, different day. No wonder her mother had left.

Cranking the knob on the stove to off, Andrea pictured her mom's bloodshot eyes and dilated pupils that day she'd left with her younger-drug-dealing-less-of-an-asshole loser boyfriend. *After* shooting all the money in their account into her veiny arm leaving nothing left to pay the bills. Yeah, 1985 was a *banner* year in the Wilkinson household. Now in '86, she had no idea where her mom was. Whatever.

Ignoring the tightness in her throat, Andrea grabbed the strainer and drained the noodles over the sink. *Dad may be a bigger asshole but at least he didn't abandon his kids. Yet.*

She poured in milk and added the powdered cheese, skipping the butter since they didn't have any. She mixed it, grabbed two bowls, and spooned a helping for each of them, wishing, for the hundredth time, that she needed a third bowl for Tim. Her older—and goofier—brother.

Picturing his face, she smiled a little. Mac-n-cheese was his favorite and he'd usually eat twice as much as her, but he always wanted more. He'd found ways to get it, too.

"Annie-banannie, let's thumb wrestle to see who gets more noodles."
"How 'bout a race instead?"
"No way. Last time you kicked my ass. I can't run as fast as you."

His ridiculous taunts always made her laugh. They weren't about the food. It was his way of helping her out of a bad mood when she'd had a crappy race at a meet or when their dad gave her a hard time for getting second. Again.

She took a breath to fill the emptiness in her chest. Her brother was the only one she could depend on—until he left, too. Not that she blamed him for finding an out with the Army, but she had nowhere else to turn. At seventeen with no place to go, everyone had left *her* stuck taking care of Mister Father of the Year.

The timer on the oven beeped. She removed the broiler pan of hot dogs using the old stained and torn potholders she'd made. She rolled her eyes at the faded words *I love you, Mommy* scribbled on the fabric in her kindergarten handwriting, then stabbed two hot dogs with her fork and put one in each bowl.

"It's ready." She set her dad's bowl on the end of the rickety card table closest to him and took the seat across from it. After pouring herself a glass of milk, she wolfed down bites of the food and glanced at the clock. She didn't have time for self-pity.

Her dad pushed up from the couch and stretched. Lifting his arms above his head, his faded Black Sabbath t-shirt slid up. Andrea rolled her eyes at his hairy beer-belly. He limped the ten steps it took for him to come into the kitchen, sending a wave of stale sweat and beer in Andrea's direction.

She wrinkled her nose but kept eating. The previous week, she'd suggested he take a shower and her sore jaw had finally healed from the slap. She didn't need a repeat performance. If he wanted to smell like a pig farmer, whatever. She could get fresh air at college.

"This shit *again*?" He pointed to his bowl. "Can't you learn to make anything else?"

Andrea swallowed a bite, pushing the angry comeback down her throat with the food. "Nothing else in the cabinet. I need to go to the store."

"Then go. I'm tired of eating like a five-year-old." He stabbed his hot dog with a fork and ate half of it with one bite. "Get some steak or hamburger for Christ's sake."

"Sure. Give me some money and I'll go after school tomorrow." She checked the clock again. Ten minutes.

"You got money. I ain't giving you shit." He shoveled a heaping bite of noodles into his mouth. "I don't get my disability check for another week."

Small pieces of pasta flew from his mouth as he spoke. Andrea frowned as they collected on his beard.

"But I'm..." She cleared her throat. "I need to save money for college, Dad. Steak is pretty expensive."

"College, shit." He laughed and waved his hand at the fridge. "You ain't goin to college."

"That's my plan. Once I get the scholarship." She retrieved a beer from the fridge and handed it to him.

"Plans don't mean crap." He pointed his fork at her. "And you definitely won't get a scholarship. You're not good enough."

"Well, I'm going to drop time then—"

"Don't give me your bullshit. You lost every race last year to what's-her-face."

"Molly."

"Yeah, knew it was some stupid girly name." He popped the top on his beer and took a long gulp. "She's gone but you still can't win."

Andrea pushed her food with her fork as flashes of last year's cross-country season went through her mind; Molly winning every invitational, Molly beating her at every home meet, Molly getting second at state while Andrea sat at home recovering from the beating her dad gave her after getting suspended for fighting.

She had deserved suspension for fighting Molly's best friend Cindy and missing state. But her dad's abuse? He hadn't left marks anywhere that would show, and at least had left the extension cord out of it that time. Still, he'd added to her motivation to improve her times and get the hell out of there.

She glared across the table. "I tried my best. I ran faster *this* season."

"Still wasn't good enough was it?" He drained the can and crushed it with his fist. Taking another bite, he shook his head. "You best plan on finding a better job. I ain't gonna support a slacker after high school."

I already have a job, asshole.

She pushed away her half-filled bowl. It wasn't her fault a new upstart freshman came in to replace Molly, leaving Andrea in second place... again. Her dad's empty threat didn't scare her, she'd do whatever it took to get away from him anyway. As much as she hated school, college seemed like the only answer.

Better than ending up like him.

"I have to go. Gotta be at work in half an hour." Standing, she grabbed her jacket and slipped her arms into the sleeves. At the door, she turned back to him. "You might want to think about doing that someday, too. Once I'm gone, nobody will buy your damned food for you."

She rushed out slamming the door, laughing at the muffled sound of the crushed beer can hitting the metal behind her.

PREORDER TODAY!

A YA fantasy romance from B.B. Swann.
Coming September 2020!
PREORDER TODAY!

OUT OF THE WOODS
(Sneak Peek!)

(Note to self: Not all change is good.)

I wake in the dark with the white plaster "popcorn" of my ceiling stabbing my bare back. My ceiling. I float nine feet *above* my bed, wearing nothing but my too-small American Eagle boxers and my messy brown hair.

Voices whisper inside my head. My parent's voices chanting… in Latin.

Wait. Since when do they speak Latin? The words get faster, like a wind in a storm, stirring the fear in my chest until I gasp for breath.

Heart racing, I dig my fingertips into the plaster and stare into the darkness at my bed below. It's like I entered *The Matrix*. My messed-up navy-blue comforter looks like a still life photo of a wave on the stormy ocean. Dust rains down, bringing it to life for a moment. My book lays open on the floor next to my bed where I must have dropped it when I floated–

No. I'm not awake. I'm still dreaming.

Closing my eyes, I try to remember my dream. That's right, I was climbing the rope in gym class. After finally making it to the top for the first time, I had plummeted toward the floor. Only then, the gym turned into a real mountain and the rope a real cliff. The fall stretched on for hundreds of feet. In my dream I'd screamed, terrified, arms flailing like I was flying. That's when I woke up.

On my fucking ceiling.

No, I'm not awake. I'm NOT awake. Sucking a breath in through my clenched teeth, I nod once.

"Okay. When I open my eyes, I'll be in bed. One, two…."

The chanting returns to my head, louder than before, followed by a surge of white-hot energy that vibrates through my bones. I picture myself like those old-time cartoons where the cat shakes hands with the mouse and gets electrocuted and you can see his skeleton through his skin. The power surges through me and at its peak, my teeth crash against each other and I drop. Hard.

The support boards of my full-sized bed crack with a loud snap from the force of my body slamming into it. Bouncing off my mattress and onto the floor, my loud yelp is quickly muffled by the thick gray carpet. Heart pumping fast, I lay there for a minute trying to catch my breath.

The sound of feet pounding in the hall grows closer, and my bedroom door flies open. My parents run in, wide-eyed, grinning ear to ear. I flip over onto my back, like lying on the floor in the middle of the night is normal.

Invisible ropes pull against me, urging me toward them. I dig my fingers into the carpet.

"Everything okay, Zaidyn?" Mom brushes her wild black hair off her face. Dad stands right behind her in his red plaid pajama pants and white sleep shirt. Light from the hall spills into the room and I squint against the brightness.

Pushing myself up, I stand next to my bed, locking my knees to keep them from shaking. Or from taking me closer to them.

"Uh, yeah. Bad dream I... uh... fell."

Not a complete lie.

Crossing his arms, Dad leans against the doorframe, grinning at Mom like they just won the lottery. "It worked this time."

She claps her hands together and holds them over her mouth.

"What worked?" I ask. "What are you talking about?" My breath speeds and the Latin words come back to me. My cheeks tingle as the blood drains from my heated face.

"Want to talk about your dream?" Mom walks toward me smiling.

(Note to self: I want to spaz out alone. I just fell off my freaking ceiling!)

"No." I run a hand through my bed head and dust flakes off. "What is Dad talking about?"

Mom brushes pieces of ceiling off my shoulders.

"What *is* this stuff?" She grabs a chunk of white plaster and frowns, lifting her gaze above our heads. "Is this from the ceiling?"

Dad's smile grows. "You owe me ten bucks, Diana."

Their voices were in my head. They're a part of… whatever this is. Glancing between them, goosebumps cover my body. "What's going on?"

"Your father thinks he's being funny." She smirks at him. "Must have been some dream. Why did you scream?"

Dammit. I've never been able to lie to my parents. Mom always seems to know when I do. She'll stare into my eyes like she's reading my soul and I'll cave. But how can I tell her *this* truth? I look at her and try to think of something to say that doesn't make me sound like I need a first-class ticket to the psych ward.

She sighs. "Sorry, Zaidyn. I hate to do this without permission, but I need to know."

She puts her hands on either side of my face and my body locks up. I can't look away. Can't blink. Can't *move*. My stomach clenches and I have the distinct and highly unpleasant sensation of a finger stroking my brain. The room seems to warp and I'm back in Matrix mode again. Or maybe it's Dr. Strange. Whatever it is, my heart has bypassed racing and gone on to massive heart attack mode.

The light from the hall melts into my brain then my brown eyes replace Mom's green ones. My breath freezes like my blood and I see myself from *her* point of view. My short hair sticks up at odd angles, my eyes so wide my long lashes touch my eyebrows. Every muscle outlined on my bare chest and arms as I struggle to breathe.

(Note to self: Who the hell is she, and when the hell did I start looking like that?)

Images from my dream scroll through my mind, like I'm watching a game replay. I fall from the cliff again and my stomach lurches until I'm gaping at Mom's eyes again. I haven't moved an inch. The only thing moving is my dizzy brain.

Before I can ask her what the hell is happening, her voice reaches me—*inside* my head.

Relax.

Oh. Sure. No big deal. It's just my mom—*crawling through my cerebrum.*

I do the opposite of relax. Every cell in my body tightens. With cold sweat coating my body, I swallow hard and instinctively push back at the finger, imagining my fist punching its tip.

Mom releases my face, winces, and presses a hand to her temple. Finally, I can blink. Breathe. Move, shuffle backward until I bump my heels into the wall next to my window. When did aliens replace my parents?

"Ha!" Mom smiles at Dad, still rubbing her forehead. "Did you feel *that* power? You owe *me* ten dollars."

"He has *ceiling* in his hair." Dad uncrosses his arms, shaking his head. "The Mitchell traits came out first."

Mom laughs. Dad joins her. I scrunch my eyes.

"I'm really kinda freaking out here."

"It's okay, honey." Mom takes a step toward me and I press my back into the cold wall.

Dad nods. "Sorry, we don't mean to be vague. We'll tell you everything."

They smile like I just won my first spelling bee or hit a home run in t-ball, not fought off my mother's brain attack after levitating out of bed in my freaking underwear.

Clenching my fists, I glare at them fighting the urge to throat punch my parents. The magnetic pull of their nearness sets my teeth on edge and clouds my thoughts. As freaked out as I am, I want to get closer to them.

"It's okay." Mom takes a step toward me and I flinch, looking at her from the corner of my eye. "We finally unlocked your abilities."

"Abilities? What the hell?" She moves closer and my stomach rolls, but I have to grab the window ledge to hold myself back from her. I shake my head. "Stay away from me."

She frowns and stops moving. "I'm not going to hurt you."

"You already did." I rub my forehead.

"I'm sorry. I didn't mean to." Mom's voice breaks on the last word.

Dad steps into the room, moving to her side. "He doesn't understand yet, honey."

Sure. Comfort Mom, not the son freaking out because his parents turned out to be from Mars.

I grab yesterday's t-shirt from the floor at my feet. Can't run away half-naked. They block my access to the door, so I turn my eyes to the darkened window behind me. Yanking the shirt over my head, I consider the drop to the cement patio at least twenty feet below. The steep slope to the backyard used to be my favorite part of our house, but now I wonder, will the fall break my leg or just my ankle?

Keeping my eye on them, I slide on my board shorts. Not the best get-away clothes, but they're the closest.

Mom leans her shoulder into Dad's side. "Zaidyn, don't leave. Let us explain."

She knows what I'm thinking? Chills race along the back of my neck. I glance again at the darkness outside my window.

"I know you're hurting. That's normal." Dad holds his hands out and takes a step toward me. "We need to complete the cycle and you'll feel better."

I slide a step closer to the sill. "Don't come near me. And I'm not staying here. I don't even know who the hell you are."

Dad follows, moving closer to me. "Nothing has changed. We're still your parents."

Fire explodes in my chest. "*Everything* has changed. I woke up on the ceiling! Mom talked inside my head!" I rush to the window, ignoring Dad's gasp. "And I don't know what the hell is going on, but you are *not* my parents."

Feet catching in the pile of dirty clothes on the floor, I stumble then grab the window.

"Zaidyn no!" Dad yells. He dashes toward me.

I lift the sash and tear the screen, leaping out into the muggy late summer air. Mom's frantic scream follows me.

"Help him, Greg!"

Falling, I brace for the painful landing, covering my head with my arms and wishing I'd thought enough to go feet first. Or to leap far enough to land in our pool.

(Note to self: Next time you want to get away fast from your freakishly warped parents, use the damn door.)

It's like time slows down to half speed. Flipping in mid-air to take the worst of the fall with my shoulders, I force my eyes open and my heart

217

stops. Every small detail explodes in my vision. Stars glitter on the black sky. Warm humid air instantly clams up my skin. And Dad rushes out the window toward me, his vibrant red hair almost brown in the darkness, arms spread wide, brows mashed together over his eyes.

Flying.

Flying.

I suck in a breath and throw my arms to the left, hoping to cushion my fall or block Dad from grabbing me or... something. Instead, I stop falling, and my body sails to the side, following the direction of my arms. I sail through the warm air, over the stamped concrete surrounding the bean-shaped pool, arms wind-milling like in my dream, the electric tingle of adrenaline prickling my skin.

"What the hell?"

Now I'm flying.

Jerking to a stop, I hover ten feet above the dark water for a moment, Dad laughing behind me. The jolt of adrenaline fades as I exhale.

"Oh shit."

(Note to self: Plug your nose. You're about to get wet.)

Glancing from Dad's face to the darkness below, I gasp and drop into the water with a splash.

PREORDER TODAY!

ABOUT THE AUTHOR

B.B. Swann wanted to be a writer when she realized writing words was easier than saying them out loud. Still, somehow, she became a teacher, too, and talks quite a bit.

B.B. Swann lives in Southern Illinois with her two- and four-legged family members. She loves to run, binge watch Netflix health documentaries, and talk to her three grown children when they have a minute to spare.

Most nights you can find her reading or writing into the wee hours of the night. She believes in the almighty power of caffeine and battling old age with purple hair and lots of sarcasm.

Visit B.B. on her website and social media platforms by clicking here!

OTHER BOOKS BY BB SWANN

BREAKING THE BRO CODE- Read about Molly and Hayden and how it all began!

KATIE COMMA- The teacher opens a window and Katie Comma is blown from her book! She dodges the curious children, diving into their books to hide. But the sentences aren't afraid to tell her she's in the wrong place. Alone and scared, Katie perseveres, determined to find the place where a lost comma belongs. (Pelican Publishing Company; Illust. by Maja Andersen)

www.ingramcontent.com/pod-product-compliance
Lightning Source LLC
Chambersburg PA
CBHW070454260626
47161CB00004B/1304